A WHISPER ON THE BREEZE

ELLEN GOUGH

APS Books
Yorkshire

APS Books,

The Stables Field Lane, Aberford, West Yorkshire, LS25 3AE

APS Books is a subsidiary of the APS Publications imprint

www.andrewsparke.com

First published worldwide by APS Books in 2025

A WHISPER ON THE BREEZE

CHAPTER ONE
1927

She lay across the fresh mound of soil, her face streaked with tears and dirt. Her arms ached from hours of toil. She had not expected it to take so long, or to be as arduous to dig a dog-sized grave. There was no-one to help her give her beloved Laddie a proper burial. She had chosen this spot beside the horse chestnut tree, because it was one of her happy places. Violet had been eight years old when Flossy, her father's collie dog, had given birth to four pups and her father had allowed her to choose one. The smallest of the litter had a white patch over one eye and he whimpered when she stroked him, and from that moment, he held a special place in her heart. Laddie had been more than just a dog. He had been her loyal companion, her shadow. It was to him that she told her tales of woe. He had been the only joy in her otherwise, miserable existence, the only one left who truly loved her. Now he was gone. She would never forget the day that she found Laddie lying near the backdoor, cold and stiff. Her tears had soaked his soft fur, but when her mother had found her sobbing over his body, she dismissed his death as a part of life. Violet placed some primroses and red campions on his grave and told him that she'd never forget him. She walked away with a heavy heart, but she had to go before her mother berated her for shirking. Although she was only seventeen years old it seemed to her, as if she'd lived a lifetime already, it felt as if she had the weight of the world on her shoulders. Her workload seemed never-ending as her mother became ever more demanding. Violet particularly hated wash days; her hands were red and sore from scrubbing clothes and the steam caused her long, dark hair to go frizzy.

As predicted, her mother was angry with her, "Where have yer been? There's work to do!"

"I've been laying Laddie to rest." Tears filled her eyes as she spoke.

"Well, it dunna tek that long to bury a dog. Stop yer fussing, me gal, It were only a dog." She thrust a bucket at her, "Here, tek this, I'm waitin' fer some water."

At the water pump, the sun was burning down on Violet's back as she filled another bucket of water, her fifth so far. She carried it into the scullery and spilt some of it as she poured it into the copper. She put the bucket down and stopped to wipe the sweat from her brow with the sleeve of her brown dress, before picking it up again. She needed to keep going, before her mother, Mabel, complained. The fact that the buckets were heavy and made her arms ache would hold no sway with her. When the copper was ready, Violet fetched the washing dolly and dragged the wooden contraption across the floor; it almost came up to her chin. She cried out as one of its three legs hit her ankle. As she lifted her skirts to look at it, she noted that she still bore a bruise from the last washday, albeit yellow now.

She climbed onto a stool at the side of the copper and called to her mother for help. Mabel silently took the legs of the dolly whilst Violet gripped the cross-handle as they lowered it into the hot water. After she'd finished agitating the washing, her wrists and back ached. She rubbed her wrists then put her hands on her lower back, but her mother paid no heed.

"Gerra move on. I need yer to help me wi' this."

Violet dutifully turned the mangle whilst her mother fed the washing through. "Couldn't we buy a washing machine, Mother?" she asked timidly. "It would make wash days a little easier for both of us."

"Where do yer think the money's comin' from? They cost a ruddy fortune!"

"But it would soon pay for itself because we would be able to do the washing quicker, so we could take on more work."

"I dunna trust them new-fangled things!" Mabel retorted.

"But Mother, we need to move with the times." Her frustration at her mother's short sightedness was evident.

"Watch yer tongue, me gal and gerron wi' yer work!"

Mabel still wore long dresses with an apron that came down to the bottom of her hem. She refused to show her ankles, believing that only indecent women wore them. She had lines on her face and wore her hair in a tight white bun, which made her look much older than her fifty-seven years.

As Violet walked across the weed-ridden garden to the washing line, she was mindful to stick to the flattened trail to avoid the nettles and the tall thistles that were growing in abundance, waiting to inflict pain on unsuspecting limbs. It bore no resemblance to the once thriving garden which had been alive with vivid coloured flowers and the sweet aroma of roses when her father was alive; it had been his pride and joy. Violet took a wide pair of Long Johns from the washing basket and hung them on the line, shuddering at the thought of Henry

2

Johns wearing them. His father, Judge Johns, was their most lucrative customer but he was a mean and unpleasant man. In spite of his inherited wealth, he only employed two staff: a gardener and an elderly housekeeper who also did the cooking. It was cheaper to pay Mabel to do the washing than to employ more staff. She remembered vividly the first time she'd delivered the washing on her own, three years before; the day she met her nemesis. Her mother used to deliver the washing, but when she turned fourteen years of age, that task befell to her. Her mother had warned her not to *dilly-dally* and the responsibility had weighed heavily on her mind.

The air too had been heavy and humid and the black clouds that loomed overhead foretold of a storm brewing. Thunder rumbled in the distance. When the storm broke, the heavens opened up. A clap of thunder was followed by a bright flash that lit up the dark sky and she'd been thankful that Lady knew the country lanes, had travelled that route many times and plodded on regardless of the weather.

By the time Violet had reached her destination, the rain had stopped and the sun was shining. She'd been in awe at the sweeping driveway which led up to a beautiful red-bricked Victorian house, with its tall chimneys, grandly called, The Manor House. She had been a very bedraggled figure when she met Henry, the magistrate's son, for the first time. He'd been very kind to her and had helped her to remove the rain-sodden tarpaulin tied to the back of the cart. He'd complimented her on her *enchanting eyes* and had pushed two pennies into her hand. She had blushed and thanked him for his kindness. Her face clouded over as she remembered her mother's wrath.

"He gave you two pennies? What did yer do?" She'd eyed her daughter suspiciously. "Did yer steal 'em? Tell me!" She'd shaken her. "What did yer do? Did yer flutter yer eyelashes at him? Tell me the truth or else I shall get me horsewhip to you, me gal!"

Violet remembered that, in spite of her mother's fury, she had still pocketed the money while ranting that, "All men are animals! They're all after one thing."

Her thoughts were interrupted by her mother's harsh voice. Mabel passed a basket over to her and ordered her to take the food to the workers adding, "Hurry up about it. There's still work to be done!"

There was no point complaining about all the tasks she was set because there was no-one else to help her mother. However, today she was particularly tired and wished that her mother would give her a break.

Mabel saw the reluctance cross her daughter's face, for which Violet received a clout round the back of the head.

Violet was aching all over and she kept swapping the heavy basket of food from one arm to the other. As she trudged towards the top field, bemoaning her life, little did she know that fate was about to lend a helping hand and that her life would take a surprising turn. As she walked, the sun was shining and a gentle breeze wafted the golden corn and barley in the fields, tickling her legs. She smiled as she tilted her head towards the cerulean sky and watched as the fluffy white clouds took on a golden hue, as the sun peeped behind them. On the horizon she could see her beloved horse, Ned, pulling along a cart loaded with hay towards the old baler at the end of the field.

Violet was a welcome sight to the little workforce of neighbouring farmers who were gathering in the hay. Farmers often pooled their resources and helped each other with gathering in the hay or when reaping the harvest. As she approached, the workers stopped what they were doing and gathered around as they accepted the proffered refreshments, which consisted of cheese and homemade bread and cake. They also had a choice of milk or water from the pump. On the periphery of the group, Violet spotted a shy-looking lad that she'd seen occasionally over the years, but never in close proximity. Ted peeped over at Violet at the same time that she looked across at him and they shared a shy smile. He wasn't usually shy, but he was awestruck by Violet's beauty. She had long dark hair in unruly curls and the most amazing violet-blue eyes. She was the most beautiful creature he had ever seen and he just had to get to know her.

That night, Ted was unable to sleep and he tossed and turned, thinking of Violet, for what seemed like hours. He was thankful that he no longer shared a bed with his two brothers, Frank and Bill. His mother Mary told him he should have a room to himself once she considered him an adult. His young sister Lillian had never had to endure the aggravation of sleeping top-to-toe. Ted threw his covers off his bed and sneaked outside to the barn. He thought that the cool night air might help him to sleep. He could see the stars in the clear night sky as he made his way across the yard. As Ted tossed and turned, unable to sleep on his makeshift bed of straw, he could hear the sounds of the nocturnal animals, every sound magnified in the still night air. The incessant sound of crickets trilling in their quest for a mate, owls hooting a warning and the occasional melancholy moo from the cows in the nearby field, assailed his ears. In the distance he could hear a dog barking. Whenever, he closed his eyes, all he could see were those beautiful eyes and her sensual, full lips. He couldn't wait to see her again.

A couple of miles away, Violet also had trouble sleeping as images of Ted's shy smile kept invading her thoughts. She felt a flush on her face, every time she thought about the way his blond hair stuck out from under his cap, and the way his blue eyes lit up when he looked at her.

The next morning Violet rose at five and lit the gaslights and then the fire, before going outside to the cowshed where she milked their four cows. As she squeezed the milk into the pail her hands were cold; the sun had not yet permeated the clouds. They used to have thirty cows but most had been sold to raise much-needed cash. Next, she fed the pigs, who guzzled down their food noisily. As soon as she opened the door to the chicken coop the birds rushed out, clucking loudly as they pecked at the scattered grain. She collected nine eggs, some still warm, and put them in her basket.

She opened the top half of the stable door and took an apple out of her pocket for Ned, who gently took it out of her hand and ate it. She unbolted the bottom half of the door, nuzzling his white nape that contrasted with his black, shiny body, before gently pulling the bridle over his head. He plodded by her side as she led him to a nearby field. He'd been just a colt when her father had brought him home and she treasured him as she did that memory. He was a gentle giant and a valuable asset to the farm.

It was now time for her mother's breakfast. She filled up the kettle and put it on the range and as she broke two of the freshly collected eggs into a pan, her mother lumbered into the kitchen. She'd become cumbersome of late and her hands were getting more gnarled and painful by the day.

"Yer late wi' me breakfast today. Gerra move on, you've got work to do," she snapped.

The impatience of her mother did nothing to dampen Violet's high spirits and she could barely keep the smile off her face. Over the next few days, whenever her mother told her to take refreshment to the workers she did so willingly. She plodded across the yard with her basket, careful not to arouse her mother's suspicions but as soon as she was out of her sight she ran, longing to see the boy who had stolen her heart.

When haymaking was finished, the young couple took every opportunity to snatch a few minutes together. They would meet when Violet was out with the horse and cart or, early mornings in the cowshed whilst her mother was still in bed. She felt a joy in her heart. Even though they had only known one another a short time, and nothing had been said, Violet felt she was in love, and was sure Ted felt the same way.

Mother and daughter ate their light supper of bread and cheese in silence. It seemed to Violet as if her mother was being deliberately slow that evening. She could barely contain her impatience and the light changed to dark before she could carry out her nightly duties. As Mabel opened the back door to pay a visit to the toilet, Violet placed her hand on her shoulder.

"Wait, Mother put this on." She reached for the shawl that was hanging on the back of the door and placed it round her shoulders, "It'll be cold out there."

Violet looked surreptitiously about as she filled the pail from the outside pump. The night was still and there was a nip in the air. She sloshed some water on the floor as she carried the pail inside and placed it near the hearth. Next she filled a stone hot water bottle with the water from the kettle and placed it in her mother's bed. She then poured warm water into the large flowered jug and put it next to the matching bowl by her mother's bed, and as she placed the clean chamber pot underneath the bed she heard the back door bang. The stairs creaked as Mabel slowly lumbered up them and into her bedroom, where Violet helped her to wash and settle into bed. She carried the wash bowl into the kitchen and tipped the water away, before she set about washing the supper dishes. Her mother was taking longer than ususal to settle that evening; it was as if she had a sixth-sense. Eventually loud snores drifted downstairs from the bedroom. Violet quietly mounted the stairs, taking care to avoid the creaky third step, but she had forgotten about the last one which creaked loudly as she stood on it. She held her breath, for a few seconds then slowly released the air from her lungs as she heard the snores getting louder. As she opened the bedroom door quietly and peered in, she could see her mother's chest rise and fall as she lay on her back with her mouth open, her long white hair spread across her pillow. Violet smiled as she closed the bedroom door quietly.

Violet's hands trembled as she lit a gas lamp and wrapped a shawl around her shoulders before heading to the barn. Her heart skipped a beat when she spied the barn door slightly ajar and smiled when she saw Ted sitting on a bale of hay with his long legs crossed, twisting his cap between his hands. The light of the lamp cast shadows across his face and as their two bodies stood close to one another, she could see a longing in Ted's eyes, but it was a longing that would have to wait. She knew he had too much respect for her, as she had for herself.

He lifted her hand to his lips and said, "Vi, I want to say sommat." He looked into her eyes as he spoke. "You know that I love yer, don't yer? Please will yer marry me?"

Violet's voice was a whisper as she said, "Yes."

He said, "I will love yer and treasure yer for the rest of me life."

Their first kiss was tentative and gentle which ignited their passion and they clung to each other with a fever, something Violet had never experienced before. But their embrace was interrupted by a loud crack! Violet held her breath as she turned to face her mother standing there in her white nightgown, grey shawl around her shoulders, her grey hair hanging down her back, and red-faced, a horsewhip in her hand.

Mabel's face was contorted with rage, "You filthy little whore! I'll teach yer to cavort wi' men!" She raised the horsewhip in the air, but as quick as a flash, Ted ran towards her and snatched it out of her hand.

"You're mad!" he yelled. "And I'm telling yer, that if you EVER touch her again, I'll fetch the constable! If you even as much as threaten her, I'll not be responsible for me actions! Do I make me sen clear?"

They glared at each other until Mabel turned and stormed out of the barn. As Ted took Violet in his arms he could feel her trembling.

"Don't be hard on her. It's not her fault," whispered Violet.

"How can yer say that? She treats yer worse than a dog!"

"She's suffered terrible losses."

"So have you!"

"You have no idea how hard her life has been," she said sadly.

Violet had felt sadness in her heart for so long but now her heart was full of joy. She was going to become Ted's wife: Mrs Edward Higgins.

CHAPTER TWO
1889-1894

Mabel's father was vicar at the local church where he was well known for his rousing sermons. Mabel would sit dutifully at the front of the church, along with her mother and remaining siblings and watch him in the pulpit with a bible raised in his hand, before a spell-bound congregation. Mabel longed to have some fun, but her parents did not believe in frivolity and always took the moral high ground. Mabel was the youngest of ten children, although there were only seven of them now.

Albert Smith went to church every Sunday, but not to hear the teachings of the bible, nor to save his soul. With his cap folded over in his hand, Albert sat at the back of the church, and when the service was over he'd watch as the church emptied from the front, and watch as the minister's family walked down the aisle. Reverend Edwards was an old school fire and damnation kind of preacher and everyone knew that he'd raised his children in a dour and strict household. Albert remembered his ma telling him about how three of the Edwards' children had succumbed to Scarlet Fever in one outbreak. Reverend and Mrs Edwards had bore their loss stoically, Albert's ma said, but they'd worn mourning dress ever since - although that wasn't very different from the vicar's long black cassock that he wore for the services. Six of the seven remaining Edwards' girls were all prim and proper-looking in their Sunday best. The exception was a girl with black curls springing from under her bonnet, and dark eyes that were full of mischief. Albert and she would exchange furtive glances and her mouth would curl up into a smile whenever she saw him. He wanted to kiss those lips so badly. After months of longing, he could wait no longer. His heart was racing as he boldly knocked on the vicar's door; although the Reverend Edwards was small in stature, Albert knew that he was a very intimidating man.

Albert was shown into an office, which was dominated by a large mahogany desk littered with sribbled notes alongside a large, leather bound bible, which he noted was open on Revelations. The reverend sat in a large leather chair, but he did not invite Albert to do the same and he remained standing.

"Please, Sir, I would like your permission to escort your youngest daughter to church."

"I have to admire your nerve, young man, but what makes you think I would allow such a thing?" Mabel's father said, looking up at Albert.

"My intentions are honourable, Sir. I wish to get to know her with a view to her becoming my wife." Albert held the minister's gaze.

"What do you think you can offer my daughter? Would you be able to keep her in the custom to which she is accustomed?" He stroked his grey beard thoughtfully.

"Sir, I could offer her love."

"Love?" he sneered. "Do you think that love will feed her or pay the bills?"

"I am an honest, hard working man. I labour on my parents' farm and one day, I will take it over. I feel that I can provide quite adequately for your daughter."

The minister scowled, but Albert fancied that he could see a twinkle in the older man's eyes.

It had been six months since Mabel had stood behind the door, listening to Albert muster up the courage to ask her father for permission to court her, and now she was Mrs Mabel Smith, a farmer's wife. As the sun shone down on the newly weds, the bride was smiling broadly at a husband who looked at her adoringly. She was just nineteen years old and, Albert at twenty-four, was five years older. They made a handsome couple, with Mabel's long dark hair and brown eyes and Albert the exact opposite, with blond hair and the bluest of eyes. Mabel had made her own wedding dress which was a delicate shade of beige and made from silk taffeta. The only embellishment was on the embroidered band on her veil, which went across her forehead. Albert wore a dark, slim fitting jacket that came to just above his knees.

Mabel's parents refused to wear bright colours, even on such a joyous occasion and their wedding attire was more appropriate garb for a funeral. Her mother kept a stiff back and remained impassive throughout the ceremony. Mabel could hear her father preaching to anyone who was unfortunate enough to stand near him. She didn't care that only two of her siblings came to her wedding since she wasn't close to any of her family.

She was bursting with joy at the prospect of starting a new life, one filled with love, and although Albert had warned her about the realities of being a farmer's wife, she didn't care. She'd had her first reality check when he'd taken her to the farm to meet his parents. The smell of cow manure had made her eyes water, and a black and white dog had come bounding at her, leaving muddy paw prints on her skirt. However, any niggling doubts had quickly been quelled when her future in-laws embraced her on sight.

Albert had referred to their future home as a farm labourer's cottage, but when she saw it, she knew that he was stretching the truth; it was little more than a hovel. It was a single roomed outbuilding at the farm which Albert's mother had divided in two by hanging a curtain across the middle. On entering the abode Mabel covered her nose with a handkerchief, but it did little to deaden the smell, which reminded her of rotting wood. The whitewashed walls failed to hide the dark patches of damp in the corners of the room and under the small windows, which were situated at both ends of the cottage and which rattled in the wind. In the soot-blackened grate, a hook hung down for boiling the kettle and heavy, blackened pans and a copper kettle, dull with age with dents on the side, lay on the hearth. Next to the cold grate was a wooden fireside chair and in the opposite corner of the room another chair which had horse hair sticking out from the hole in the arm. Behind the curtain was a double bed with a jug and bowl on top of a wooden chest. Her breath furled out in front of her, like puffs of smoke. As she stepped outside, she squinted as her eyes adjusted to the daylight.

As the newly weds stood side by side on the church steps, she knew that she could live anywhere with her husband by her side.

After the celebrations, Albert carried his bride over the threshold and straight to the bed. As he slowly lay her down, he cast her veil aside and kissed her gently at first and then with more fervour. He fumbled with her buttons and kissed the top of her breasts as he exposed them. When he rolled her wedding dress up to her thighs, she tensed and as he entered her, she cried out and the consummation of their marriage was over very quickly. Albert lay on his back, panting, staring at the ceiling, but when Mabel reached over and touched his face reassuringly, he gathered her in his arms. She helped him to lift her dress above her head and and cast it on the floor. Together they touched and kissed, delighting in the revelation of two bodies uniting as one. Enjoying intimacy with her handsome husband felt like a private rebellion against her mother, who had not told her what to expect, just warned her that sex was to be endured, an ordeal only to be done for the purpose of procreation and a duty she would have to endure as a wife.

Mabel grew to love Albert's parents and wider family very quickly. They were so warm and welcoming. She often played tricks on them and they embraced what her parents referred to as *her rebellious nature*. Sometimes she would knock on the door and hide and jump out to frighten whoever opened the door. On one occasion, she stuck dark paper onto her beautiful white teeth and went round to see her mother-in-law, holding her mouth. Ena fell for her joke and was horrified when she thought her beautiful daughter-in-law had lost her front teeth. Mabel was unable to stifle the giggle that was bursting to come out of her mouth and they both fell into spontaneous laughter. Ena and Sam loved to hear their daughter-in-law laughing and singing and Sam often said that he wondered how two such miserable buggers managed to produce such a happy child, but they worried whether she would cope with a life so different to the one she'd been used to in the long term.

The smells of damp and cooking permeated every part of Albert and Mabel's little home. The fire in the living room was not only used for cooking, but was the only source of heat. A copper kettle, hung on a hook over the fire to keep the water hot, which now shone after Mabel had brought it back to life. The water came from an outside pump which had to be carried indoors in pails. Mabel made colourful mats from rags and sewed curtains out of material brought from her previous home, to brighten up their abode. She tried to make the best of it, but it was a difficult life. She knew she should be thankful because whole families lived in the same conditions or worse. Her daily chores seemed never-ending and although she participated in all aspects of working on the farm, it was the milking she found particularly arduous, especially at half past five on a cold winter's morning. However, the thing she hated most of all was the incessant mud which clung to the bottom of her skirts.

Mabel quickly became pregnant and happily relayed the news that she was expecting to her parents. Her father showed little emotion and her mother's face actually showed distaste.

"Hmm, you'll soon see what being a parent's like! More chores and an extra mouth to feed," her mother said.

Mabel didn't let her mother's words dampen her joy and glowed as her belly grew bigger. Her arms ached to hold her baby, but a few weeks later Mabel was sweeping the kitchen floor when she was gripped with a pain so intense that she collapsed on the floor. Her in-laws called for the doctor, and he advised her to rest after the loss of her baby. She had not been allowed to see the little soul but was told that it was a boy. For weeks, Mabel was inconsolable and took to her bed. She knew her Albert's heart was full of sorrow at the loss of their child and how helpless he felt at easing her pain. Ena sat with Mabel and comforted her, her plump face etched with sorrow. She was steadfast in her devotion, mothering her in ways of which her own mother had long proved incapable. Albert's sisters came back to stay in the farmhouse and help with the chores and they took turns to sit with a grieving Mabel. However, one of them was pregnant herself, which only added to Mabel's grief, and the other had young children to look after.

Her own parents were unsympathetic and simply told her that it was *God's will*.

Gradually, Mabel climbed out of the deep abyss that had engulfed her, but had two more miscarriages, each one as painful as the last. She found it difficult to be the wife that Albert deserved, because she was scared of it happening again. Perhaps her mother was right when she'd insisted that sex was to be endured, not enjoyed, but she had enjoyed it. The realisation struck her like a bolt of lightning! She'd brought this on herself. She dropped to her knees and made a pact with God.

"Please God. Forgive me for I have sinned. I've enjoyed the pleasures of the flesh too much, but I repent me sins! Please God, if yer let me keep a baby, I promise I will love me baby wi' all me heart, amen."

Nine months later and five years after their marriage, Mabel's prayers were answered. After a long and arduous labour she gave birth to a bonny baby boy. As his cherub mouth opened, searching for food, she kissed the top of his downy dark head and made him a promise, "I'll love yer forever and I promise that I'll NEVER let any harm come to yer." She held her baby to her breast and as he rooted for the nipple, she knew that she'd not feel like this for anyone else, ever again.

There is an old saying, one in and one out, and this came true when Mabel's father passed away suddenly at the age of sixty-nine and didn't get to meet his new grandson while her widowed mother showed little interest in him. Arthur Edward Smith was christened in his grandfather's church and brought into the Lord's fold by Reverend John Browning who was somewhat gentler than Mabel's zealous father had been. When her mother passed away two years later, Mabel showed very little emotion. Her love for Arthur was all-consuming and she had little interest in anyone else, including her own husband.

Albert tried to make love to his wife, but she rejected him.

"For God's sake, woman, I'm your husband, it's what married people do!" he shouted.

"Don't you dare take the Lord's name in vain! Sex is fer procreation not fer pleasure and I dunna want any more children."

"Well, it's only right that Arthur should have a brother or sister." He stressed this point since Arthur was a few months old, but it always ended in an argument.

"I dunna want another child. What don't you understand? I've told you that I will never love another child like I do Arthur!"

CHAPTER THREE
1894-1898

Mabel fashioned her hair in a tight bun and wore dark-coloured clothes. Her belief in living a clean and Godly life was unshakable and the mischief and fun had gone out of her. Mabel's love for her son was all-consuming; it was as if mother and son were one, two parts of a whole. In spite of Arthur eating well, she insisted on nursing him and continued to breast feed him until he was six months old.

She snuggled him next to her breast and he sucked loudly, his teeth caused her to wince, but after only a few minutes, he would wriggle to try and free himself. Mabel hung on to him pleading for him to come back to his Mam.

"Leave the lad alone, you're smotherin' him. He dunna need his Mam's milk, he's gerrin too big fer that."

"He's my son and I know what's best fer him."

"And I'm 'is father and I dunna want 'im growing up a cissy. Yer 'ave to stop mollycoddling 'im." He scooped his son up and wrapped him in a blanket. "I'm teking him to see me Mam and Dad" and before Mabel could protest, he was out the door.

She ran outside and yelled after them, "Bring me son back! He dunna need them, he needs me!"

She scuttled back inside and threw a log on the fire. It hissed as it hit the warm embers. She slumped into the fireside chair and watched the tendril of grey smoke go up the chimney. Silent tears ran down her face as she pressed her breasts once gorged with milk, mourning the fact that she could no longer suckle her baby.

A few days later another argument ensued when Albert carried a hand me down cot through the door.

"My son inna goin' in that thing!"

"Why not? Me Dad made it and it were good enough for me and me sisters to sleep in," retorted Albert.

"He sleeps wi' me. He dunna need a cot and he inna sleepin' in that thing!"

"He's too big. The bed anna big enough fer the three of us."

"Well, you move out then," retorted Mabel.

"You canna kick a man out of his matrimonial bed and home because of a baby! I'm your husband, the head of this house and yer need to show me some respect!"

Mabel sneered, "Yer might be me husband but Arthur is me son and he comes first. I dunna need anyone else."

Albert grabbed his cap and jacket and stormed out the house, slamming the door with a bang.

Arthur wimpered and Mabel put out her arms to him, and he snuggled into her chest. "There, there, stop crying, yer mam's here, yer dunna need anyone else," she soothed.

Albert could see the willowy figure of his father with his trusted Shire horse, Daisy, gathering in the harvest in the distant fields. The weather had been generally kind to them, but the days were getting colder and the ground was hard beneath their feet. Albert noticed as his father stopped working, and walked towards him, that his movements were cumbersome. His steps were shorter and slower and his stoop was getting more pronounced.

Sam simply said, "Yer late, Son."

"I'm sorry Pa, I didna sleep very well last night. Let me tek over now. You gerroff home and get yersen warm."

Sam shook his head, "Nay, Son, we'll get the job done quicker together."

The light had faded by the time father and son sat by the open fire, nursing mugs of hot tea. Ena put a plate of cold meats on the large wooden table, followed by bread and cheese. As she pulled a chair out to sit at the table, she felt the pain again. She gripped the table with one hand and held her stomach with the other, and was thankful that the men were facing the fire with their backs to her.

As they sat eating their supper, the subject of Mabel came up. "Why don't yer bring her round for Sunday lunch? It anna healthy to keep hersen cooped up like she does," said Ena.

"Thanks, Mam, I will ask her but yer know what she's like. She anna got time fer anyone but Arthur."

"I'll pop round again tomorrow and see how she's doin' but I hardly got two words out of her last time."

"I think you should be taking care of yersen Mam. You look very pale lately. Are yer feelin' alright?"

16

She brushed his concerns aside. "I'm gerrin older, Son. We both are. Dunna you worry about me. I'll be as right as rain once I can gerra good night's sleep."

As Albert walked the short distance to home, his thoughts lingered on the parting hug he had given his mother, and the shock he'd felt on feeling that her shoulders were turning to skin and bone.

Mabel was sitting in the fireside chair with Arthur asleep in her arms when Albert reluctantly came home. He took him out of Mabel's arms and laid him in the cot and she made a futile attempt to snatch him back.

"See he fits it good and proper,"observed Albert, as Arthur carried on sleeping.

That first night without her son in their bed, Mabel insisted on keeping the candle burning in the window so she could watch her sleeping baby, the flame flickering in the draft, casting shadows across the wall. She woke early from a fitful sleep and lay staring at Arthur, willing him to wake up. When he eventually opened his eyes and saw Mabel leaning over him, he responded with a big, toothy grin. She kissed his chubby cheeks and carried him over to the fireside chair where she sat him on her lap by the glowing embers of the fire and snuggled him to her. After washing and dressing him, it was time to give Arthur his breakfast, and he opened his mouth willingly to feed on poor porridge, consisting of flour, butter and water, and guzzled the milk from their cows.

Mabel changed into a long black skirt, which was her Sunday best and placed a straw bonnet on her head. As far as she was concerned, Sunday had arrived far too quickly.

"Yer need to be kinder to me Mam than you were last time," Albert warned. "She thinks the world of yer."

"Well, I'm tellin' yer, that if she mentions me 'aving another baby one more time, I wunna hold me tongue" she snapped.

The driveway up to the farmhouse was uneven with potholes, which were full of muddy water after the downpour of rain that had fell in the night. It was difficult to lift her skirt up to avoid it getting wet whilst carrying Arthur in her arms, but she refused to let her husband carry him.

Ena welcomed them with a smile and held her arms out to Arthur, but Mabel quickly walked away with him in her arms. Sam just nodded his head in acknowledgement. As his mother busied herself in the kitchen, Albert noticed how much slower her movements had become and the dark circles under her blue eyes, were getting deeper by the day. When they sat at the large wooden table, Mabel sat Arthur next to her.

"Let 'im sit next to his grandparents," said Albert

Mabel glared at him and leaned in closer to Arthur, but after a little tussle, the infant was seated between his grandparents, much to Mabel's dismay. She hardly touched her food and instead spent the time when the others were eating, glowering at her in-laws as they fussed over their grandson. Immediately, after the food was eaten, Mabel stood up and snatched him out of his chair and clung on to him possessively. Albert whispered to her that she was being childish.

Arthur was growing fast, and his mother was dreading the time when he would have to go to school. She rarely let him out of her sight. He learned to do tasks with gentle coaxing from her and he would laugh when the chickens ran across the muddy ground, bobbing up and down as they pecked at the scraps he'd thrown down. His squeal of delight on finding the eggs and passing them into his mother's basket always brought a smile to her face. One of his favourite things to do was to offer Daisy an apple and feel her lips tickle the palm of his hand as she gently took it out of his hand, showing her enormous teeth as she crunched on her treat. Arthur stirred the mixture when his mother made cakes and he especially enjoyed licking the contents of the bowl, and she would laugh as the mixture formed a moustache above his lips. He helped to sweep the floor of their abode and put logs on the fire, but their close bond often caused arguments between husband and wife. Albert accused Mabel of being selfish and too possessive with their son, and on one of those occasions he physically tried to prize him out of her arms.

"I'm taking the lad wi' me. It inna normal to have 'im hanging round yer skirt all day. He's my son as well as yours! He'll be a farmer when he grows up, a proper man, not a namby-pamby."

"He's got plenty of time fer all that. He's stopping 'ere wi' me!"

Albert did not pursue the argument as he had other more pressing concerns. As he strode up the path to the farmhouse, he saw the local doctor leaving. He raced up the stairs and found his mother sleeping, her face a pale shade of grey, and his father sitting by her bedside sobbing as he clung onto her tiny hand.

"It's bad news, Son. I didna tell yer before, but the doctor came by a week ago. He says that he believes that she 'as cancer and that he thinks it's too late to do owt. He's going to try and gerr her into the cottage hospital where he does voluntary work, but he canna promise. He's a good man. He wudna tek any money but he accepted the meat I gave him. If it weren't fer the likes of him, us poor buggars would be in the workhouse or the infirmary when we took ill."

Gladys and Ethel, Albert's sisters, came to stay at the farmhouse and took turns to nurse their mother and do her chores, in the house and on the farm. Gladys, the eldest by eight years, took it upon herself to chastise Mabel. She was an imposing figure as she marched up to Mabel's door and banged on it until she opened it.

She poked a podgy finger at Mabel, "You know me mam's dyin' but you dunna seem to care. Why aren't yer helpin' to look after her?"

Mabel looked up at her sister-in-law and took a step back, "Of course I do, but I've got Arthur to look after."

"You anna the only one that's got children and husbands to tek care of, so get yoursen round there now, and yer canna use Arthur as an excuse. He'll be fine playin' wi' his cousins."

Mabel did indeed take her turn to help, but she insisted on Arthur being within her sight at all times and she hardly spoke to her sister-in-laws. Thanks to the care given by the women, Ena was able to remain in her own home until she passed away, surrounded by her loved ones.

The funeral was a solemn affair which took place at their local church. None of Albert's three brothers were able to attend due to the after-effects of wartime injury. However, his sisters and their families came, as did the local community of neighbouring farmers and friends, who came out in force. It was a bitterly cold day and a steady drizzle fell from a grey, melancholic sky as the coffin was lowered into the ground. Mabel watched Arthur with concern and admonished herself for not standing her ground with her husband earlier. She had not wanted Arthur exposed to the damp weather, but Albert had warned her about mollycoddling their son.

Over the coming days and weeks, Mabel gave her husband scant comfort as he grieved the loss of his mother; she was too preoccupied with her own worries.

As Albert rested his head on Mabel's shoulder he felt her body tense up. "I've just lost me Mam, and yer dunna care. A man should be able to turn to 'is wife for a bit of comfort."

"I know what comfort yer after and it inna goin' to happen," she snapped.

Mabel tossed and turned in bed, listening to her husband snoring and envied his state of sweet oblivion whilst her own mind was in turmoil. What would she do when Arthur went to school? The fear consumed her.

Gladys stirred the tea leaves in the brown teapot and set it on the large kitchen table, along with mugs and milk in a jug, straight from their cows, and a bowl of sugar. As the family sat around the table, they looked anxiously at their father.

"What can we do fer yer Dad?" Gladys spoke first.

Sam cut a said figure as he sat with his head in his hands, his broad shoulders hunched over. "Let me die, that's what." His voice was a whisper.

"Dunna talk like that Pa. Me Mam would be vexed wi' yer if she heard yer talk like that."

"But she wunna hear me, will she Son? She's gone and I wish I could have gone wi' her."

Gladys glared at her diminutive sister when she suggested that Albert and Mabel ought to move in the farmhouse.

Mabel sat silently in her chair, watching her son playing marbles with his six cousins, oblivious to the unfolding drama around the table. She jumped when her husband touched her on her shoulder,

"Are yer harking? We're just talkin' about me Pa. Ethel 'as just asked if we could move in 'ere and look after me Pa."

"I dunna think I could look after 'im. I've got me hands full wi' Arthur," she exclaimed.

No-one missed the look of horror on Mabel's face.

"Dunna talk so daft, we'd 'ave more room and me Pa's no trouble," protested Albert.

"I dunna want to be a burden on anyone," muttered Sam.

Gladys glared at Mabel, "If yer anna going to contribute anythin' to this discussion, then it's best yer go 'ome," she snapped.

Mabel was met with protests from her son, "But Mam, I'm enjoyin 'meself.Why don't yer just leave me 'ere?"

"Yer comin' back wi' me and that's final."

An argument ensued, which resulted in Mabel leaving by herself and slamming the door on her way out while Albert gave his son a conspiratorial wink and they laughed.

After much discussion, Gladys spoke firmly, "I'm tekking yer back wi' me, Pa. It's clear that yer canna stay here on yer own and there is no way that I am letting that witch look after yer!"

"I think it'd do yer good to go wi' our Gladys, just till yer feel like comin' back," agreed Albert.

Ethel nodded her head, "It will be nice fer the children to see more of their grandpa and p'haps when yer feel up to it you might want to come back and work on the farm, even if it's just part-time."

Sam shook his head. "I canna do it anymore; none of it! It's not the same now that yer Mam has gone. You were always goin' to tek over the farm one day, Son. It'll be berra for yer to live 'ere."

Albert was cautious. "Yer might change yer mind when you've had a rest."

"Well if he does, he inna stayin' in the same house as her!"

Albert knew that it was futile to reason with Gladys. Once her mind was made up nothing would sway her. It did not go unnoticed that he did nothing to defend his wife.

CHAPTER FOUR
1899-1901

Albert beamed as his wife wandered from room to room, "This will be better for yer won't it? And Arthur will be able to have his own room. He's gerrin' a bit big to share wi' us."

Mabel glared at him, "But I dunna like Arthur sleeping in another room. He's stayin' wi' me!" she declared. "There's room for another bed in 'ere."

Arthur followed his parents round and on reaching the smallest bedroom, with the blue curtains he quickly sat on the bed. "Can I 'ave this room?" He looked longingly from one parent to the other.

"Of course yer can, Son. That used to be my room and I were very happy in there."

Mabel exploded, "He anna sleepin' in there. It's the furthest away from our room."

Ignoring his wife's protests, Ted confirmed with his son that he was indeed being allowed to have his old bedroom.

"Dunna you think that because my son is in another room that you can fornicate wi' me."

"We anna done that fer years so why would I would want to now? Besides it would be like fornicating wi' yer bloody mother!"

Mabel sat on the side of her bed and took the silver locket she'd inherited from her grandmother, from her neck. She kissed the soft dark curl nestled in her hand and gently placed it inside the locket before placing it back around her neck. She delved into the wooden chest at the foot of their bed and reluctantly brought out the trousers she'd made some weeks before. Silent tears rolled down her cheeks. Arthur was growing up too fast.

The big day when Arthur was breeched and had his hair cut short, had finally arrived. Mabel flatly refused to have the usual celebration that took place on the day a boy stopped wearing girls' clothes and started wearing trousers. How could she be joyful about marking Arthur's first steps into manhood?

Albert stared at his son with a huge grin on his face. "Let me 'ave a look at yer. My yer a big boy now, you'll soon be me right-hand man on the farm."

Mabel retaliated, "Dunna get talkin' like that. He's nowt but a baby and still needs his Mam."

Albert shook his head at Mabel. The woman was impossible.

Mabel served Arthur his porridge in silence and her hands shook as she poured out a mug of tea. She kept glancing at the mahogany clock on the mantle shelf. It seemed to her as if time was ticking away more quickly than usual. When the clock reached twenty-five to nine, Mabel felt as if she were going to faint. How was she going to get through the day without her beloved son by her side? Arthur on the other hand, was excited about starting school and was standing near the door, hopping from one foot to another.

She insisted on holding her son's hand as they walked into the village towards the parish school. There were two other boys and four girls from neighbouring homes, starting school on the same day and Arthur tried to pull his hand away from his mother's tight grip and join the other children who had free rein to walk in front of their mothers' or older siblings.

When a teacher came out carrying a heavy brass bell in his hand, Mabel's heart beat quickly. As the peals of the bell rang out, the children were ordered to line up and to walk into school in a straight line. Arthur did not look back to see her waving, and did not see the tears that ran down his mother's cheeks.

Mabel returned home feeling bereft and alone. She carried out her chores in a daze. Even Daisy nuzzling food out of her hand, failed to bring a smile to her face.

The school was not an inviting place to be, its atmosphere austere and cold. The large windows were high up on the wall to prevent the children from looking out and getting distracted. The ice had formed delicate, lacy patterns on the cold glass. There was a gaslight on the wall, next to a display of maps of different countries. Children sat at wooden benches and were given slates to write on. The classroom was one large room and children of varying abilities were taught alongside each other. Girls were taught sewing and home-making skills and boys were taught woodwork and gardening. At the front of the classroom, next to Mr Sadler's desk, was a wooden cane which left the children in no doubt about the consequences if they misbehaved.

Every school morning, Fred and Sam called for Arthur to walk to school with them, but Mabel insisted on walking with him and staying until he disappeared into school even though Arthur refused to hold his mother's hand, instead, chosing to run in front with his friends. Every morning she gave him a kiss, but as the weeks went by he did his best to avoid it.

On one such morning, she puckered her lips and said, "Give me a kiss, then Arthur."

"I dunna want to. The others laugh and call me a Mammy's boy," he protested,

She stopped trying after that, but she would take every opportunity to make up for it when he got home. On the days that Arthur went to school, she would count down the hours until it was time for him to return home.

When the door knocked and she saw two scruffy looking little boys standing there, she glared at them and said, "Clear off!"

Arthur came running downstairs. "Where 'ave they gone?"

"I've told 'em to go."

"Why did yer do that? Why do yer keep on embarrassing me? It's a wonder I've gorr any friends left!" He rushed outside and ran after them.

When the three boys returned, Fred the smallest of them sidled past Mabel to join Arthur and Sam, as they ran up the stairs. Moments later she entered Arthur's bedroom, and opened her arms to him for an embrace, glaring at the boys when they sniggerd.

"Gerroff, will yer?" exclaimed Arthur and turning to his friends, he said, "Come on, let's gerrout of here!"

Mabel found her husband ploughing the fields with Daisy, his trusted shire horse. "Have yer seen Arthur?" she enquired.

"No, I anna. Stop bloody mitherin' the lad! It's time yer let 'im grow up!" he warned.

Mabel made her way to a neighbouring farm and banged on the door which she noticed was in need of a good clean. When a woman answered her knock, she could see muddy boots cluttering the porch, and the woman's clothes were dirty. She shuddered at the thought that Arthur might frequent such a place.

"Is me son 'ere?" Mabel enquired abruptly.

"Yes, come in. He's just 'aving his tea."

To Mabel's dismay, Arthur was seated at a cluttered, dirty table with Sam and Fred, eating bread with homemade jam and drinking from a brown stained mug.

"Yer dunna need to give me son food. He gets plenty at 'ome. It's time yer came home Arthur."

"Dunna fret; the lads are enjoyin' themsens."

"I dunna like yer attitude, Beryl Taylor! I know what's best for me own son," she snapped.

"I doubt that. Yer making 'im a bit of a laughing stock round 'ere. Yer canna even let 'im play out wi' his friends."

Arthur had only been at school for a few weeks when he witnessed Mr Saddler's brutality first-hand.

One of the girls, who had started school on the same day as himself, was unable to grasp sums and Mr Saddler called her out to the front. "You canna be that stupid Ethel Watson! What does eight and three make?"

"It-it meks ten, Sir" she stuttered."

"Ten! Ten! We've been working on sums for weeks. Have yer not listened to a word I've said? You know the punishment for gettin' it wrong, child." He walked slowly up to his cane and held it up in the air for all to see. "Let this be a reminder to all you dimwits and ne'er do wells that dunna care about learning. Hold out yer hands child!"

Ethel was shaking and sobbing and as Mr Saddler raised the cane, a wet patch spread across the back of her dress and formed a puddle on the floor. His handle-bar moustache jiggled up and down as he brought down the cane with force and struck her hands.

Arthur stood to object, but Bert, one of the older boys yanked at his top and pulled him down with a heavy thud. "It'll mek 'im worse and he'll give yer more than just four strokes. There anna a thing we can do about it, but I'll tell yer sommat, the day I leave this place, I will give 'im the thrashing of 'is life."

On the last day of term, attendance was low, but the children that did turn up to school were excited and talkative. However, Mr Saddler made no allowance for the fact that the children were excited about breaking up for Christmas.

"Come out here Bates!"

"What—what have I done Sir?" stammered the frightened young boy.

"You were talking, and you will get an extra stroke for your insolence!"

Bert balled his right hand into a tight fist making his knuckles white. At the last stroke of the cane he stood up abruptly, sending his slate clattering noisily to the floor. Heads turned and an ominous silence spread across the room. Children watched in awe as Bert stormed down towards the teacher. Miss Evans stood at the back of the classroom watching the tableau unfold. She tentatively clutched her neck with a scrawny hand and the lines on her forehead formed deep furrows as she frowned.

"Leave 'im alone! Yer bully."

Mr Saddler stood still with his cane suspended in the air, as if frozen in time. "Sit down Evans or you will get the same!"

Bert squared up to him. "I'd like to see yer try!"

Mr Saddler looked up at Bert and lowered his arm. "Sit down now Evans, and you Bates!"

You could have heard a pin drop as the exchange took place, but once the boys were back in their seats, chaos ensued. Children were hooping, shouting and sniggering. Mr Saddler picked up the fallen cane and walked in front of his desk. Glaring around the classroom with the offending weapon in his hands until silence fell once more, he sat back down and surreptitiously placed the cane under his desk.

Snow fall in 1900 was severe causing attendance at school to be at an all time low. Mabel made no attempt to get her son to school and was content to have him at home with her.

Albert stared out of the window. "It's been snowin' for two weeks now. When's it goin' to stop?"

"I'm running out of logs. You will have to chop down a tree or sommat. I've gorra a young lad to try and keep warm."

"I'm more worried about how long the food stock will last if this weather keeps up," he stated.

Not everyone was perturbed by the snow and Arthur's friends were excited when they knocked on the farmhouse door, sporting rosy cheeks and runny noses. Fred and Sam helped Arthur to rummage through all manner of things in the shed, until they found what they were looking for behind some old tools and a tin bath, which was corroded and rusty. Albert had made the sledge for his son, but Arthur had not had the pleasure of using it until now. The boys dragged it out the shed excitedly and made their way to a steep hill in one of the fields and spent a few hours pulling their sledge up the hills and flying down, landing in a heap at the bottom.

A few days before Christmas Day, Albert brought in a large fir tree and put it in the corner of their living room," It looks as if the snow 'as gone, but I reckon there's more to come; the sky is full of it."

"Stop mithering about the weather; there's nowt you can do about it," snapped Mabel, and turning to Arthur said, "Come and help me wi' the tree."

Mother and son decorated the tree with coloured fir cones and dried fruit and a few baubles that had seen better days, and finished it off with tinsel and a star on the top. Mabel welcomed Arthur's help, which had been sadly lacking of late as he preferred to go out with his friends or help his father round the farm.

It was time to choose the bird for Christmas and Mabel asked Arthur to help her catch one. As he approached the geese they ran at him, honking and flapping their wings but undeterred Arthur ran between them and managed to corner one so Mabel could grab it. As the unlucky bird wriggled in Mabel's hands, she very quickly wrung its neck, carryied the limp bird into the kitchen and, after cutting its throat, hung it above the sink to drain the blood.

Christmas morning arrived and much to Albert's relief there was just a smattering of snow on the ground. A stocking hung over the hearth for Arthur, which had been patched up at the bottom. Inside it was an orange, a few nuts, a homemade miniature cake and sweets. Under the tree was a parcel with Arthur's name on it and he quickly tore off the paper. He shrieked with joy when he opened it and found a wooden train with a carriage, which had been lovingy crafted by his father. Arthur passed his mother a present wrapped in plain paper, and when she opened it tears sprung to her eyes.

"It took me weeks to try and gerrit right Mam, but me teacher were pleased wi' it."

"He canna be more pleased than I am wi' it." She turned the mis-shaped wooden spoon this way and that. "I will treasure it always," she declared.

A couple of days after Christmas, Albert's worst fears were realised when heavy snow fell. They had barely recovered from the previous harsh winter, and this cold snap looked as if it was set for a longer duration. His marriage was already under strain, without adding financial woes to it, so Albert kept his worries to himself.

Snow and gales caused havoc across the country and roads were blocked by heavy snow fall. Communications were down and the railways came to a grinding halt, in fact it snowed on and off until March.

CHAPTER FIVE
1901- 1906

The weather became milder by the end of March and Arthur was helping his father with the many chores on the farm. He'd assisted with the weaning of the calves earlier in the year and was keen to do the lambing, but his mother had other ideas.

"Yer canna stay up all hours like yer father. Them ruddy sheep keep gerrin him out of bed all hours of the night. It inna suitable for a young lad like yerself."

"I'm norra baby anymore, Ma. I'm almost seven! I will be leaving school soon. He drew himself up to his full height and was only an inch or two smaller than his mother. He was very mature for his age and with his broad shoulders, could easily pass for ten.

"Yer wonder be leavin' school for another five years, more's the pity!" sighed Mabel.

Albert entered the kitchen with a lamb wrapped in a blanket in his arms. "This little fella, 'as lost his mother so I need yer to tek good care of 'im." He lay him down by the fire. "He needs to keep warm."

Mabel quickly filled a bottle with milk and attached a long teat on the end. "He needs feeding, but you'll have to hold onto the bottle tightly," she advised.

Nurturing orphaned lambs was a task that took many hours. She smiled in the knowledge that it was something they could do together as she knew that all too soon he would be off with his father across the fields. Mabel knew from his demeanour that her husband took great delight in taking her son away from her. She imagined that he was trying to turn Arthur against her, but she knew he wouldn't win because nothing could break the bond of mother and son.

Arthur was in fact feeling suffocated by his mother's possessiveness and enjoyed spending time away from her with his father. The tasks he'd previously shared with his mother, he could now do independently and he refused to let her follow him. Arthur was learning alot about farming and he particularly enjoyed gathering in the hay which would be a community task. Neighbouring farmers and their children worked together working long hours until the task was done.

When the chidren returned to school, a new teacher greeted them. Miss Hayworth was a prim and proper lady. She kept her grey hair in a tight bun and wore a long black dress that hung loosely on her tiny frame.

"Pl- pl-please Miss, will Mr Saddler be coming back?" stammered Ethel Watson.

"No dear, he will not. You will be having me from now on." Her face crinkled when she smiled and a slight flush crept up her face.

Rumours were rife about the whereabouts of their former teacher. Apparently the last time he was seen, he was sporting a black eye and had his arm in a sling. The coalman was known to share idle chit chat to his customers, and he passed on the fact that Mr Saddler's terraced house was empty and that he and his family had vacated it.

Miss Hayworth took a much gentler approach to teaching than her predecessor but even so she did not suffer fools gladly. She would turn her steely eyes on any child who was not paying attention. However, they were rewarded with one of her kind smiles when they tried hard to do well with their lessons.

Over the years, Arthur excelled at school, particularly with maths and English but he couldn't wait to leave and work full-time on the farm with his father and that time had come. Farming was in his blood and he never doubted that it was his destiny.

Haymaking was in full swing, and Mabel walked over with refreshments to where the workers were gathering in the hay. She could hear giggling close by and followed the sound. To her horror she came across Arthur and a girl throwing hay at one another. The girl looked under her lashes at him with her head tilted to one side and giggled, her cheeks flushed when Arthur whispered in her ear.

Mabel snatched up a rake that was lying on the ground nearby and raised it in the air. "Gerraway from me son, you little harlot!"

Arthur attempted to snatch the rake from his mother as the girl froze like a statue, berating his mother and screaming in her face. "Why can't yer leave me alone? What's wrong wi'yer?" Arthur was red in the face. You canna stand me 'aving any friends!"

"She inna after bein' yer friend. Anyone can see what she's after, and it inna a crime to want the best for me son!" exclaimed Mabel.

The girl took her chance and made a run for it, calling over her shoulder, "I'm goin' to get me dad. You're mad!" She ran towards a little crowd of people and into the arms of a man bult like a prize bull.

He strode across the field towards Mabel, "I dunna like men that hit women, but I'm warnin' yer, that if yer ever threaten me daughter again, I will gi' yer a taste of yer own medicine!"

Albert grabbed his wife by her elbow and advised her in no uncertain terms, to go home. It took all of Albert's powers of persuasion to pacify his irate neighbour and to calm his son down.

Later when father and son returned home, strong words were spoken. "Yer lucky that Big John didna fetch the constable to yer. Yer made a show of yersen and of me, and embarrassed Arthur. It anna normal to be so jealous. Yer need to let 'im grow up. He's left school, he anna a baby anymore."

Mabel tried to retaliate but Albert refused to listen. She had the same response when she went to Arthur's bedroom.

"I'm sick of yer, Mam! Me friends dunna want to come over 'cos of you and yer stupid jealousy! Just gerrout me bedroom and leave me alone! And shut the door on yer way out!"

On the other side of the door, Mabel cried silent tears. She was losing him. Her resentment towards her husband grew and she thought, not for the first time, that he was responsible for turning her son against her.

By the time Arthur had left school at twelve years of age, he was able to carry out almost all of the work which farming entailed, independently. He helped to milk the cows and was able to herd them back into the field by himself. He could even harness Daisy, their shire horse and tether her to the plough, although it would take many months for him to perfect the art of ploughing in a straight line. He prepared the pigs for market by scrubbing them with a wire brush and continued to look after the chickens, often beating his mother in collecting the eggs.

Mabel's joy was short-lived at him leaving school because she saw less of him now that he was working with his father on the farm full-time.

The bond between father and son was unbreakable and Arthur would say that they were brothers in arms!

CHAPTER SIX
1909-1914

Arthur was fifteen years of age and although he had worked full-time since leaving school at twelve, Mabel was still reluctant to let him grow up. She remained possessive and jealous of anyone who spent time with him and resented the hours he was with his father. Regular confrontations took place with Mabel accusing her husband of deliberately keeping him from her. On one such occasion, Mabel yelled, "Yer just canna stand it that he prefers 'is mother, can yer?"

"Dunna talk so stupid, woman. It's your possessiveness that's turning him against yer. It inna bloody normal! No wonder he dunna want to come 'ome from working. For God's sake, let the lad grow up! We've 'ad enough of this. We're off to the pub."

"How dare yer corrupt him? He ain't old enough to be goin' drinking! You'll bring the wrath of God on us!" she wailed. She grabbed her son's arm. "Don't go Arthur, please!"

Arthur pulled his arm away and looked at her in disgust. "Stop treating me like a baby," he implored.

Albert called over his shoulder, "Yer sound like yer bloody mother. Give it a rest!" He slammed the door on their way out.

Mabel was beside herself with anger and fear. She had one of her headaches coming on and knelt at the side of their bed and said a short prayer. "Please God be merciful. Please don't let the sins of his father pass on to my beloved son!" She swallowed two spoonfuls of a potion she'd bought off a local woman and lay on the bed.

Albert wasn't used to drinking and was feeling melancholy when he returned home. He found his wife sound asleep on top of their bed. On the bedside table was a blue bottle with the stopper lying next to it. He sniffed the pungent potion and it made his eyes water. He looked longingly at his wife, her long black curls spread over the pillow and her nightdress hung over her shoulder, exposing the top of her breast. His desire for her was overwhelming. He climbed on the bed and lay next to her tentatively stroking her hair. She murmured softly when he kissed her neck and unbuttoned her nightdress. It had been so long since he'd kissed her soft breasts and his emotions got the better of him, and unable to stop himself, he thrust inside her until he was spent.

Afterwards he fastened her buttons and pulled her nightdress down and gently eased her under the covers before snuggling next to her, his tears wetting the pillow.

Mabel was sweeping the yard when she stopped in her tracks at what felt like a kick in her stomach. She frowned, how was that possible? Then she thought back to that night a few months before when she thought she'd been dreaming. On waking she had prayed to God to forgive her sins for having had such a dream; a dream where her husband had been undressing her. She had assumed that she was going through the change of life, but it was evident to her now that she was with child and the obvious fact that her husband had taken advantage of her. How could he have behaved in such a way towards her? He was no better than an animal, in her opinion. She was now facing the consequences of his actions.

Five months later, after a particularly traumatic labour, Mabel gave birth to a bonny baby girl. When the unofficial midwife of the village placed her on Mabel's breast, she said, "Tek it away!" The venom in her voice shocked everyone present. She was too old to have another child! She did not want another child! She now understood how her mother must have felt. She could never love another child like she did Arthur. She felt nothing for this creature born from an evil deed.

It took a while to name her. Albert insisted on calling her Violet, on account of her beautiful eyes. He flatly refused to let her be called Maud after her pious grandmother and although his in-laws had passed away some years before, their influence had long tentacles although Albert had rebelled against any sort of religion. He'd stopped going to church some years ago and he refused to allow his daughter to be baptised, a fact that alienated Mabel even further from her husband and daughter.

Violet's father and brother tried their hardest to make up for her mother's lack of warmth. Mabel was unjustly harsh with Violet, especially if she showed her rebellious streak, history repeating itself once more.She was strong-willed even at two years of age when she would have temper tantrums if she didn't want to do something. Violet adored her brother, who in spite of being sixteen years older, relished in playing childish games with her. They climbed trees together and whenever he went fishing he would take her with him and she would happily sit quietly beside him. Her favourite game, however, was Hide and Seek, with the farm providing many hiding places. By the time she reached four years of age, Arthur showed her a ways to protect herself from assault. She was a beautiful child and he knew that as she grew up, she would attract unwanted attention from men and he worried that he might not always be around to protect her. Those times were precious and would provide treasured memories in the dark times ahead, snatched moments between the long hours working on the farm.

Meanwhile, Mabel's resentment grew as the bond between the siblings grew ever deeper.

Soon Mabel had had more serious worries about her son, than him spending too much time with his father, as political unrest swept the country. There was widespread speculation that a war was brewing, and in the workplace, and especially at the pub, people talked of little else. Women were worried for their menfolk, and Mabel was no exception. If, indeed there was a war, Arthur might get called up. She would not be able to bear that.

CHAPTER SEVEN
1914-1920

July 28th 1914 saw the start of what was to be known as *The Great War*. The British government gave Germany an ultimatum to get out of Belgium, but when they gave no such undertaking, Britain declared war on Germany. Mothers feared for their sons, husbands, brothers and fathers. A propaganda campaign began and posters were pasted all over the towns, telling Britons, *Your Country Needs You* and a misconception became prevalent that the war would be over quickly with the enemy easily defeated.

Six months after the start of the war, Arthur left the farm early without telling anyone and disappeared for the whole day.

Mabel turned to her husband for reassurance. "Where can he be? Yer dunna think he's gone to volunteer, do yer?" she asked anxiously.

"He wuddna be that stupid! Try to stop worrying. I'm sure he'll tell us when he gets back. Perhaps he's gorra girlfriend. It's about time he did." Albert hid his own anxieties from her.

She grimaced over the word *girlfriend*.

Arthur arrived home late at night and rushed through the door excitedly. "You'll never guess where I've been!" and before they could answer he said, "I've been to join up."

"Yer canna do that! Your place is here on the farm!" Mabel almost fainted on the spot and had to reach for the smelling salts, which were in her apron pocket. "You don't need to go. Yer more use 'ere! Your father needs all the help he can get and besides, we're doing our bit for the war producing food for the troops."

For once, Albert was in agreement with his wife and tried to reason with him. "Your mother's right. The government want more food and I need help." In spite of seeming calm on the outside, his insides were doing somersaults. He was gripped with fear. He knew that in all likeliness, his beloved son would be injured—or worse! He'd seen many of their neighbours go through the devastation of losing loved ones over the last few months.

"Fred and Sam have signed up today! All me other friends have already gone. They were all helpin' on the farms, but their parents are proud of 'em!" he protested.

"They're just stupid! Peasants!" his mother said in a derogatory tone.

"Those peasants are our friends, people who have helped us whenever we've needed anythin'! Do you think their lives are less worthy than mine?" he yelled at her.

In desperation, Mabel resorted to blackmail. "What about yer sister? She's goin' to miss her big brother. How can yer be so selfish?"

Arthur stood up to challenge his mother, his dark eyes flashing, so like her own. "You're a hypocrite! Since when have yer cared about me sister's feelings? You don't care about her at all!" he snarled.

"Of course I do!"

"You're a liar! If you care about her, why haven't yer ever shown her any love? Most of the time, you treat her like she dunna exist. In fact the only time you speak to her, is when yer mean to her. She is not responsible for yer miserable life! Why can't you see her for the beautiful little girl she is?"

"No, yer right. It's yer father that's responsible for me miserable life, as you put it. I never wanted another child, especially at my age! Why don't you ask 'im how he took advantage of me?" she said defensively.

A huge argument ensued which left Violet cowering behind a chair.

"Now look what you've done!" Arthur turned to look at his mother as he stormed towards the door. "I'll be glad to go, to gerraway from you! Any road, it's too late. I've told yer, I've already signed up."

Mabel beat him to the door and knelt on the floor in front of him, begging on bended knees for him not to go. She grabbed hold of his legs and clung onto them tightly, to prevent him from leaving. "I love yer!" she sobbed. "I'll die if I lose yer!"

"You dunna know the meaning of the word! Your love is possessive and suffocating! By leaving I can finally be a man!" He released himself from her clutches and slammed the door as he left.

The next morning, breakfast was a silent affair. Mabel and Albert didn't touch their breakfasts, so Arthur scraped the food off their plates onto his own and said, "Well, if you dunna want it, I'll eat it. I might as well fill up 'cos I dunna know when I might get a decent meal."

Violet nibbled the corner of her toast, too afraid to leave it. She had to wash it down with a drink of milk to get it past the lump in her throat.

Their journey to the train station was silent apart from the clip-clop of the horse's hooves. Mabel gripped Arthur's fingers tightly. she didn't want to let go. Albert felt sick to his stomach as dark thoughts filled his mind. What if he never saw his son again? He took hold of his daughter's trembling hand. The scene at the station was chaotic with the platforms awash with people. Some of the volunteers looked like they should still be at school. Men and boys were hanging out of the windows and mothers and loved ones were trying to hold onto their hands as the train pulled away. There was cheering and waving of flags and many tears being shed. Mabel held onto her son's fingers through the open carriage window and ran along with the train as it juddered out of the station, fearing to let them go. As the train gathered speed their fingers slipped apart and Mabel screamed her son's name as they watched the train disappear in a cloud of smoke.

Albert took her in his arms and they cried together, Violet standing in bewildered silence, clinging onto her father's leg, too young to fully comprehend the reality of war.

Mabel missed Arthur every day, as did his father and sister. She could barely eat or sleep. Her weight plummeted as she struggled to eat the smallest of morsels. She had dark circles underneath her eyes as sleep evaded her, most nights. When Mabel did in fact drop off to sleep, she saw Arthur lying on the muddy ground, wounded with bullets flying around him. She would inhale the metallic smell of gun powder and the rotten stench of decaying flesh as bodies were strewn about, arms and legs hanging off. Then she would wake up shaken at how real her nightmare had been.

It did in fact take several weeks before Arthur could take part in active service. Only once he'd completed his basic training in warfare, was he transported to France by boat, along with hundreds of other recruits.

A month later, on a particularly cold and misty morning, Mabel and Albert were working in the field adjacent to the farm, when someone caught their attention. A young man in uniform was walking up the path to their farmhouse. He was tall and dark. They failed to see his cycle leaning against the hedge at the bottom of their path. Mabel cupped her work-weary hands, above her eyes, squinted and then started to run in his direction.

"Arthur! Arthur! You're back!" she screamed. Tears ran down her face as she stumbled through the mud with her arms outstretched towards him.

She stopped in her tracks. He was a stranger, a mirage; an apparition. The boy reached in his bag and took out an envelope; Albert reached over the fence and reluctantly took it out of his hands. He tore it open and read the words. *We deeply regret to inform you, that a report on the 2nd March 1915 has been received that Arthur Edward Smith has been killed in action. The army council desire to offer you their sincere sympathy.*

Albert stood with the telegram gripped between his hands. He had turned to stone; a statue. Their beloved son was dead at just twenty-one years of age.

Mabel stared at her husband, grief etched in every line of his ashen face. She felt her body go numb. She couldn't breathe. Her heart died in that instance. Her legs could no longer support her and she collapsed in the mud and the dirt, oblivious to the bitter, cold March wind.

The grief seemed never-ending. Mabel cried for hours, weeks, months upon end, until her tears were spent, only to be replaced with a constant dull ache in her chest. Her heart felt as if it had been crushed into a thousand pieces. She had promised to never let any harm come to her son. She had broken that promise. She was eaten up by guilt; devoured by it. She was oblivious to the shared pain felt by her husband and daughter, who had lost a beloved son and brother. Mabel clung to her husband, like a drowning man would cling to a life raft.

Albert kept his emotions hidden and a stiff upper lip as he supported his wife and daughter, but in the moments when he was alone, he would cry, releasing the tight coil of grief that threatened to choke him at times. On more than one occasion, he took his shotgun and fired indiscriminately at squirrels or birds, creatures that were alive, whilst his son was dead. He would take his axe and swing it purposefully as he chopped up logs for the fire, each swing more vicious than the last.

Whenever he saw his young daughter, looking forlorn, he would snatch her up in his arms and hold her tightly against his chest, reassuring her that things would get better. Mabel on the other hand did not seem to notice her daughter's bewilderment. Nor did she care.

In fact she was unable to care about anything much as the days went by in a haze. She went about the daily grind of chores as if in a trance, devoid of emotion.

Together, husband and wife struggled through the dark days as best they could. Mabel had no friends and her siblings lived miles away, not that they were close. Besides they had troubles of their own. Albert's family siblings also lived quite a distance away and two of his brothers were badly injured. Every family had their own problems due to the war.

They kept expecting Arthur to walk through the door, or to see him working in the fields. They had fleeting moments when they forgot that he was dead, especially when rousing when the mind hadn't fully dragged itself from slumber. Some nights, sleep would evade either one of them, or they would dream that Arthur was doing some mundane task on the farm, only to feel the pain all over again on waking, as reality set in. They had no closure, no body, and no grave where they could visit him. They longed to visit his final resting place, to be able to talk to him and feel close to him, but they would never be able to afford to go to France where he was buried along with countless others.

Mabel lost her faith in God and berated him for taking her precious son away and husband and wife became closer, united in grief and working in tandem as they tried to keep up with the demands of growing the extra food required by the government.

The war was still raging, and in 1916 the German Empire and their Austrian allies put the clocks forward to save on artificial light, thus saving fuel for the war. The fact that Britain was about to follow suit enraged Mabel.

"The stupid government are like sheep, just following others. We shouldn't 'ave to do what other countries do, especially the Germans. It's their fault that we're in this mess!"

"Well, it means that we will 'ave more daylight and will save on fuel. We're not the only ones following suit; other countries are too," Albert said.

"That means that you'll be out fer more hours!"

"Well, I've got help comin' soon."

"That's another stupid idea. The government's full of 'em."

She was referring to the formation of the Women's Land Army, which had been set up to fill the gaps left by men going off to war.

Farms had become more mechanical as the government provided tractors to replace the horses sent to war. Tractors were quicker than horses, thus providing more food while Albert's beloved horses, Bonny and Bess, were requisitioned to go to the war. He had been dreading that day, and when it finally arrived and he saw a big wagon drive up to their farm, he rushed out and stood in front of it.

"They're mine! They're goin' nowhere!" he yelled.

"Sorry mate, but these papers say otherwise. They belong to the government now." The driver wafted the papers under Albert's nose.

"The bastards have already had my son!"

The man's tough demeanour, softened a little when he saw Albert's anguish and gave him a moment to say his goodbyes. He'd witnessed this many times.

Albert stroked their brown manes and nuzzled their faces with tears streaming down his face. He couldn't bear the thought of the traumas they would face. Bonnie and Bess whinnied as they were loaded into the wagon.

Violet gripped her father's fingers as they stood transfixed watching the wagon drive away, taking their beloved horses to the port, where they would be shipped off to France. They both cried until the horse wagon was little more than a speck in the distance.

Mabel hung her head; the war had brought them nothing but heartache.

Albert frequently swore at the tractor and would shout, "The bloody thing's broken down again," but fortunately he had a right-hand woman to fix it. Edith had done a mechanics course when she joined the land army. She shared Violet's bedroom and was like a big sister to her, chatting to her when they were in bed.

"My mother nearly fainted when she knew I was signing up." She imitated her mother's cultured voice. "Oh Edith, what on earth possessed you? Working on a farm is so unbecoming!" They giggled together as Edith copied her mother's mannerisms and cocked her little finger.

Mabel was less friendly towards her, but Edith was thick-skinned and let Mabel's barbed comments go over her head. She'd say, "It's like water off a duck's back."

Violet cried when Edith returned home after the war came to an end in 1918. After four years of war and millions of lives lost or ruined, many families were depleted having lost so many of their loved ones. They were also hit with financial hardship when food prices dropped, causing many tenant farmers to pack up and leave.

Mabel and Albert continued to work side by side on the farm, united in saving their livelihood. Mabel couldn't bear to lose their home, a place where Arthur's bedroom remained untouched: a shrine. She was prepared to do whatever it took to keep it.

Violet fed the chickens and collected their eggs, she swept the floors and washed the dishes and generally helped with the chores, but no matter how hard she worked, her mother barely acknowledged her. Her father on the other hand, never let her down and demonstrated his love with tight hugs. Whenever he saw her coming towards him, he would open his arms and Violet would run into them. He was so proud of her. She had such a sweet nature and she was doing very well at school. He hoped that she'd have a bright future. He wanted more than anything for her to be happy. It brought him great joy when Flossy, his trusted collie, gave birth to four pups and he let her choose one for herself. He knew only too well how comforting a dog could be. He watched as the pups were tumbling over each other to gain his daughter's attention, the runt of the litter getting left behind. He smiled when Violet picked up the smallest and held him to her chest. He could have wagered that she would choose the weakest; his daughter had the kindest heart. He was not to know that later, a dog would be her only source of companionship.

Violet's childhood changed again. Five years later, tragedy struck once more when her father was crushed by a bull. The doctor was called and he treated Albert's wounds but warned that the next forty-eight hours would be critical. A woman from the village brought various potions, purporting to be a cure for all ills and Violet never left her father's side as she steadfastly tried to get him to sip the potions.

Laddie lay at Violet's feet, comforting her in his own way. She prayed with all her heart for God to heal her beloved father, but it was to no avail. He never fully regained consciousness, and, two days later, passed away.

Violet refused to let go of his body as she clung on to him, screaming, tears running down her face. "Don't leave me father. Don't leave me!"

However, it was a neighbour rather than her mother who took her in her arms and held her tightly as she sobbed. Mabel just stood passively by her husband's bedside, too numb to deal with the shock. Later, as the enormity of being a widow and keeping the farm going sunk in, it was as if she'd been struck by lightning. The thought that was uppermost in her mind was that she had to keep Arthur's bedroom at all costs.

It was the same neighbour who suggested that Violet would be better returning to school but Violet's school days came to an abrupt end, only weeks after her father's death. She was just ten years old.

She'd been reading out loud to Mr Smith, when there was a commotion in the corridor. Miss Adams' voice was high-pitched as she called, "You can't go in there!"

The silence in the room was deafening as Mabel marched into the classroom brandishing a horsewhip. Her clothes were dirty and her long apron had blood on it. With her white hair hanging in strands over her face, and malevolent, dark eyes flashing, she looked the epitome of a lunatic. The children shrank back from her and as she advanced towards her, Violet curled up in her chair but Mabel grabbed her by her collar, yelling, "Gerr' home! You've got work to do!"

Her teacher, Mr Smith, protested, standing up to remonstrate but quickly backed down when Mabel raised the horsewhip in the air.

There were feeble attempts by officials to send Violet back to school. After such visits, she would return to the classroom but whenever Mabel needed extra help, Violet was kept off school. When her attendance remained poor, another official came but after he was threatened within an inch of his life by Mabel, no further actions were taken. No-one reinstated Violet at school and no-one helped her to navigate the adult world into which she'd been plunged. There was no-one to alleviate the loneliness she felt, except for her beloved dog, her faithful companion; her comforter.

CHAPTER EIGHT
1928

Violet and Ted spent weeks planning their wedding, snatching time away from their chores at every opportunity and one of their biggest decisions was deciding where to live.

"Mum and Dad have offered us the worker's cottage on their farm. It's not much. It's only got two rooms but it's a start. We'll look for sommat better later on."

"But where will me mother sleep?" Violet enquired.

Ted looked puzzled when he said, "Well, she's gorra own house!"

"I can't leave her on her own! How can you be so thoughtless?" She glared at him.

"Well, what do yer suggest?"

"We could live here. There's more room."

"Vi', I'm sorry but I canna live wi' yer mother," he shook his head as he spoke.

Violet turned her back on him and when he touched her on her shoulder, she shook his hand off. When Mabel heard the door bang, she went into the kitchen to her daughter.

"What was all thar about?"

Violet told her that Ted wanted them to live in the worker's cottage. "I don't want to live in a hovel!" she declared.

In an unexpected show of solidarity, her mother agreed, "I dunna blame yer. Me and yer father started our married life in one of 'em. Why don't yer carry on livin' here?" If truth were told, she didn't want to live on her own.

Ted was miserable; all he could think about was Violet and how she'd reacted to him when he'd suggested they live elsewhere.

"I canna live wi' her mother. I just can't!" Ted sat with his head in his hands.

"Yer need to start as yer mean to go on," advised his father. "Yer need to show her that you're the boss. If yer let her gerr her own way before yer even married, well you'll be under her thumb fer the rest of yer days."

"Yer mean like you are, Jack?" Mary shook her head at him and gave him a smile. Mary took an entirely different approach to her husband. "Dunna listen to yer father, what yer need to understand is that she's very loyal to her mother. She loves yer both so, dunna mek her choose between yer. Marriage is about compromise, son. Yer dunna want to lose her."

His parents' words went round and round in his head and when he shut his eyes to sleep, all he could see was Violet shrugging his hand off her shoulder.

The next morning Ted was still determined to get his own way. He had to make her see that he couldn't live with her mother but when Violet opened the door to him, her eyes were red and puffy and his resolve disappeared instantly. He knew that he'd rather live with Mabel than live without Violet.

Violet couldn't wait to get married. She hoped that she would be able to stop taking in washing once Ted was managing the farm. Then she'd never have to see Henry Johns again. However, for now she had no choice but to carry on doing her weekly deliveries of washing and today was one of those days.

Violet's hands were sweaty as she drove the horse and cart up the long drive to The Manor House. She said a silent prayer. "Please, please God, don't let Henry Johns be there!" The tongue lashing she'd had from her mother for accepting two pennies off him, when she was only fourteen, still haunted her.

She hadn't understood what her mother had meant by him *wanting sommat in return* but Henry Johns unnerved her. He would stare at her through the window whenever she delivered the washing and sometimes he would follow her to the horse and cart although she tried to keep her anxieties to herself because they needed their custom.

She saw Mrs Brown the housekeeper bustling about in the enormous kitchen, rattling pots and chopping up vegetables. The wind was lifting Violet's long skirt, as she carried the heavy baskets of washing, back and forth from the cart. She was unable to hold it down with her arms full. "Good morning, Mrs Brown," she said in no more than a loud whisper. "Are you on your own?"

"Speak up, I canna hear yer."

Violet repeated her question.

Mrs Brown shielded her mouth with her hand. "I wish! The young master's here." She screwed her nose up as she spoke of him.

After Violet had exchanged the clean laundry with the dirty laundry and secured it on the cart, she went back to the house and accepted the money, which she put in her skirt pocket. If Mrs Brown noticed her trembling hands, she didn't say so.

Violet rushed along the path towards Lady, holding her skirt down as she went, but she had her head bowed against the howling wind, which prevented her from hearing a twig snap nearby.

Henry had watched Violet's every move. Seeing her legs on show as the wind played havoc with her skirt had aroused him. He knew that he evoked fear in her and the thought excited him. He had a misguided view that he was entitled to have whatever he fancied, a result of being over indulged by his mother. He was a terrible snob and thought that *a lowly wench* should be flattered by the attentions of her superior. Oh, she could play hard to get as much as she liked, it only added to the thrill of the chase. He would have her sooner or later—in fact, sooner rather than later! He knew what loose morals working class girls had. After all, they didn't have his breeding, he thought.

He laid in wait for her and as Violet rushed by the bushes, he jumped out at her, taking her off guard, grabbing her wrist to pull her into the bushes. "Come on! Don't be shy, just a little kiss," he sneered. She'd been too young when he first noticed her, but now she was just right for the taking! He shoved her down to the ground, confident that they were hidden from view by the foliage.

"Get off me!" she screamed.

He silenced her by kissing her with fat, wet, rubbery lips forcing his tongue inside her mouth. His body emitted a pungent smell of sweat. He pushed her long skirt up her slender, white thighs as she bucked and tried to throw him off. He hadn't expected her to be so strong. He had to admit, that she put up a good fight. He loved it! He held her down, unable to wait any longer, but as he tugged at his trousers she kicked him between the legs.

As Henry rolled over in agony, she took her chance, jumped up, and started to run, but he rolled over, reaching to grab her ankle and she fell heavily on her face.

"Henry, where are you, darling?"

"Coming, Mother," he called. He snarled at Violet, "You'll keep! Don't you even think about telling anyone! I'd just say that you tripped. Who do you think they would believe, an upstanding citizen like me, or a working class little whore like you?"

Violet lay there listening to Henry's mother soothing her son. "Darling, whatever happened to you? You look very dishevelled."

"I was doing a bit of gardening and I tripped."

"Why in Heaven's name would you be gardening? We wouldn't even expect Tinker to tend to the garden in this weather. Come on in, before you catch your death of cold. I will see that Mrs Brown gets you a hot drink."

Violet could barely hold Lady's reins steady and not for the first time, she'd been thankful that her trusty horse knew her way home. As the horse and cart came into the yard, Mabel stood rooted to the spot at the sight of Violet's face bleeding and was then taken aback as her daughter, uncharacteristically, ran towards her and flung herself into her arms.

Violet sobbed out her sorry tale and taking their earnings out of her pocket to give them to her mother, she lamented that she had also lost one penny, but her mother did not acknowledge it.

Something stirred deep within Mabel's broken soul and an anger rose to the surface, erupting like a volcano! "I'll kill 'im! I'll kill 'im with me bare hands!" she exploded.

"No, Mother, you can't do anything. No-one would believe me!"

Mabel's eyes blurred with tears and she felt a softening of her heart that she had not felt for years. Her mothering instincts had finally kicked in. Her dark eyes flashed with anger as she said, "Men think they have a God-given right to tek advantage of women." She tentatively held her daughter to her chest.

Violet cried even louder as she buried her head on her mother's breast and heard her mother's heart beat next to her ear for the first time in her life.

CHAPTER NINE
1928

Ted was shocked to see the state of Violet's face and even more so to see her mother bathing her sores. It was the first time he'd witnessed Mabel showing any sort of kindness towards his wife-to-be. He gently cupped Violet's face between his large hands, tenderly kissed her sore face and asked, "What happened to you?"

"She tripped when carryin' the washin' and hit 'er face on the ground," Mabel lied. She exchanged a look with her daughter and gave an almost imperceptible shake of her head.

Ted held Violet close to him. She felt so tiny in his strong arms. He hated the thought of her lugging heavy bags of washing and vowed that things would change when they got married.

When he'd gone, Violet said, "I don't like lying to Ted."

"Well, what do yer think will happen if he knew the truth? He'd go round there and thump 'im and then he'd be in trouble and we dunna want that. We will just have to think of summat to teach him a lesson. I will tek the washing next time. You can gerron wi' the work here. I'll try and find out when he's there and then we can tek care of him ourselves."

Mrs Brown smiled when she saw Mabel. "Well, what brings yer here? Is Violet not well? Come in and have a cuppa wi' me, whilst I've got five minutes," she said. "It will be really busy when the young master comes home from London in a day or two. I wished he'd stay there. He wants waitin' on hand and foot and honestly, I dunna know how much longer I can keep this pace up. They seem to forget how old I am!"

Mabel sat at the large rectangular table and took in her surroundings whilst Elsie Brown busied herself making tea. She couldn't help but compare her own damp, cold kitchen to the light and spacious one she was sitting in. The large stone tiles were covered with expensive mats, unlike theirs which were made from rags. The embers glowing in the fire made the kitchen warm. She was envious of the huge black range which gleamed, reflecting the light from the window, unlike hers which was small and blackened with smoke. Shiny pots and pans hung from beams.

As the housekeeper sat down, her ample bosom rested on the table and her chin wobbled as she talked. Mabel sipped her tea from a china cup and saucer, her thin body taut as she listened to Elsie bemoaning her lot in life.

Over tea and biscuits, the talk returned to Henry and his rudeness. "He's the rudest young man I ever did see. His mother 'as spoilt him rotten and his father dunna seem to care about anyone else but himself. He's an arrogant man! To tell yer the truth, I've about 'ad enough on 'em."

By the time Mabel left, she knew what day Henry would be returning and she made arrangements for the washing to be returned a day later than usual. By way of explanation, Mabel said, "It'll tek me longer to do it on me own. I ain't as fit as I used to be."

Mabel and Violet worked on their plan. It was imperative that they worked closely. They had an extra day to return the washing, a day longer to perfect their plan.

On the agreed date, mother and daughter put the washing on the back of the cart and covered it with tarpaulin, to keep it clean and dry. They didn't speak on the way there. Violet's hands felt clammy on the reins and her mother sat with her hands clasped on her lap, looking at the passing countryside and the trees that were turning red and gold.

They were sure that Henry would want to finish what he started, but that would depend on his mother's whereabouts. They might well have to bide their time, but they were prepared! They had a foolproof plan, or at least they hoped it was.

When they neared the last bend in the drive, before they veered off to the tradesmen's entrance, they put the first part of their plan into action. Mabel got off the cart and crept around the back. She looked surreptitiously around her and was relieved to see no signs of life. Violet, meanwhile, followed her usual routine, but her legs were shaking as she went round the back to the kitchen door. After the usual exchange of clean and dirty laundry, she could see Henry hovering around in the adjacent dining room, looking her up and down. She hurried away, but Mrs Brown called after her.

"You're in a bit of a rush. Are you feeling poorly? You look a bit peaky."

Henry grinned. He heard every word. He made haste through the kitchen almost knocking the elderly housekeeper off her feet. He went round the back of the garden to block her exit and Violet shook when Henry jumped in front of her. She tried to steady her breathing. They had a plan; it was time to set the second part of their plan into motion. She and her mother had gone over it many times but she was still anxious something could go wrong.

"If you come near me, I'll scream!" she yelled.

Henry sneered and said, "No-one will hear you. The old dear is as deaf as a post." He cupped his ear with his chubby hand, to emphasise the point. "Tinker has gone on an errand and will be gone some time. Father is in court, dealing with thieves and good-for-nothing criminals and mother is doing her civic duties, visiting the sick." With a sickly grin he said, "So go ahead; scream as much as you like; it won't do you any good. In fact I find it rather exciting. It's like when a fox is cornered and you can smell its fear."

Violet ran and he gave chase but unbeknownst to Henry, he was being stalked. The figure moved in and out of the shadows like a lionness. Mabel's anger had peaked, releasing adrenaline through her body and making her unusually agile.

Violet was aware of her mother's presence and was reassured by it.

It was time to implement the last part of their plan, and she stopped at the side of the pond to regain her breath. Henry stood on the south side of it watching her. He was sweating and red in the face but was smiling. He could see that she was tiring. She was no match for him, but he was so intent on catching his *prey* that he was unaware of what was happening in the shadows of the house.

Mabel was behind him, creeping silently towards him. The almighty push she delivered in his back came as a complete shock and he splashed into the water face down, spluttering, cursing and bewildered by the turn of events. "What? What? What just happened?" he stammered.

"ME!" boomed Mabel.

"You stupid, old bitch! You'll pay for this!"

Violet's mother stood with her hands on her hips. "I dunna think so!" she said sarcastically. "You've already said there anna any witnesses." She sneered as she repeated his words back to him. "Funnily enough, I'm dealing wi' a good-for-nothing criminal meself. What yer did to my daughter is criminal!"

Henry was thrashing about in the water. "I will tell!" he shouted childishly. "You're crazy if you think you can get away with this!"

"Let me tell YOU summat! If you ever try to touch me daughter again, ye'll see just how crazy I am!" she growled.

"YOU, are threatening me? That's a joke." He was gasping for air, "My father will have you in court and get you locked up! And when I become a Judge, I won't be as lenient as my father and not only will I lock up mad people like you, but I will throw away the key as well!"

"I'd get away wi' it because, like you said, I'm crazy. Everyone knows me as *the Mad Woman* that lost her mind wi' grief!"

Henry was attempting to climb out of the pond when Mabel whacked him on his knuckles with a big stick, her face contorted with rage. He fell back into the water, yelping with pain. His brown clothing clung to his bulbous body and pond weed hung from his hair. His rubbery lips were quivering like a child's.

"Stay where yer are," said Mabel.

As they trotted off up the road they burst out laughing.

Even Lady had left a deposit on the immaculate path.

They laughed as they recalled the sight of Henry floundering in the murky pond and Mabel laughed louder still when her daughter likened him to a *big, fat toad.*

Violet's eyes sparkled as she praised her mother. "You were wonderful Mother. You were so brave!"

Their triumphant laughter did not last long and it was soon replaced with trepidation. Every time there was a knock on the door, they peeped through the window before answering it.

"Do you think we've gorra way wi' it?" asked Mabel.

"I think the constable would have called by now, if we'd been reported," soothed Violet. They both started to relax. That is until the next delivery day.

They rode in silence and Mabel sat at the side of her daughter as Lady trotted up the drive. She remained seated at the front of the cart in full view, with her shoulders back and her head held high. Her heart was beating quickly in her chest as she watched Violet meekly tap on the kitchen door.

"Are yer OK, Violet? Yer look troubled. Where's yer lovely smile gone?" Mrs Brown looked closer at her.

"I'm fine, thank you," she replied quietly.

Violet breathed a sigh of relief when they exchanged the money and the washing. She smiled as she walked away, but her relief was short lived when Mrs Brown called after her.

"Violet, I nearly forgot, but the Mistress asked if you could bring yer mother next time. There's summat she wants to discuss wi' yer both."

Although they prided themselves on doing a good job, they paid particular attention to the Judge's washing. They were sure he was going to terminate their services, or worse! Mabel took the heavy iron off the fire and pressed the creases out of the clothes, a task that was becoming too much for her gnarled fingers. She hoped that her future son-in-law would keep his promise. She couldn't go on like this for much longer.

The drive to The Manor House seemed endless. Mabel sat rigid with her hands in her lap, but Violet chatted incessantly inspite of getting no response from her mother. When the Manor House came into view, Violet stopped talking and they drove up the long drive in silence.

They knocked on the kitchen door and were greeted by Mrs Brown who showed them into an elegant parlour, which had fine furnishings and curtains. A piano sat in the corner of the room and a fire roared in the grate. They were shocked to be greeted by the Judge himself; they had been expecting his wife.

He was a foreboding figure as he towered above them, but he was uncharacteristically polite directing them to sit in the armchairs.

He spoke directly to Violet. "I understand that you had an unfortunate accident and I trust that you have fully recovered. It's hardly surprising that you slipped with the ground being so uneven round the back. It must be awfully heavy carrying washing so far, especially for such a young woman." He smiled at her. "So from now on to make it easier you will ring the bell and deliver it to the front entrance. We wouldn't want you to have any more unfortunate accidents or misunderstandings." He stood up to indicate that they were being dismissed and added, "Good day, Ladies."

Mabel knew that he knew and there had been no misunderstanding. She had seen his momentary hesitation and quick recovery when he saw Violet's face, which bore yellow bruises. He didn't care about her daughter's welfare. He was just covering up his son's behaviour! Well, she wasn't going to be dismissed as easily as that.

Mabel stood up, closely followed by Violet, determined to have the last word. "That's a good idea. I did notice that yer pond is deep. Yer could easily drown in it!" she said defiantly.

Violet took a sharp intake of breath and looked at the floor.

The judge's face remained a mask, "Yes, one could easily drown and I think we understand each other, Mrs Smith. Thank you for coming to see me. My wife is very satisfied with your work, so perhaps it's time we increased your fees. We would hate to lose you. How does an extra three pennies sound?"

That's blackmail! Well two can play at that game! Mabel stubbornly refused to kowtow to him. "Sixpence sounds better." She held her head high and looked him in the eye.

His long grey beard wafted up and down as he spluttered, "That's extortionate!" He thought for a moment or two before answering her, "I trust that our new arrangements are satisfactory and we need not speak of it again!" He held the door open for them. He was going to be firmer with Henry from now on. *Damn the boy!*

They dared not look back and walked quickly towards their horse and cart, but as Lady trotted back up the drive, they had huge smiles on their faces. Violet had nothing but admiration for her mother, seeing her in a new light.

Later the stunned Judge relayed the events back to his wife. "The cheek of the woman!" he retorted. "But it was a small price to pay to buy their silence."

"No-one would have believed them! Why would anyone take their word over our son's? I still can't believe that you don't believe him!" She said indignantly. "She should have been prosecuted! He could have drowned, the poor love!"

He looked at his wife in her finery, wafting her fan against her face, red with indignation and shook his head at her. "It's time you stopped mollycoddling him, woman!" He stamped his foot. "You have overindulged him for years and he thinks he can do whatever he likes! You know that I'm waiting to be promoted to a senior judge and I cannot afford to have even a sniff of scandal! You only have his version of events."

"What do you mean, only his version of events? Who else's do you need? You surely can't believe that woman over Henry? She pushed him in the water. She needs punishing!"

"I'm sure she had good reason. Why do you think her mother started to accompany her? She is a pretty little thing, and he's clearly noticed. Have you ever wondered why he hangs around whenever she comes? The servants certainly have. I've heard them gossiping!" He put his hand in his pocket. "I found these where Henry was *gardening*." He put a penny and a bow on the shelf above the fireplace.

She started to protest, but he put his hand up to stop her. "Henry knows that if he as much as glances in her direction, I will cut him off without a penny! I don't want to hear another word about it!"

CHAPTER TEN
1929

Violet and Ted married with a simple ceremony in the village church. She was honoured to have Ted's father walk her down the aisle, which brought thoughts of her own father. The weather was unusually warm for the time of the year and as they made their wedding vows, dust motes swirled in the shafts of light as the sun shone through the stained glass window.

Violet had made her own wedding dress from imitation silk, which came above her ankles. It had a dropped waist just below the hips, long sleeves and a round neck. She wore it with a cloche style headdress with the veil attached to the back of it. She had been respectful of her mother's wishes not to have any flesh on show, but it had taken all her powers of persuasion to agree to her hair being styled in a looser bun than she was accustomed to.

Ted wore a two-buttoned modern jacket which was shorter in length, and casual trousers.

Ted's sister, Lillian was the only bridesmaid and her blue dress was a more simplified version of the bride's.

The mother of the bride wore a long navy dress with long sleeves. Mabel had not had the occasion to dress up for years and felt out of place. Seeing the happy couple smiling on the church steps, her daughter petite with dark hair and amazing violet blue eyes, and Ted tall with blond hair and deep blue eyes, brought back memories of her own wedding. She felt melancholy when she thought of Albert; he should have been here for their daughter's wedding. She reflected on her own marriage and wished she'd been kinder to him, but more than anything she longed for Arthur to be by her side.

The church hall was decorated with bunting made by Violet. Their neighbours had brought round old curtains and clothing and various remnants of material with which to make it. Their neighbours also contributed to the food and the feast spread out on the table consisted of pies and cakes and jams to put on bread. There were also various meats and pickles and fruits.

A good time was had by all as they danced and made merry until the small hours.

When the newlyweds tiptoed into Violet's bedroom, they half expected Mabel to wake up and come out brandishing a horsewhip but nothing of the kind happened. When they both lay on the bed, it squeaked and Violet held her breath, her heart pounding. Had her mother heard them? They were both naive, and Violet in particular was very shy and they made love in the dark, tentatively and quietly afraid to wake Mabel who, asleep nearby, was the spectre at the feast.

Sunday lunch with the in-laws was a regular thing and it was always a noisy affair with good natured sibling rivalry, something Mabel had not experienced before her daughter married into the Higgins family. Although she always offered to wash up, Mary and Violet worked as a team and would decline her offer in the knowledge that Ted and Jack would call Mabel over to join them by the fire.

As Mary and Violet washed and dried the pots, Mary touched her on the shoulder and nodded towards Mabel, "How long do yer reckon it'll before yer ma starts snoring?"

They chuckled as no sooner was it said, than Mabel's head lolled back in the fireside chair.

Although life was easier for Violet with Ted by her side and she was now part of a loving, supportive family, who accepted her mother and her eccentric ways, it took Mabel much longer to accept the changes. In particular it took several months for Mabel and Ted to adjust to living in the same house. Although she wouldn't admit it, Mabel enjoyed having a man about the house, especially one who was respectful.

One night when they were having their supper, Ted gave her some good news. "Ma, you can retire now. It's time that yer did. I can take on a bit of help now and Vi doesn't need to do so much on the farm."

Violet had never seen her mother smile so broadly. She would make sure that her mother's retirement would be a happy one. Unfortunately Mabel's fingers had become more gnarled and she had pains in her knees and hips and at times she got people's names mixed up, and called Ted *Arthur*.

Ted purchased a washing machine, which enabled Violet to do the washing on her own, but he hated the fact that she still needed to do it. "I canna wait till yer give it up Vi. It ain't right yer slaving fer other people."

"Well, we need the extra income and the washing machine has made it a lot easier."

"Well, it ain't right, you've gorr' enough to do wi' out yer taking in bloody washing!"

One day he was bemoaning their lot to his mother, "It ain't right, Mam. She works too hard!"

His mother had an idea and wasted no time in putting that idea to her beloved daughter-in- law. "Yer wonderful wi' a needle and thread. Yer could put an advert in the shop window offering yer services. It wunna be back-breaking work like washing."

Violet was unconvinced, but before the week was out she had her first order.

Mrs Smythe, their landlord's wife, came to see her. She was quite beautiful with a slender figure and she was charming, unlike her husband.

When Violet's father died, Frederick Smythe had called, concerned about his rent. Mabel had been unable to pay the full amount of rent at first and he'd shown her no leniency whatsoever. He'd been taken aback when Mabel had paid up her arrears in full. She couldn't bear him and she'd say, "I dunna trust 'im further than I can throw 'im!" She shuddered whenever she saw him. It brought back memories she'd rather forget, and the lengths she would go to just to pay her rent. Memories of clandestine meetings and coming home and scrubbing herself clean. Forty-odd years before, she wouldn't have been allowed to take over the tenancy, but in 1870 the government passed The Married Woman's Property Act, ensuring that women were more protected.

Violet showed Mrs Smythe her wedding dress and her mother's navy blue Mother of the Bride outfit, and the lady gushed.

"They're lovely. I must say that you are wonderful with a needle and thread. Do you think you could make me an evening gown for a very important function? We've been invited to Moreland Manor."

Violet made Alice Smythe a beautiful silk gown in peacock blue, which was inset with glittering beads. The colour complemented Alice's blue eyes and fair skin. It had taken many hours to complete, but the financial rewards had been worth it, which gave Violet great satisfaction. Apparently, Alice Smythe had been the belle of the ball, but Violet preferred helping their neighbours, who hadn't got lots of money to spend. They would work on the farm or provide meals in lieu of money, which meant that she got a reprieve from back-breaking work and was able to spend more time with her mother.

Violet's dressmaking services were soon in demand which meant she was able to give up her washing round: a chore she'd always hated and she gave her customers the courtesy of putting the termination in writing. It gave her particular satisfaction to put the envelope into Mrs Johns' hand as she was leaving the house. Mrs Johns looked at the envelope with the beautiful italic writing with disbelief. *How could a pauper write like this?* She was in shock when she opened the letter and rushed into the house, calling for her housekeeper.

"Mrs Brown, what am I going to do? She's not doing our washing anymore!"

CHAPTER ELEVEN
1929

When Lady Fitzroy asked her to make several outfits for her daughter, Violet knew it was because her Ladyship was too mean to pay the higher prices in London. Violet realised a long time ago that people who were well off wanted to pay as little as possible for services. The Fitzroys, like many aristocrats, had a London residence, as well as one in the country. During the summer months they resided in their country manor organising shooting parties and dinner parties. On their return to London they would then attend high-class social events, with the intention of finding suitable husbands for their daughters.

Mabel accompanied her daughter to Moreland Manor and they were in awe of their surroundings. The drive which seemed never-ending was lined with imposing dark conifers contrasted with the white trunks of silver birch trees. The manor had monumental, tall chimneys and ivy-clad walls.

They drove the horse and cart round the back to the servants' entrance, tied Lady to the railings and rang the large brass bell which hung above a double oak door. They were made to wait. It was a few minutes before a servant in a long black dress and white frilly apron came to the door.

"Yes, can I help yer?" She looked them up and down.

"We've come to see her Ladyship." Violet held her head high. "She's expecting me."

The door opened into the boot room which was almost the size of their kitchen and living room put together. There were coats hanging on pegs and boots and outdoor shoes lined up on the stone floor. As they were shown into the hallway, Mabel's mouth fell open at the splendour of the huge chandeliers which hung above a wide, sweeping staircase. The mahogany and black floor tiles shone and Violet thought about how many hours a poor girl must have spent on her knees, polishing them.

After several more minutes, the same surly servant came back and showed them into an elegant room which had dark green wallpaper with a bold pattern on it. In the corner was a small table with an overgrown Aspidistra and large fireside chairs sat either side of a roaring fire. Lady Fitzroy sat on a plush settee that had a high back, the epitomy of sophistication. Her grey hair was styled in waves to her sharp cheekbones and her pale pink dress had a band just below her slim hips. Her daughter, Beatrice, sitting alongside her, in sharp contrast wore a knee-length pleated skirt in grey and blouse and her mousy-coloured hair was scraped into a roll at the back of her head and she cast her eyes down, her hands resting in her lap.

Lady Fitzroy dismissed the servant with the wave of her hand. Violet took Beatrice's measurements discreetly; she had a somewhat round figure and Violet wondered if that contributed to her shyness; that and her mother's dominance. After the designs and fabrics had been discussed, and Violet's fees determined, her Ladyship had a condition of her own.

"I cannot possibly let my daughter come to your farm. You will have to do your dressmaking here. I will send my driver to collect you. It's not appropriate you coming here on your horse and cart," she said haughtily. "I trust this will not be a problem to you." She rang the bell to summon the servant and with the wave of her hand, they were dismissed.

Violet walked out with her head held high after nodding in agreement. She squeezed her mother's arm as she propelled her forward.

Ted was furious. "I agree wi' Ma, you should 'ave told her that we dunna want her money. People like them, think they can do whatever they want to the likes of us. Yer good enough to save her money, but our farm inna good enough! Tell her that you're not doing it!"

"I don't like it any more than you, but the farm only just pays enough and its better than me taking in washing." She touched her tiny belly which was starting to expand, "It's only until I've had the baby."

Violet watched as the limousine drove slowly up the farm drive and came to a halt on the yard. The chauffeur stepped out looking gingerly at his feet. She felt uncomfortable as he held the door open and helped her into the car. Although they drove in silence, she noticed that he frequently glanced at her in his mirror.

When she arrived at Moreland Manor, the servants were standoffish and stared as she made her way to the Blue Room, which she was to use as her sewing room. They resented it when Lady Beatrice rang for refreshments to be brought to them and that behaviour continued throughout the time Violet was working there, and unpleasant gossip was rife in the servants' kitchen as they expressed their resentment at waiting on her. They said mean things about her like, "I dunna think its right to wait on the likes of her!" and, "Who the blooming heck does her think her is? She ain't nobody. She's just a farmer! Lower than us!"

Then someone added that, "Even Maurice is put out 'aving to drive the likes of her about. He thinks it's beneath 'im; says he 'as to wash the car every time he goes to the farm and 'as to drive back wi' the windows open to get rid of the smell," and, "She's got ideas above 'er bloody station. She even talks hoity-toity."

Violet's school teacher had always corrected her grammar and taught her the importance of speaking correctly. He'd realised how clever she was and thought that she had the potential to improve her life; that was until that dreadful day when her mother had dragged her out of school. Even her own mother would correct her if she said words like "summat" in spite of speaking with a local accent herself. Violet also always took pride in her appearance and when she went to the Manor, she fashioned her hair into a neat chignon and wore smart clothes, which she'd made herself. She was glowing as an expectant mother, which made her more beautiful than ever evoking even more jealousy amongst the women.

Violet spent weeks going backwards and forwards to Moreland Manor and during that time she gained one admirer. One evening when her work was almost complete, she saw Lord Fitzroy talking to a tall dark haired man outside, whom she recognised as Mr Smythe, their landlord. Although the aristocracy tended to stick to their own, there was some movement between classes if business deals were to be done. When he came into the house, he heard Lady Fitzroy say that she would order the car for Violet.

"You don't have to do that, your Ladyship. I can drop her off on my way home."

"There's no need for that, Mr Smythe. I can walk."

He put his hand up to protest and looked towards Lady Fitzroy. "No, I won't hear of it. You cannot walk in your condition. Besides, the weather is changeable and you are likely to get caught in a downpour."

Lady Fitzroy said, "Quite, Smythe." She looked disdainfully at him as she spoke.

Mr Smythe had a green saloon car which wasn't easy to get in and out of, due to the running boards that ran along the car from the front to the back wheels so he held Violet's arm to help her into the car. On the way home he kept chatting to her despite her monosyllabic replies.

"How's married life? You're still a newly-wed; you're still learning. You could do with a man to show you a thing or two." He had a sickly grin on his face as he looked across at Violet.

"Stop the car! I want you to let me out!"

"Now don't be like that! I'm only having a laugh. Relax." He put his hand on her knee. "You don't know what you're missing," he chuckled.

Violet pushed his hand off and yelled at him, "Let me out!"

"I'll let you out if you give me a little kiss." He laughed at the horror on her face.

She tried to open the door but he was leaning over her and as his lips got near her face, she could smell the stale tobacco on his moustache. She balled her fist up and punched him hard in the face and he was completely taken aback. How could a tiny little thing pack such a hard punch? He'd been taken off guard and was unable to stop her climbing out the car but she fell onto the wet ground and hurt her knees.

As Frederick Smythe got out of the car, Violet shouted at him, "If you come anywhere near me, I'll scream and the people in those nearby houses will hear me. I'll tell them what you are, and everyone will gossip about you and you won't be invited to join any more shooting parties and no-one will want to do business with you. You've got no class. You should be ashamed of yourself! You wait until my husband hears about this!"

"That wouldn't be a good idea. I'm your landlord, or more precisely, your mother's. What a shame that your mum is getting too old to rent the farm! I must look over her tenancy agreement," he sneered. He then got back into his car and drove away.

Violet hobbled to her in-laws' house which was close by and was relieved to find Mary there alone.

"What on earth has happened to you? Your pretty dress is wet and dirty and yer knees are bloody!" Mary held her arms out to her.

Violet ran into her mother-in-law's embrace and burst into tears as she told her the whole sorry tale.

Mary fetched her dressing gown from her bedroom and brought it into the kitchen.

"Tek yer wet dress off and put this round yer. I'll make us a nice cup of tea."

Whilst the tea was brewing, Mary bathed Violet's knees. "I would've loved to 'ave seen his face when you punched him! He wudna have expected that. Yer right about 'im having no class. He married into money and it's his wife that holds the purse strings. I've never trusted 'im!" She poured the tea into a mug and passed it to Violet. "You mustn't tell our Ted cos he'll thump 'im and end up gerrin into trouble." She hugged Violet tightly and added, "I'm that proud of how yer stuck up fer yoursen today."

"I know you're right, but it's not the first time I've had to lie to Ted. It's not right. He's my husband!" Once she started to talk, she kept nothing back. She told Mary all about Henry Johns. It was a relief to share it with someone she could trust.

"Yer mother has gone up in my eyes. Good old Mabel!" She chuckled. "I didn't know that she'd gorrit in her. I would've loved to have seen her hit 'im wi' a stick! Yer too beautiful and that can be a burden. There are some men that think they have a God given right to tek advantage of women. Life is unfair. The rich have all the power, but we've got summat more precious than money. We've got love and yer canna buy that." She hugged Violet to her even more tightly and added, "Dunna worry about Smythe, he'll trip up one day. Now, yer said that you've only one session left and that should only tek an hour, so I'll come wi' yer and catch up wi' me old friend, Edith."

Mary couldn't keep the smile off her face. She felt like royalty as the chauffeur opened the car door and helped her out. Mary strode boldly up to the door and rang the bell and the same maid let them in, curling her lip as she did so.

Edith and Mary hugged each other tightly; they had seen little of each other since Edith had become cook, a necessity to make ends meet. When her employers were in residence Edith worked long hours, but when they went back to their London residence, she only had to cook for the skeleton staff that looked after the Manor in their absence. She was not expected to go to London with them, as they employed a cook there, and this arrangement suited her nicely.

Edith invited her friend in for a cup of tea. Her employers were out and, as Lady Beatrice would be otherwise engaged, she could take a little break.

"I've seen your Violet comin' and goin'. She's a bonny little lass. It's made tongues wag, I can tell yer." She chuckled, "The servants are more stuck up than their employers. It's all about class and the pecking order wi' them."

They chatted about family and the subject came round to Mr Smythe. "He meks me skin crawl, that man!" Edith's large shoulders shook as she shuddered. "How such a nice lady ended up wi' the likes of him, is beyond me. He's comin' here more and more and I can tell that her Ladyship dunna like 'im, but he's ingratiating himself wi' his Lordship. He struts around like he's the lord of the manor!"

They gossiped for a while before Edith had to get back to her duties, but she reassured her friend that she could wait for Violet in the servants' kitchen despite which as the servants came in and out, they gave her disparaging looks.

On their drive home, Violet's relief was palpable. She was glad that she didn't have to be picked up in a chauffeur-driven car anymore; she felt like a fraud. No wonder the servants were hostile towards her. She was much more comfortable with her normal mode of trans her horse and cart. She had excelled herself with the outfits for Lady Beatrice though and the money she had earned would come in very handy, particularly as she'd soon have to cut down on her chores as her pregnancy progressed.

"No wonder Her Ladyship is pleased. The ruddy skinflint! It would have cost her a small fortune if she'd paid London prices. The rich are obsessed wi' saving money but for the likes of us, money is a necessity to make ends meet and they know that, which is why they exploit the poor. It meks me blood boil!" Mary fumed.

"I'm glad you've finished up there." Ted snuggled up closer to Violet in bed. "I dunna trust any of 'em! They ride roughshod over the likes of us! They think they're entitled to whatever they want!" He put his hands on her growing belly, and felt the baby move. "I'm the luckiest man alive and I'll always protect yer. I'd kill anyone if they ever hurt yer!" he said earnestly.

Violet knew then that she'd been right not to tell him about Frederick Smythe and Henry Johns. She felt aggrieved that Judge

Johns passed judgement on others, but happily paid hush money to keep them quiet, knowing full well that they couldn't turn the money down. She felt a sense of injustice that his son had escaped any punishment for his actions. Sleep continued to evade her as recent events played on her mind. Mr Smythe disgusted her, not only was his behaviour inappropriate—he was old enough to be her father—but he was also a bully. His veiled threat left her in no doubt that it was blackmail. She knew without any shadow of a doubt that men like that had neither shame nor remorse and that their prestige and money gave them all the power. She'd learnt this knowledge the hard way and it was something she'd never forget.

CHAPTER TWELVE
1930

On a bitterly cold January morning, Violet gave birth to a son, weighing in at 8 lbs 2 ozs. Ted stared in awe at the wonder of new life as he gently held him in his arms.

"He's gorra lot of hair," Ted laughed. He walked over to Mabel and placed his new born son in her arms, and tears ran down her face as she held him to her bosom, reluctant to pass him back to her son in-law's arms.

"Come on now Ma, he needs 'is feed. He anna goin' to grow if he dunna 'ave his milk."

A few weeks later, John Edward Albert Higgins was brought into the Lord's fold when he was baptised in their local church, where Mabel's father had preached before he passed away. Mabel had not been to that church for many years but she showed no emotion. She only had eyes for the baby, and took him from his mother's arms as soon as the service was over.

"It's good to see Ma smilin' Vi."

"Yes, it is but she's getting a bit too possessive with John, for my liking. You haven't even had a hold of him this afternoon."

"It dunna matter, let her enjoy 'im. Bein' a grandma has purra spring in her step."

John was a healthy baby with a hearty appetite and his parents doted on him, as did the extended family. There were always helping hands to babysit. Violet thought she would burst with joy. Motherhood really suited her and Ted was the proudest of fathers but the change in Mabel was a joy to see. It was as if she'd come alive. She kissed and cuddled John at every opportunity and proved a willing and capable babysitter, meaning that Violet could help out more on the farm.

After a few weeks, John started sleeping through the night and waking about seven in the morning. This enabled Violet to help with the milking at 5.30 a.m. Ted had bought a few more cows which proved a good investment and she'd work for a couple of hours and then pop home soon after her son was awake. She knew that he was in safe hands. Her mother loved to see John's smiling face cooing at her from his cot on waking. This arrangement worked well and she was grateful for her mother's support and ignored her growing niggles when Mabel often referred to her baby as *Arthur*.

"If it gives yer mam comfort, then it dunna really matter," Ted soothed. "She's happy and we should be glad about that. I'm sure she knows he's ours, but she's gerrin' old and sometimes forgets names. She's a Godsend to us, especially now that the milking teks longer. Me mam and dad are always busy on the farm, so dunna get much time to come round, so let's just be thankful for yer mother's 'elp."

"I suppose you're right, just as long as she doesn't get too possessive like she did with Arthur, otherwise I won't get a look in with me own son!"

Life was good and Violet became a bit complacent; less guarded. However, when John was five months old, her old nemesis re-entered her life. Violet was busy doing housework when a familiar car turned into the yard, but thankfully *he* stayed in the car. It was Alice Smythe who tapped on the door.

"Is it OK if I come in? I was just passing and I thought I'd pop in to see how you're doing."

"Come in. I'm fine, thank you. Just busy with this little one." She smiled at her baby snuggled on her mother's shoulder.

Alice Smythe gave John only a cursory glance, before asking, "Please can you make me a gown?"

"I'm sorry but I've stopped taking on commissions for now."

"Oh no, that's a shame, I was hoping you'd do it for me. I'll make it worth your while." she gave Violet a beaming smile.

How could she refuse? "Well, I suppose it depends on what you want."

"Well, that's marvellous! Do you think you could come to ours? Only I'd like some curtains making too and I'm no good at measuring up, and you have such a good eye for these things. I'd really appreciate it if you could oblige." She clapped her gloved hands together with glee.

She noted the look that crossed Violet's face and mistook its meaning.

"Don't you worry about the travelling, Frederick will pick you up. It looks as if your little one would be in good hands for a couple of hours."

Violet had no choice but to be firm and insist on making her own way. She would never get in his car again. She dreaded the thought of going to his house, but she would take her mother with her. They could do with the extra income and Alice Smythe was so charming. She didn't make her feel inferior like Lady Fitzroy did. She knew that Ted wouldn't be happy but she wouldn't be taking on any more customers.

She was right about Ted. He was furious, "Can't yer see that she's tekkin' advantage of yer? Bloody money talks! You've gorr enough to do here."

Three weeks later, Violet, accompanied by her mother set off on the horse and cart, on a fine but misty morning. When John snuggled into Mary's arms, Mabel glared at her; Violet almost expected her to snatch him back. Mabel spent the journey with her arms folded and didn't utter one word.

When the Smythe's house came into view, Violet could barely breathe and her hands were shaking as she held Lady's reins.

The house and gardens were beautiful, albeit not on the grand scale of Moreland Manor. Huge iron gates with intricate finials on the top opened onto a long gravelled drive up to the house, which had a pointed window at the top and tall chimneys. There was a veranda on the front and the cream-coloured climbing roses that clung to the walls were out early, exuding a sweet smell. She closed her eyes for a few blissful moments as it evoked a memory of long ago. The house reminded Violet of the wooden doll's house her father had made for her when she was little. The garden had a big expanse of lawn, edged with flowering borders and Laurel and Rhododendron bushes in glorious shades of pink.

Alice Smythe spoke discreetly to the elderly gardener, "Please will you collect any horse droppings, Tink? We don't want them left on the drive," and added with a laugh, "I hear they're very good for the roses."

Tinker touched his cap. He knew how everything had to be kept spick-and-span, and how important appearances were to the *posh nobs*. He saw and heard a lot as he discreetly went around gardening from house to house, unseen and unheard.

Violet was relieved to see no car on the drive and relaxed further when her mother gently smelt the roses and smiled.

Alice Smythe led them in to a large parlour decorated with bold flowered wallpaper and adorned with expensive works of art. "We're going to a dinner and dance in London, where Frederick will be hoping to seal a business deal, so it needs to be very sophisticated. One has to dress to impress, if you want someone to do business with you," she laughed.

After taking Alice's measurements, Violet discussed the style of dress and which material to use, "Silk velvet is expensive and may be hard to come by. Perhaps we could use rayon velvet instead. No-one will know."

"But I would know," she wafted her hand in Violet's direction. "Oh, don't worry about silly little things like that. Daddy can get me the best of everything London can offer."

This only reaffirmed Violet's view that money could buy you anything.

Next they were shown into an elegant dining room which had a high ceiling and large windows on either side. A huge chandelier hung above a dark wood table, casting prisms of light around the room. They were in awe that the house had electricity, a luxury that millions of working class people couldn't afford. Violet was measuring up for the curtains and was still standing on the steps when Frederick Smythe popped his head round the door. She hadn't heard the car draw up and the shock made her wobble on the steps.

"Hello darling, you're back early." Alice spoke cheerily to her husband, but she couldn't fail to notice the look on Violet's face, nor the look in her husband's eyes when he caught a glimpse of Violet's ankles as she stood on the steps. However, she quickly dismissed it because she knew that Frederick was a terrible flirt.

CHAPTER THIRTEEN
1932

Violet and Ted were struggling financially and at times it was difficult to pay their rent. Their neighbours were too; they were all in the same boat. Farmers in particular suffered the after-effects from the war, which ended in 1918. Then when the stock market crashed in America in 1929 it added to the financial woes of the country.which lasted for years. Many tenant farmers struggled to pay their rent to their landlords, and had no choice but to pack up their belongings and leave. Frederick Smythe paid regular visits to the farm to *keep an eye on his investment* but Violet knew he was more interested in her than his money and his enquiries about her mother's health were patently false. On one such visit, he became more threatening.

"Clearly, your mother is not well. I'm not sure that she even knows what decade she's in," he sneered. "I think it's time we reviewed her agreement." He stepped nearer to Violet and said, "Of course, it might help if her daughter was a little kinder." He looked her up and down as he spoke.

"If you come near me one more time, I will tell me husband!" she said in a sharp voice.

He mimicked her and repeated her words in a childish voice. "You're so naive! Principles are all well and good, but they won't get you what you want in life. Times are hard and they are going to get worse. You won't be so high and mighty, then. You'll soon change your tune! Mark my words!"

He gave Violet a lingering look as he left. *By God, he did love a woman with spirit.* His wife's calm demeanour and willingness to please him was so boring. He wished she was as accommodating in the bedroom!

Later on, Smythe's words would come back to haunt her but, at that moment in time, in spite of being poor, she was happy. She had a loving husband and a child who was contented and adored by everyone. Violet loved to hear his deep chuckle when she tickled his tummy, and how he would shriek whenever she hid her face and then called, "Boo!" She couldn't live without him. She could only imagine the pain her mother had gone through when Arthur died, and although she was happy to see the sparkle back in her mother's eyes her behaviour was rapidly changing and was becoming more of a concern.

Mabel's behaviour had been deteriorating over the past two years and her possessiveness with John was causing problems. She was repeating herself more and would often ask the same question many times over. She was very forgetful and kept losing things. She was also becoming paranoid, particularly towards Violet. She would frequently cry, and accuse Violet of stealing. "How could yer? You've robbed me of all me money! I've got nowt!" Then she'd tip her purse upside down to show that it was empty. Sometimes Violet would be able to hold her mother close and she'd sob on her shoulder, but other times this approach wouldn't work and Mabel would lash out at her. Later, the contents of her purse would be found in various places, such as the tea caddy, or under her bed.

It was impossible to rationalise with her, as her mind was confused and her memory fragmented. Mabel often became emotional as she relived an event that had clearly affected her. She would be accusatory to Ted, saying that, "Yer took advantage of me, you bastard!" failing to recognise him as her son-in-law. Sometimes she said, "I'm sorry, Mother, I had no choice. I'm so sorry."

Violet had no idea why her mother was saying such things and she had never heard her use strong language before. Violet cried when her mother was in that distressed state of mind and she was unable to pacify her. She'd no idea if it had been a real event or not, but it was real to her mother and happening in the present! She would tremble and cry, rocking backwards and forward. Violet had a nagging memory of that day, when she'd hidden behind a chair, as a young girl. She remembered only fragments of an argument that she hadn't understood. She couldn't recall any details, but she remembered the intensity of it.

On one occasion, she had to intervene when her mother picked the iron up off the hob near the fire, to test if it was hot, on the palm of her hand. Mabel would have periods of being lucid and they could have a proper conversation, but then she would drift off in the middle of a sentence and talk about something totally unrelated.

Mabel's behaviour had an impact on their working life as Violet felt that her mother wasn't capable of looking after John anymore, especially because he could run off at great speed and he didn't see danger in anything.

Violet arranged for the doctor to come, although they could ill afford his fee.

"I'm afraid that there's nothing that can be done; it's senility. Just carry on as you are. She needs stability, but if she gets too unmanageable, then we'll have to look at sending her away."

"How can she have senility? She's only sixty-two years old! And there's no way I would send her away!" she protested.

That night, after Mabel retired to bed, Violet told her husband about the doctor's diagnosis, and reiterated that she would never send her away.

"If she gets any worse, yer might have to. She's becoming more difficult to manage."

She retorted, "I won't ever send her to one of those places! They might call them hospitals now, but it's not long since they were lunatic asylums! It's not fair. My mother has had a very hard life. Now's the time that she should be enjoying life, not living like this!"

As always, Ted soothed away her worries and they talked well into the night. They decided life needed to change and that Violet wouldn't be able to work outside anymore.

"I'll just 'ave to do the milking on me own. P'rhaps our Bill will give me a hand, but that can only be a short term solution."

A few weeks later, Violet woke up in the night, a mother's sixth sense kicking in. She went to check on John and discovered that his bed was empty! She rushed into her mother's room but her bed was also empty! The front door was open, but their coats were still hanging up beside the back door. She woke Ted up in a blind panic and they rushed outside, pulling their coats on as they ran. They checked the barn, frantically calling out their names and searched the outbuildings, the milking parlour and the stables. They looked in every nook and cranny, getting more desperate with each failed search. It was dark and they only had a gaslight to show them the way, although the light from the full moon helped a little.

Violet was crying hysterically and screamed, "John, John! Mother! Where are you? What have you done with me baby?" Tears streaked her pale face. Her voice seemed to be coming from elsewhere and she felt as if she were detached from her body. Her heart was pounding so loudly that she could hear it echoing in her ears.

Ted felt fear gripping his insides, but he managed to keep a calm demeanour. He tried to soothe his wife, "She canna have gone far, not wi' her bad legs. Dunna worry so much, she wouldna do owt to hurt him."

Violet screamed at him. "How can you be so calm? It's the middle of the night and they haven't got their coats on!'

They continued shouting their names, getting more and more desperate as they exhausted the search of the farmyard. As they went through the farm gate and out on to the road, Violet was screaming John's name, when Ted put his hand on her shoulder and put his finger to his lips. They heard a little voice calling, "Mummy, Mummy!"

They followed the sound of his voice, and found them near a pond adjacent to the farm, in their night attire, shivering from the cold. The full moon shone into the water, reflecting the image of her mother smiling, her long, grey hair hanging over her shoulders and John with tears running down his face.

"What the hell were you thinking of? It's the middle of the night!" screamed Violet. She was inconsolable.

"I was tekkin' him to see the ducks," Mabel yelled. "Who do you think yer yelling at? It's got nowt to do wi' you! Yer just jealous, 'cos I've gorra beautiful baby. Go home and leave us alone, or yer'll be sorry!"

Violet lunged forward in an attempt to grab John out of her mother's arms, but Mabel refused to let him go and hung on tightly to him. Violet became hysterical and clung onto John's leg for dear life. A tussle ensued, causing John to cry even louder. Finally Ted stepped forward and wrapped his coat around Mabel's shoulders. She was shivering hard. He spoke quietly to his mother-in-law and gently took the crying infant out of her arms, passed him to his mother and cajoled Mabel into coming back into the house with him.

Violet opened her coat and snuggled John inside it. He was as cold as ice. She cuddled him to her chest and could feel his heart beating rapidly next to her own as they clung on tightly to each other. She followed Ted and her mother into the house, but she couldn't bear to look at Mabel. She gave John a warm drink and went straight upstairs with him where she put him in their bed and snuggled up to him to get him warm. She was afraid to let him out of her sight. She knew that her mother had lost her grasp on reality and that she wasn't to blame, but all the bad memories that she'd buried, resurfaced and she felt pure resentment towards her mother.

Ted stoked up the fire as Mabel sat in the fireside chair and he made her a cup of warm milk, and when she became drowsy he assisted her back to bed. He sat on the end of her bed until she was snoring.

That night, with John snuggled up between them they decided that drastic measures needed to be taken.

The next morning, Mabel didn't seem to have any recollection of the drama that had taken place during the night. As she sat in the fireside chair, drinking her tea, Ted went to see his parents and discussed their predicament with them.

"Violet canna leave her wi' John anymore, but if she canna work, how do we pay the rent? We're only just managing to pay it as it is!"

"You will have to give up the farm, Son. I could do wi' the help and you could do wi' the support."

Ted looked at his father's weary face and he knew that it made sense.

"I know you turned it down before, but the cottage is empty. I know it inna what you want, but yer won't have to pay any rent," Jack soothed. "At least it will give yer a bit of breathing space."

When Ted relayed their conversation, he held her close to him, "I'm so sorry Vi, you dunna deserve this. I feel as if I've let yer down."

She could feel his cheek wet as he kissed her forehead. "We have to do what we can. You haven't let me down. You're a wonderful man, Ted Higgins. You are doing this because of me mother."

They gave three months' notice to their landlord and they took their stock, machinery, animals and anything else that they could use to Blackberry Farm. Ted and his youngest brother Bill had cobbled together an extension to the side of their new abode, made with stones and insulated with wattle and daub and it created a bedroom for Mabel and one for John. Violet scrubbed the black patches off the walls, and cleaned the place with vigour and made a fire to warm up the cold, dark space that was to become their home.

They only had room for a settee, a fireside chair and a table and chairs in the living area while the bedrooms were just big enough to take a bed and wardrobe so they stored their excess furniture in the barn.

Violet took a last look round the barn where Ted had kissed her for the first time, the place where he had proposed. It was a bittersweet moment when they left the only home she had ever known, the place where she'd lived for twenty-two years, one that was filled with memories of a beloved father and brother. Her eyes filled with tears when she stood by the big Horse Chestnut tree in the nearby field, where she and Arthur had collected conkers from the ground and climbed its large branches so many times. As the soft leaves rustled in the wind, she could have sworn she heard him calling her name; a whisper on the breeze. She rubbed her fingers over their names, Violet and Arthur and the date - March 1914 - which her brother had carved into its trunk almost exactly twelve months before he gave his life for his country. She knelt by the side of Laddie's grave and as she bowed her head, the unspilled tears, ran down her face. She was leaving fond memories behind.

However, she felt relief that her husband's family were close at hand to assist her with her child and her mother and she would also be free at last of Frederick Smythe's threats.

Mabel seemed blissfully unaware that she was leaving her home behind, the one where Arthur's bedroom was exactly how he'd left it; the shrine which she had been prepared to do *anything* to keep. Even though their new home was a replica of the one she'd started her married life in, she showed no reaction to it.

CHAPTER FOURTEEN
1933

Annie was born on a cold January evening, a sister for John just two days after his birthday. She was only six pounds in weight and was almost bald when she arrived. Ted chuckled at her lack of hair and screwed his face up as Annie screamed. "That's a loud cry for a little 'un," he said.

Ted took the screaming infant out of Violet's arms and stepped towards Mary, but his mother declined, raising her eyebrows and casting her eyes towards Mabel, foregoing the privilege of nursing her first granddaughter.

"There yer are, Ma, yer little granddaughter," he said, and placed Annie on her lap.

Mabel stared at her, repulsed, and yelled, "Tek it away!"

Mary picked John up and showed him his sister and he kissed her on her head but Mabel snatched John out of her arms and it was only down to Mary's quick reactions that Annie was prevented from rolling onto the hearth.

Tears slid silently down Violet's cheeks as she said quietly, "She thinks the baby's me. I told you: she hates me."

Mabel had developed a hacking cough, as a result of that fateful night, when she had taken John on a late night excursion. She was now unable to carry out the most menial of tasks and was completely dependent on Violet for all her needs. What made life even more difficult was that Annie was so completely different to John. She was a fractious and demanding baby and it seemed as if every time Violet was tending to her mother's needs, she would start screaming, leaving Violet feeling exhausted.

At first it had been difficult to adjust to their new abode, especially as she had to cook and live in one small room. She missed her range. However, it was easier to keep a watchful eye on her three dependants, and there was less financial pressure on them. Ted looked more relaxed and he was less tired.

Mabel was in her favourite chair, sleeping by the fire, John was playing quietly with his toys in the corner and Annie was asleep in her crib for a change, which lulled Violet into a false sense of security. Her eyes were getting heavy and she was fighting the urge to sleep, but she was instantly alert when her mother stood up. The back of her dress was wet, but she was oblivious to it and then, as if on cue, Annie started to scream.

"Come on Mother, let me help you to get changed," Violet soothed, talking gently to her, repeating her instructions. Annie was left to scream.

Mabel resisted, yelling, "Gerroff me, yer dirty swine!"

Annie's screams got louder, adding to Mabel's agitation but after a struggle, she was finally washed and changed.

"Lift your foot up Mother. That's it. Let me put your clean slippers on, and then you can sit by the fire and I'll make you a nice cup of tea."

Mabel lurched forward and grabbed a handful of Violet's hair and refused to let go. Annie's screams got louder.

"Hello, what's all the commotion about?" called Mary. Her mother-in-law had popped in for her usual afternoon cuppa and Violet breathed a sigh of relief.

Mary took charge of Mabel and helped her back to her chair and chatted away, although it was a one-sided conversation, and within minutes the older woman fell off to sleep.

Mary poured the water out of the kettle and made a pot of tea. "Drink that and then I can read yer tea leaves whilst yer feeding Annie."

As usual, Violet humoured her mother-in-law and let her stare into her cup, turning it this way and that, but Mary stopped abruptly and said that she'd do it another time, when Annie was settled.

"That will be never!" laughed Violet.

Mabel spent hours sleeping in the chair by the fire, but when she was awake, she would often have a faraway look as she retreated into a world of her own, and Violet wondered if she was thinking of Arthur, or perhaps her husband. She was refusing to eat and her weight was plummeting quickly and consequently she was becoming very weak.

It was now late autumn and the weather had turned cold, their bedroom window was iced over and Violet snuggled under the blankets for a few minutes longer, but she didn't have the luxury of staying in bed. She needed to stoke the fire before taking her mother a cup of tea in bed. She took care not to wake Annie who was sleeping in her cot. She peeped round John's bedroom door and he was sleeping soundly, his chubby little cheeks squashed up against his teddy. When she pulled the curtain across to the living room, she was surprised to see her mother up and sitting in the fireside chair.

"You're up early, Mother. Can't you sleep?" she enquired. "You must be cold sitting there in your nightdress. Never mind I'll soon get the fire roaring."

She picked up her mother's old woollen cardigan that had fallen on to the floor, but as she slipped it round her shoulders, she froze, stifling a scream as she touched her mother's cold, lifeless body.

Violet knelt in front of her mother and put her head on her lap as she cried big, silent tears. "I'm so sorry, Mother. I'm so sorry. I should have heard you get up. You shouldn't have died alone!" She rubbed her mother's hands, already cold, and added, "Please forgive me!"

Ted came in from milking, remonstrating about the cold. When he saw his wife clinging to her mother's lifeless body, he immediately took charge. He held Violet in his arms and smoothed her hair as she cried on his shoulder.

"I should have been with her," she sobbed.

"She passed away in her favourite chair, in her favourite place. That's a lovely way to go," he soothed.

"Why couldn't she have loved me like she did Arthur? Why couldn't she see that I loved her? Why?" she sobbed.

"She didna have a loving childhood and her life was shaped by her parents' religious views. She suffered great losses and it made her a bitter woman. You've been a wonderful daughter and I'm sure that yer mum appreciated yer care, even if she cudna express it. Now, I'm going to lay yer mother on her bed and get me mam and our Bill to come round. They can sit wi' yer and help wi' the children."

Ted eased Violet into a chair and then picked up the frail, little body of his mother-in-law and carried her into her bedroom, where he laid her gently on her bed. He covered her with a blanket and as he stroked her hair from her face, he whispered, "Rest in peace, Ma," before rushing round to his mother's for help.

Mary made Violet a warm, sweet cup of tea and Bill helped take care of the little ones. Mary's heart went out to her beloved daughter-in-law. She'd been such a good daughter but had received little love in return. A few hours later, they watched the mortuary van take away Mabel's body. Silent tears rolled down Violet's face as she whispered, "Goodbye, Mother."

Two weeks later, they held Mabel's funeral. The cold, grey day matched Violet's mood. It was a simple but moving service, where she was laid to rest beside her husband in the local churchyard. When Violet looked at the flowers, she noticed a small bunch of red roses, which simply said, "With love from H xx." She had no idea who H was, but she was pleased that someone other than their family had remembered her with affection.

Violet was left with an ache in her heart which she thought would never pass. She missed her mother even though her life had become easier without having to care for a frail old lady, but she felt guilty when those thoughts crept into her mind.

CHAPTER FIFTEEN
1933

A few weeks later, Mary came rushing into Violet's house and said, "Put the kettle on. I've got summat to tell yer!" Over their tea, she continued, "There's trouble in Paradise. Me friend Edith told me that, our landlord's missus has been checking up on that slimy husband of hers. As yer know, Tinker does the gardening for the local posh nobs, so he sees all their carryings on. Well, according to 'im, Mrs Smythe paid him his wages and told him that she no longer required his services. Olive Walker's been in Alf's shop crying that she's lost her cleaning job and she said that a For Sale sign has gone up." She stopped to take a sip of her tea. "Anyway, I dunna think he'll be bothering yer again. The bloody cheek of the man, keep turning up 'ere, he never did that before you came 'ere. I thought you'd got rid of 'im when you moved to our farm." She gave Violet a big hug. "I'd love to know what happened. It's about time he got what was coming to him."

They chuckled when they recalled the prank that Frank had played on him. Violet remembered it vividly. Frank was very astute and when he'd spotted Smythe's car again at their farm, he guessed that he wasn't there on business. He'd never visited his parents before; he didn't need to because they had always paid their rent on time. Frank thought it was a good job that Ted was working whenever Smythe called. He hated how anxious Violet became whenever he turned up, so he decided to teach him a lesson. Frederick Smythe mysteriously developed car trouble and the local garage charged him an extortionate fee to get his car going. They never let on about the potato shoved up his exhaust.

"That mechanic Len, said that it couldn't have 'appened to a nicer bloke," laughed Mary

Mary was right, they never saw him again. All the rents for the farms were taken over by an agency as the Smythes vanished overnight. Alf's shop was the hub of the village and the gossip mongers were having a field day.

"Well, I heard that he's run off wi' another woman and she don't want to stay here."

"Well, Ada, people dunna do a bunk unless they're runnin' away," said Alf.

"Old Bill reckons that she's buried him in the garden."

Alf laughed loudly, "She's only a tiny little thing. She's no match fer him! Besides she's a lady."

"Hell hath no fury like a woman scorned, Alf," Ada put her hands on her ample hips and gave him a knowing look.

I wuddna like to get the wrong side of her, thought Alf.

"Besides, Bill said there's a fresh patch of garden that's been dug, which he thinks is enough proof."

"Well perhaps they were spies," Alf chuckled.

The truth never reached the locals' ears because when the affair between Frederick Smythe and Lady Beatrice was discovered, both families returned to London. Alice Smythe went to live with her parents' and the Fitzroys to their residence in Mayfair.

Lord Fitzroy had found out about their affair, quite by chance.

Lady Beatrice travelled to London, under the pretext of meeting her cousin, Lady Ursula Fitzroy. She gave the two retained staff, at their Mayfair home, the rest of the day off. Her father unexpectedly went to London to sort some urgent business out and after meeting with his business partner at the gentleman's club, The Berwick, he took a chauffeur driven car to his Mayfair residence.

On entering the hallway he called out, "Roberts, where are you? Mrs Jenkins! Beatrice! Beatrice!" His tone was curt. He stormed across the long hallway, opening doors as he went, muttering "Where is everyone?" He impatiently climbed up the long winding staircase, but stopped in his tracks. He could hear a man's voice talking to his daughter. He followed the sound to Beatrice's bedroom and forewent the usual etiquette throwing the door open, just in time to hear Doctor Bennett, telling his daughter that she was *with child*. He was consumed with rage and demanded to know who the father was. He did not speak one word on their journey home and on arriving he went to his gun cabinet and unlocked it. He loaded a shotgun and actively sought out *the filthy swine*. Lady Fitzroy pleaded with him to calm down. She did not want him in prison for murder. Neither did she want the servants to find out. She was relieved when he told her that *the bird has flown.*"

The truth might never have come out if Alice Smythe hadn't taken a walk into the village on that fateful day. It was something she'd never done before. She entered the local shop, to find that her husband was the subject of gossip.

"It's a bloody disgrace, harassin' people when they're struggling," said Alf to his customer. "His car's been seen up at that farm so many times, an' let's face it, yer canna mistake that flash car, can yer? As if that family ain't been through enough! That farm's been in their family for generations and that little gal has worked her fingers to the bone ever since her lost her dad. I heard they were strugglin' a bit wi' her mother bein'ill and that's why they packed up and moved. It was a bit of a come down for 'em though. I hear that Smythe's been going up there, too! Now why would he be doing that, unless of course, Mary and Jack ain't paying their rent?" He carried on weighing out cheese as he spoke. "This country's goin' downhill, there's that many people goin' under, its time the bloody government sorted it out!" He shook his head. "Any road, he shouldn't be giving 'em grief. It just ain't right! Why can't he just leave 'em alone? It's not as if they're short of money!"

"You're right there Alf. She's a lovely lady but I dunna trust him, he's shifty," the rotund woman said with a shudder. "She probably knows nowt about it. He's a dark horse that un! You've got to count yer blessings, ain't yer? Cos some people have rotten luck! The poor little mite has just lost her mother, too."

Alice Smythe slipped out of the shop unnoticed. She'd been standing behind the shelves at the back of the shop and heard every word! She was still shaking when she returned home. She went to the drinks cabinet and poured herself a drink of brandy and then sent her cleaner home. She needed to be alone. Alice sat in quiet contemplation by the fireside, and in spite of the warmth from the fire, she felt so cold. Her face was as white as the lilies displayed in the elegant vase on the sideboard. She thought back to that day when she saw the look of horror on that little girl's face! She knew that their rent was up to date. They had always paid their rent when her father had been landlord. He had never had any trouble with them. So why was he calling there? She stood up and walked out of the drawing room, taking a hairpin out of her hair as she did so.

When Frederick came home, he found his wife in his office. She had unlocked his drawer and his papers were spread out on his desk. His insides tightened when he saw the false bottom to his desk laying in pieces, next to a hammer. Alice was eerily calm and her blue eyes bore through him. Her blonde hair hung loose over her shoulders.

"I know about your little love nest in London. I wonder how long it will be, before His Lordship finds out about it? I knew that you were trying to ingratiate yourself with the Lord of the Manor, but he only tolerated you because he thought your schemes would make him money, but don't you think that ingratiating yourself with his daughter is taking it a bit too far?"

Frederick was unable to speak.He hadn't expected his wife to put two and two together. She'd been brought up with wealth on her side and had never had to think for herself. She was very naive and unworldly and he hadn't expected her to be so devious. Her father owned a factory in London which made screws and it had profited immensely from the war by diversifying into making bullets and shells and her father's wealth had meant that she wanted for nothing.

"Always the social climber, aren't you? I should have listened to my father when he said that you weren't to be trusted and that you only wanted to marry me for money. I thought that he was being cruel, but he was right! He could see straight through you! I was so blinded by love and dazzled by your good looks that I didn't listen to him. I only wish to God that I had!"

"It's always about you! Have you ever thought what being married to you has been like for me? What it's been like, always living in your shadow? I've heard people talking, saying that I live off your wealth and that you married beneath you." His face was flushed.

"Boo hoo! Poor you!" she said sarcastically. "You've had a good life. You've wanted for nothing. Would you rather still be trying to work your way up the career ladder and still living in a two-up, two-down with your timid little mother and that drunken, good-for-nothing father? Now, let me think, what was your career path?" She paused for a moment, her blue eyes were piercing, "Oh yes, I remember, you were an odd job man. You'd already reached the peak of your career," her sarcasm continued.

"You sarcastic bitch! You're such a snob! I don't remember you complaining when we first met. You made it quite clear that you wanted me. You weren't so bloody refined then! After we got married, I found out how boring you actually are, especially in the bedroom. Why do you think that I had an affair? Wait, let me rephrase that, why did I *need* to have an affair? Do you know what it's like making love to the Ice Queen? Do you?" he yelled, his green eyes flashing. He was fighting back now. H e had a lot to lose. "Do you know that I've never seen you without your clothes? Whenever I touch you, it's under the covers, as if it's shameful! Beattie had so much love to give, she might have been naive, but she was willing to learn and so willing to please me! She was highly intelligent and we had some deep and meaningful conversations, not like you. You are only concerned with appearances.You have no idea about the world around you. *Daddy* has always protected you as he didn't want his precious little girl exposed to anything nasty. But do you want to know something? Those times spent in London were the best days of my life!"

His words were cruel and hurt her more than she could have imagined! "Now, you're just being cruel, you can't possibly love her, and stop being so vulgar! You shouldn't be talking about such things!"

"Of course not, My Lady, but what do you expect from someone that's beneath you! Do you know how patronised I felt when you created the job of landlord, when your father had someone looking after his assets already? It wouldn't look good with the locals and all your cronies from the charity board if I wasn't earning my keep, would it? And you're right, I don't love her but she made me feel good about myself, not like you do!"

"I've given you my unconditional love!" She was outraged. "I've always known that you had an eye for the ladies, but when I hear the locals gossiping about you, well that's a different matter entirely. What I want to know is why you kept bothering that little girl at the farm. I saw how pale she went that day when she was measuring up the curtains."

"Little girl? She's a grown woman and she has a spirit about her. She's got guts and by Christ, she's easy on the eye, but you don't really think I'd stoop that low. She's just a farm girl!"

"Of course, she's not in the same class as Lady Beatrice, is she? But your social climbing days are over. We will both be social pariahs when His Lordship finds out!"

All the tenancies of the farms were handed back to Alice's father who put them back into the hands of an agency. The conversation with her father was full of "I told you so" and "You should have listened to me." He immediately had their house put up for sale, wanting his money back. He reinstated his son-in-law to his prior position and reluctantly allowed him to live in their vast house. Although he was annoyed with his foolish daughter, he would do anything to make her life easier. He was happy that she was home, but he could barely tolerate his son-in-law.

Alice stoically stood by her husband, but they were no longer invited to social occasions, as Alice had foretold—Lord Fitzroy had seen to that. His Lordship made sure that everyone knew that the man was not to be trusted, but never divulged his reasons for saying so.

Lady Beatrice was sent to live with her Aunt Cynthia in Italy for a year, during which time a suitable home would be found for the baby, but finding a suitable husband for her would be a different matter entirely.

CHAPTER SIXTEEN
1939

On September the third 1939, Neville Chamberlain addressed the nation via the BBC Home Service. People gathered around their radios wherever they could, to listen to their Prime Minister announce that they were at war with Germany. There'd been growing concern throughout the country and across Europe that WWII was imminent. People had hoped in vain that another war would be averted. Many had been through the last world war, and had already lost too many of their loved ones.

Violet held her children close to her. She couldn't bear the thought of losing anyone again. The effects of losing her brother had lasted a lifetime. Although she couldn't clearly recall Arthur's face, she remembered the strong bond they had shared. Violet was glad that her mother wasn't here to relive another war; she'd barely survived the last one. Meanwhile Ted was worried for his parents, who weren't getting any younger. Farm work was already taking its toll on his father, who was getting very tired.

"Me Mam reckons that me dad never really recovered from the last war." Ted paced up and down as he voiced his concerns to Violet. "How's he goin' to get through another 'un?"

At night, in the privacy of their own bedroom, Mary cried in her husband's arms. "I canna go through it again, Jack," she sobbed, "I really can't! All those lost lives. All that hardship, for nowt!"

"Well, they never sorted it out proper the last time. We were younger the last time round and I dunna mind admittin' that it'll be harder this time. Any road, we'll get through it, lass," he said, stroking her blonde curly hair with his calloused hands.

Jack checked the air raid shelter left from The Great War, to ensure that it would survive another war. The RAF had purchased a munitions depot in the 1930s, only a few miles away in Staffordshire. They lived on the border of Staffordshire and Derbyshire and Jack feared that the Germans might try to bomb that facility. Annie and John sometimes went into the air raid shelter which was dark and damp and full of cobwebs. Annie relished the *spooky conditions* and would frighten John by telling him that *The Bogeyman* would get him. Sometimes, she'd put her gas-mask on, hide in there and jump out at him. Although Annie was the younger sibling, she was always more outgoing than her brother. She was fiery in temperament, the exact opposite of her brother, who always took the path of least resistance where his sister was concerned.

Jack was set in his ways and found the changes brought in by the government difficult to accept. "I dunna need no government telling me what I can grow an' what stock I can have. What do they know about runnin' a farm? If they send someone to inspect our farm, I'll set me bloody dog on 'em! I'll bloody well do what I want!"

"At least they've realised that if they want us to produce more food, then they canna be pinchin' our labour force. They're goin' to be payin' unemployed men and conscientious objectors to 'elp us, so that's good, ain't it, Dad? It means that yer can slow down a bit." Ted was referring to the government declaring that farming was a reserved occupation.

"Has yer mother been talking to yer? I wished you'd all gerroff me back!" he huffed. "I still dunna trust the government. The country went to the dogs the last time and we had food that we cuddna' give away and we were worse off. Mark my words, it wunna be any berra this time. They're all ruddy talk!" He went to storm off, then turned back and added, "And they needna bother to send any bloody conscientious objectors neither!"

Ted spoke to his mother, "I'm worried about me dad. He's not copin' wi' the changes we've gorra do." He looked at his mother's face and added, "Mam, yer look so tired."

"I canna sleep. I keep worryin' about our Bill. If only this useless government had made farmin' a reserved occupation when this bloody war started, he'd have been here where he belongs!" She wrung her hands. "Why wait fer nine months before mekkin' that decision? They would 'ave known from the last war, that if they want us to produce more food, they canna send our men away."

Mary cried herself to sleep most nights, fretting for her youngest son. Jack kept his fears to himself. He had seen war at first hand. He had fought in the first world war, until he was honourably discharged due to his foot being shattered, which left him with a permanent limp. Nothing could have prepared him for the horrors that he faced. Seeing his pals blown up, the exhaustion, the hunger, the noise. Fighting in muddy trenches where soldiers got Trench Foot and epidemics such as Typhus, yellow fever and the likes. Being plagued with scabies and lice.

They had both seen what war did to men. They'd seen neighbours and family who had been wounded or traumatised—that is if they weren't killed, either by a bullet or disease. Bill would have been unprepared, just like Jack and so many other young men in the last war. They were thankful that Ted would not have been accepted if he'd tried to join up, due to him having a limp; the result of a childhood accident. Their other son, Frank, worked in the munitions factory and had to live away from home, but at least he got to come home quite regularly. Mary had no idea how dangerous it was working in the munitions factory because they weren't allowed to talk about it; even the locations were secret. Their only daughter worked as a typist at the same factory as her brother so Mary was so grateful to have Violet and the little ones close by.

Violet was relieved that tanks and such like had replaced horses on the battle fields. She remembered vividly, her father crying when his beloved horses were sent to France, knowing the traumas they would face. She had always loved tending to the horses on the farm. She had been heartbroken when her dear old Ned had passed away. Although machinery was vital to deal with the increased yield, horses were still popular and more reliable.

The village shop was a hub of activity. It was where people gossiped and talked about the war and complained that goods were getting harder to come by.

"Mark my words, it wunna be long before the government bring in rations. The bloody Germans keep targeting our boats; they're trying to starve us into submission!" Alf predicted.

The topic of Moreland Manor was high on the list of gossip. The government had requisitioned it to be used as a convalescent hospital.

"I bet her Ladyship's not 'appy. I'd love to have seen her face," laughed Alf. He took off his glasses to wipe his eyes.

Mary was eager to pass on this information to her daughter-in-law. Violet wondered kindly how they'd have felt. "It can't have been easy to give up a beautiful home like that! I don't suppose they will want to stay in London with war on. I wonder where they'll go?"

"Well they've got money, so they'll have choices. They wunna have to slum it like the rest of us," declared Mary.

What they didn't know was that Lord and Lady Fitzroy had not intended to come back to Moreland Manor; their daughter and *that lying-good-for-nothing,* had put paid to that! Having their home requisitioned by the government gave them a valid excuse not to come back for the foreseeable future.

Violet felt such sadness for the evacuees. She couldn't imagine sending her children away, but it showed what lengths parents would go to protect their children. She discussed with Mary the possibility of taking on a couple of children.

"P'rhaps we can use our Frank or Bill's room?" queried Mary. "Frank wunna be coming 'ome as often now that he's savin' up to get married. Bill could sleep in the parlour, if he ever comes home on leave, but God knows when that will be. Or perhaps our Lillian can share her room, it wunna kill her to share for once. She's been lucky always 'aving a bedroom to herself just cos she's a girl. She dunna come 'ome that often anyway."

"Or they can sleep at ours, when they come back. I know it's a bit cramped, but we can work something out between us."

The following day, they went to the church hall where the volunteers and would-be hosts met the evacuees. They were determined to give a child a home where they would be loved and cared for. On opening the door, they were met with a cacophony of sound. Some children were shouting excitedly, whilst others were crying or standing quietly, huddled together. A woman stomped about carrying a clipboard and barking out orders, her green jumper hugging an ample bosom and her brown skirt clinging around her large hips.

Mary whispered behind her hand, "Ruddy Hell, she ought to wear a Nazi uniform!"

In the corner were two little girls with blonde pigtails dressed in identical blue dresses. They looked like twins, except for the fact that one girl was head and shoulders taller than the other. They clung to each other, their eyes darting round the room as Mrs Winters, the woman in charge pointed at them whilst referring to her clipboard.

Mary approached her and asked, "Can we tek those little girls home wi' us?"

Mrs Winters consulted her clipboard, "I'm afraid they've already been allocated homes."

"What do yer mean, 'homes'? Yer canna split 'em up!"

"I'm sorry, it's too late," she was striding away as she spoke.

Mary and Jack changed overnight as their son's tragedy became their own.

Eventually, Bill was allowed home and he held on tightly to his mother's arm as she guided him indoors. The horrors of war tormented him day and night and he would wake up screaming from his nightmares. He lost his appetite and was reluctant to get dressed, preferring to stay in bed with the curtains closed. Every day, Violet would tap on his bedroom door and sit on the side of his bed, and little by little she encouraged him to face the world again.

The sun was shining and he reluctantly walked to the stables with her. When Bill stroked the mane of Annie's young chestnut pony, a ghost of a smile passed his lips. When he was ready to talk, Violet was ready to listen. Raymond, the conscientious objector who'd been assigned to their farm, bore the brunt of Mary and Jack's anger and pain. They couldn't deny that Raymond was a very hard worker and an asset to the farm, a quiet, well-mannered young man, but they couldn't forgive him for not doing his bit for his country. It was as if Raymond had injured Bill himself.

To make matters worse, at this time Mary received a letter containing bad news. Mary tore open the letter, but she was unable to continue reading it for the tears in her eyes. When Violet popped her head round the kitchen door, she found her mother-in-law with her head in her hands crying. Violet gently took the letter from her hands and difficulty reading it. The words were blurred through her tears.

Dear Mr and Mrs Higgins,

It is with deep sadness that I have to tell you that my little cousins, Freda and Mavis, have been killed. The whole family were killed when a bomb hit their house, as well as half the street. The girls talked a lot about their time on the farm and how much they enjoyed it. They were hoping to come and visit you when this dreadful war is over. It gives us some comfort to know that they all went together. We can't thank you enough for what you did for them.

Kind regards,

Mrs Freeman

They cried together and John and Annie were inconsolable. The consequences of the war were becoming increasingly evident.

"Now you just 'old yer horses, Mrs! These are little children that are frightened and away from home. Yer canna dish 'em out like Jelly Babies!"

Both women locked horns, but Mary was determined to get her own way. Mrs Winters eventually backed down, on account of being called in every direction. The girls, Freda and Mavis, smiled at the two ladies with the kind faces and willingly held their hands. They were eight and six years old respectively.

It was decided that they would use Bill's bedroom. They knew he wouldn't mind giving it up for children.

John and Annie went to school with the sisters and they formed a close bond. At first, John was worried that he'd be outnumbered by girls, but they were nothing like Annie, and he was thankful that they gave him some respite from his bossy sister. John showed them how to feed the animals and they played hide and seek round the farm or they climbed trees and made dens in the woods. Sometimes John would pull them along on the wooden cart that his dad had made for him, and they would squeal with laughter, but it was a different story at night time when Freda and Mavis cried themselves to sleep.

A few months later a woman walked through the farm gate, with a battered suitcase in her hand. Her lined face lit up when the two little girls came running towards her shouting, "Mummy!"

"I couldn't stand it no longer without my little uns." She juggled the excited girls on her bony knees. "We ain't had any bombs as predicted and to tell you the truth, me and me old man, think it's a load of old baloney and it's just the government telling porky pies." Her East End accent was very evident.

Maureen Brownlow was like many others who believed that it was a phoney war. Many parents were desperate to be reunited with their children and were willing to risk the perils of Hitler's bombs in order to take them back home. "If any bombs get us, we'd rather go together."

A few weeks later, a young boy on a bicycle in a post office uniform knocked on the door. Mary's knees buckled when he put the telegram in her hand. Whatever it said, she knew it would be bad news.

She read it quickly. "It says that our Bill has been injured and is in a military hospital in France, but it dunna say what his injuries are."

Jack held her close to him, and tried to pacify her. "Well, at least it dunna say thar he's been killed in action"

Not knowing the extent of Bill's injuries, or if they were life-threatening, caused Mary and Jack to worry about the endless possibilities. The toll on them aged them and Jack, in particular, became very short-tempered. John helped around the farm, whenever he could get out of going to school. Annie didn't like working on the farm and would avoid it at all cost. She enjoyed reading and would have her head stuck in a book at every opportunity. One of the things that Annie excelled at was delegating!

They were sent a conscientious objector and, although they had no time for him, he proved to be a hard worker, and as Jack said, "Beggars can't be choosers!"

"We'd 'ave been under bloody German rule, if it'd been left to the likes of 'im! He's a bloody coward!" Mary remonstrated. She was thinking of her son.

Meanwhile, Lillian started coming home on her days off, instead of staying in the hostel provided for the munitions workers. Mary took solace in spending more time with her daughter, it compensated a little for Frank not coming home as often.

CHAPTER SEVENTEEN
1940

The dawn of another year came without any celebrations. The war was still raging and they hadn't had an update on Bill.

"Well, we anna had any more telegrams, so at least we know he's alive," reasoned Jack.

"I 'ope you're right, but you canna be sure of owt. There's that many of 'em being killed and injured, we canna be sure that they will keep us up to date," Mary fretted. "I just want to see 'im Jack! He's our youngest son, it inna right that a mother canna tek her child in her arms!"

Jack tried to comfort her but he spared her the empty platitudes. His own feelings were akin to his wife's. However, a few weeks later they received the news that Bill was convalescing at Moreland Manor.

"I canna wait to see 'im, Jack, but I'm scared."

"He'll be as right as rain when we gerr' 'im home," Jack soothed.

Moreland Manor bore no resemblance to the elegant Manor it was. Beds were lined up everywhere, except in the dining. Injured men were lying on their beds or were outside walki grounds or being pushed in wheelchairs around the garden. were playing chess or cards, whereas others were lying o staring into space. The sight of men with limbs off and of their bodies bandaged was almost too much for Ma clung on to Jack's arm as they looked around for kindly nurse directed them to Bill's bed, which the trepidation.

When Mary whispered, "Hello, Son," Bill turne

"Dunna look at me!" Bill buried his head dee

Mary made soothing noises and coaxed hi Bill was blind in one eye and part of his fac bomb. It took a great deal of willpower for gasping. One side of Bill's face was cove swathed in a bandage. Mary cupped his Jack wasn't as brave and walked awa outside, he gave way to tears; tears th

The trauma was evident in their

Violet was trying to keep up the spirits of the whole family and it was she, to whom everyone turned for support.

Shortly afterwards, when Ted and Violet were in bed, Ted asked, "Have you wondered why our Lil keeps comin' home on her days off? She used to come back once a month and now it's every week."

"Well, to support your mum and dad and to help out on the farm," replied Violet.

"No, there's more to it than that, I'm sure of it! She's never been interested in the farm before and now she canna gerr' enough of it. She dresses up as if she's on a night out, norra job on the farm. She's got her eye on someone, but I just canna think who."

Bill fell in love with his nephew and neice who were by now ten and seven years old. He laughed when Annie was direct and asked him what had happened to his face, and when she knew he was blind in one eye, she'd said, "So, you've gorra another one." He loved how children saw life so simply. He became devoted to them and whenever he saw them, they would run up to him with joy on their faces, Bill credited them and his sister-in-law for saving his life when he first came home, badly injured and depressed. Violet was a good listener and she seemed to judge his moods well. He would frequently talk to her about a nurse called Molly and he'd smile whenever he spoke about her.

One morning Bill came bursting through Violet's door, wafting a letter in his hand. "It's from Molly. She said that I ought to go as a volunteer, as I could be a great help to other men who were strugglin' wi' adjusting," he hesitated. "But I don't know, what if I don't know what to say?"

"That's wonderful! No-one knows better than you what it feels like to be depressed and traumatized and look at you now, you're an inspiration, Bill," Violet encouraged.

"I felt suicidal when I came home, and it's down to you always bein' there for me and listening. And the little-uns gave me a reason to live, and that Annie being a cheeky little bugger," he beamed when he spoke of the children.

"So think what you could do for them. Just give it a go AND you'll get to see Molly," she said with a smile.

"Molly's too good for me!" he exclaimed.

"Well, you must have made an impression on her to single you out." She smiled as his face turned pink. "I'll make some cakes and come with you if you like. It's the least I can do because you've been so good minding the kids whilst I get me jobs done."

Driving the horse and trap up the drive of Moreland Manor brought back some difficult memories for Violet, and she was pleased to have Bill by her side, but inside the house it bore little resemblance to the elegant abode of Lord and Lady Fitzroy. The sights and sounds of wounded men covered in bandages were not for the faint hearted, there were rows and rows of them lying in beds. Bill knew that many of the men had gone to war as naive boys and could never have imagined the horrors of warfare awaiting them, the noise, the exhaustion, the hunger and the fear as men lay dying around them.

Bill had been very reticent at being seen out and wore a wide brimmed hat that cast a shadow over his face but Violet's cakes were well received, and she was soon chatting with some of the men. Bill recognised some of them from his convalescence there and he started to feel more at ease. He played chess with a patient and was engrossed watching his opponent study his next move when he heard a familiar voice nearby.

"Well, that wound's lookin' a lot better now, James. We'll soon have you up and walking."

Bill knew that gentle, encouraging voice and felt his face go hot as a blush spread across his face. He felt as if rooted to the spot. His opponent took advantage of Bill's lack of concentration and laughed as he called out, "Checkmate!"

Bill tried to leave without Molly seeing him, but she spotted him on the way out and called to him, "Bill, it's so good to see you! You're looking really well!"

He felt shy as he stood before her and when Molly smiled that wonderful smile he remembered so well, he felt his heart flutter. She asked him again to think about coming as a volunteer, but he was unable then to give her an answer.

Bill did however start to spend more time at the hospital, and did indeed become a volunteer. However he ensured that it was while the kids were at school. He tried to spend as much time as he could with them. He was like a child himself when he was with his niece and nephew. Life was simple at a child's level. He played hide and seek round the farmyard with them and pulled John's cart with the kids in it, pretending to be a horse. Sometimes Violet would join in their games of hopscotch, skipping or football. Annie was fearless and would recklessly tackle her opponent to get the ball. She had never been interested in playing with dolls. Indeed, when she was four years old, they'd bought her a doll and Ted had made a cot while Violet had sewn a whole wardrobe of clothes for it, but she'd been more interested in John's toy cars.

On one such occasion, it was getting late and Annie wanted to play hide and seek and she knew that they'd soon be called in for their supper. She'd pleaded with Bill and John to play just one game with her. They were putty in her hands and it was futile to argue with her. Bill and Annie split up while John counted to fifty. She ran stealthily across the field at the back of the farm, and down towards a stream two fields away, determined to make the game last. She heard her brother shout, "Coming, ready or not!" knowing that he would look no further than the farmyard and grinned. He ought to know by now that she'd break the rules of the game.

A few days previously, while out riding her pony, she'd discovered a large bush that was hollow in parts and had some hay that had been flattened out like a bed and she knew it would make a brilliant hiding place. It seemed much farther away on foot, but as she approached it, she could hear a strange noise. She stood and listened to the panting and moaning noises coming from inside the bush. Worried that an animal might be hurt, she crept quietly towards the sound, but as she peeped through the foliage she stepped back quickly. There were two people lying naked on the hay and the man was sweating as he moved up and down on top of the woman, calling, "Oh God, oh God!" and the woman was moaning. She thought they were in pain. She was just about to run for help when the woman turned her head and she saw that it was her Aunty Lillian! The two lovers were so wrapped up in their passion that they were unaware of the child running for help and the consequences it would bring.

Annie ran into the yard shouting, "Help! Help!" She was out of breath.

Bill held on to her arms to slow her down, "Calm down! Tell me what's wrong."

"It's Aunty Lillian. A man is hurting her!" She was trembling as she pointed towards the fields.

Violet, ever the voice of reason, said, "Sit down Annie. Tell us what you've seen. I'm sure we can sort it out."

Bill and Violet passed a knowing look at each other as they tried to reassure her. During the drama, John had run off to find his grandmother. Mary was shutting the hens up in their coop for the night and quickly followed John as he hurried to the house and they entered just as Annie was telling her tale.

Lillian had been with Raymond. They were in love, but the fallout from their liaison had far-reaching consequences. The family disapproved of him, particularly Mary and Jack, who refused to listen to his point of view, his belief that it was wrong to kill and that violence breeds violence. Lillian pleaded his case and begged them to get to know *the kind, compassionate man* she knew and loved, but it was to no avail.

She packed her bags and left with Raymond leaving the whole family in shock. Not only had they lost a daughter and a sister, but also a pair of hard-working hands on the farm.

CHAPTER EIGHTEEN
1941

Lillian and Raymond married in the summer with Annie as their bridesmaid and Bill their best man. He had been a surprising ally as he understood better than anyone Raymond's reasons for being against war. He still had nightmares about young men with tortured faces knowing they were about to die.

"I anna going to the wedding and that's final!"

Mary was a pragmatist and reasoned with her husband, "I dunna want to go either. I feel sick at the thought of her marryin' that coward but she's our only daughter, Jack." She took hold of his hand and pleaded with him. "She wants you, her father, to walk her down the aisle. You'll regret it for the rest of yer life if you don't!"

"Why are you stickin' up for him? You dunna want her to marry 'im, any more than I do. You said it yourself, that he's a bloody coward and that we'd be under German rule if everyone thought like 'im!" Jack stomped across the bedroom, flaying his arms around, his tattoo of the Union Jack clearly visible on his forearm, something he'd had done when he was discharged from service in The Great War after being injured. "Why did she have to pick 'im?"

"She's in love, and love's blind. I just 'ope he treats her right. We've just gorra be happy for her."

Material was becoming increasingly hard to come by, so Violet altered her own wedding dress and made it simpler. The high-necked collar was replaced by a lower neckline and the dropped waist was made higher and cinched in, to show off Lillian's tiny waist and the hemline and sleeves were shortened. She made Raymond a navy waistcoat from remnants of cloth. He certainly was tall, dark and handsome. Violet added some pink smocking on the chest of one of Annie's dresses and made a pink sash that went round the middle with a big bow at the back. Lillian's bouquet was made from Lily of the Valley from the garden and her dark locks were swept off her face with curls rolled on the top of her head.

Jack had a tear in his eye and his limp was evident, as he walked his only daughter down the aisle. He was overwhelmed with mixed emotions. He was a concerned but nonetheless proud father as she held his arm. She looked stunning and so much like her mother did when they got married, except for the dark tresses which she had inherited from him. He smiled at his son standing proudly next to the groom with his distorted face.

The bride and groom looked wonderfully happy as they made their vows. All of Lillian's siblings had come to their wedding along with Frank's fiancée, Clara, and Bill's friend, Mollly. However, Freda, Raymond's mother, was the only member of his family who attended the wedding; his beliefs had come at a high price.

After the service Jack stood in the graveyard looking at his parents' gravestones and wondering what they would have thought about their granddaughter's choice of husband. He was deep in thought, when a woman's voice made him jump.

"Would you like a cigarette? You look as if you could do wi' one."

He quickly spun round but before he could answer, a lit cigarette was handed to him by a tiny little woman, dressed in a smart navy suit. He hadn't noticed her in church.

"Penny for 'em," she said.

"Trust me, yer dunna want to know!"

"Let me guess. You think that me son ain't good enough for your daughter?"

Jack spluttered but she quickly put him at ease. "I don't blame you for thinking that Ray's a coward. That's what most people think, including me own family but you're all wrong! It takes guts to stand by yer principles and Lillian has guts to stand by 'im. His father served in the last war and was injured, but he was a changed man. He went from being a loving husband and father to an aggressive drunk! Ray had to stop 'im from beating me to pulp and got a good hiding for it. He hates any sort of violence and believes that violence breeds violence and that differences should be dealt with diplomatically. Ray is a Christian and his faith is very important to him. He believes in the sixth commandment *Thou shall not kill*. He wants to train as a vicar. Just get to know him and you'll see what a wonderful human being he is."

Jack just nodded and offered her his arm, "We'd berrer get back inside, then."

The rest of the evening was spent dancing and singing and all talk of the war was banned for a few hours. Jack held Mary close as they danced cheek to cheek.

"I'm that happy to have 'em all together. I'm that proud of 'em," said Mary.

"We'll be doing this all again soon." Jack smiled at Frank and his fiancée Clara dancing cheek to cheek.

"I think our Bill will be next." She nodded towards Bill and Molly. "He says they're just friends, but anyone can see how they look at each other. I'm that proud of our Bill standing up at the front of the church like that. He's come such a long way."

When Lillian had stormed out the house after her disagreement with her parents, Freda had taken her in, but she had strict rules and told them that, "I don't want any funny business goin' on under my roof until you're married." But tonight they would return home as man and wife and Freda had given them privacy, by agreeing to stay overnight at the farm.

In the privacy of their own bedroom, Mary hugged her husband tightly, "I'm proud of yer!" she said. "Yer really stepped up!"

"Well, Freda put me straight! She's a good woman!"

"Should I be jealous?" she said as she held her husband tightly. She chuckled, "Don't lose yer way in the night, will yer love?"

"Dunna talk so stupid, there's only one gal fer me!" He spoke softly as he hugged her back. They talked long into the night about their families and a decision was made.

Freda had breakfast with them and looked troubled. She seemed to be in a hurry to get home. Mary insisted on her staying for another cuppa, sure she could persuade Freda to confide her troubles to her.

CHAPTER NINETEEN
1941

Several weeks after the wedding, Violet was in her mother-in-law's kitchen having a cup of tea, when Bill came rushing through the door.

"Aye up, where's the fire, son?"

"I've got summat to tell yer! A few weeks ago, when yer thought I was at the hospital, Molly and I went on the train to London to see a specialist."

"What specialist? When? Why?" His mother was alarmed.

"Me face, Ma! They're goin' to fix me face!" And he twirled her round the kitchen. "I'll need more than one operation, but when it's done I'm goin' to ask Molly to marry me." He looked thoughtful and added, "Do you think she'll say yes? What if she turns me down?"

"I'm sure she wunna do that," Mary smiled, "Anyone can see that she loves yer."

"Well I anna even asked her to be my girlfriend yet."

"Well get on with it then. Why wait until you've had your surgery? She loves you just the way you are." Violet smiled at Bill. "There's only one way to find out and that's to ask her. Go. What are you waiting for?"

When Bill had gone, Mary said, "I want to put sommat to yer. Me and Jack were talking last night and wondered if the four of yer would like to come and live 'ere? Frank ain't interested in the farm and he'll be married soon. Can yer see Clara livin' 'ere? She looks like a puff of wind would blow her away. She wuddna cope wi' farm life, she's a timid little thing, but then I anna surprised she's quiet wi' a father like hers. He seems a bit controlling to me. Any road, our family's falling apart, Frank hardly comes home and I reckon our Bill will be married next."

Violet interrupted, "I wonder if Bill's seen her yet? I hope she says yes."

"So do I. It would knock 'is confidence if she turns him down. Any road I want to keep 'im close and our Lillian will be moving further away soon."

"Moving where? Why?"

"I could see that sommat was up wi' Freda. They've had all sorts of slogans written on their door. She said that it used to happen before, but it stopped when 'e was working on our farm, but it's all started up

100

again. Some of their neighbours, resent 'im living wi' our Lillian, whilst their men canna do the same cos they're fighting. Raymond's gorra a job working fer the church and a house to go wi' it so they're all moving into it." She tipped some more used tea leaves into the pot and added some boiling water. She looked thoughtful as she said, "I'm sure that Molly will say yes and Bill will be the next to get married, so we thought that they could live in your house. It's near fer Molly's work and fer Bill to go wi' her when he's supporting the men. She'd be willing to 'elp round the farm too. It would be a start for 'em. It's gerrin' a bit small fer your growin' family."

Mary poured the tea away. "That's no good. I canna use them." She made a fresh pot of tea and used fresh tea leaves. "Drink up and I'll read your tea leaves."

Violet laughed as she thought of what Ted called her: "Gypsy Rose Higgins".

"You can laugh all yer want, but I'm always right. I was right about you 'aving another baby and that it would be a girl. I was right about a wedding and then our Lillian got wed." She held back the fact that she'd seen an imminent death before Mabel passed away.

Violet thought it was just coincidence and that it was easy to predict such things as a birth or a wedding. Nevertheless, she indulged her mother-in-law. She left a little liquid in the bottom of her cup, swirled the dregs round three times in an anti-clockwise direction, put it upside down to let the liquid drain out and left it for a few minutes. She then tapped the bottom of the cup three times with her finger and turned it over. She smiled as she watched Mary hold the cup with the handle pointing towards her heart and twist it backwards and forwards.

"There's going to be an imminent change for you," then she turned the cup to a different angle and said, "It says you'll be moving."

"Well, that's easy to predict," laughed Violet. "You know very well that Ted will say yes."

"That's it, mock me like our Frank and Ted do. Jack wunna let me do his 'cos 'e knows that I'm always right and our Bill's the same."

"Go on then, read a bit more," said Violet.

Mary turned the cup round and stared into the cup. She felt a knot form in her stomach. She got up from her chair abruptly, "I anna really got time, I think that's enough fer today." She scooped the empty cups up and swilled away the tea leaves in the cups.

Violet had a good relationship with her mother-in-law who gave her more love than her own mother had ever given her. She hoped that Ted would agree that moving in with his family would be good for all of them and the children would love it.

Bill knocked on the door of the little terraced house and waited anxiously. When Fred Smith opened the door, Bill introduced himself.

"Aah, we meet at last. I've heard all about yer, but our Molly is at work."

"I know she is. It's you I came to see," he said nervously.

"Well you'd berra come in, lad," then he called to his wife, "Put the kettle on, Iris, we've gorra visitor."

Bill removed his cap and gripped it in his hands, whilst he sat at the kitchen table. Iris put a large brown earthenware teapot on the table and offered him a slice of homemade cake. She was a well-rounded woman and she had a pretty face so like her daughter's.

In spite of being small in stature, Fred had a surprisingly deep voice. "Spit it out lad, you've obviously got summat on yer mind."

Bill said, "I'm here to ask permission fer your daughter's hand in marriage, Mr Smith. I know I ain't much to look at wi' me face bein' like this, but I'm 'aving an operation soon, and I really love her!"

Fred spoke sternly. "Dunna talk so bloody daft lad! Our Molly dunna care about yer face! Of course you've got me permission," and at that he stood up and shook his hand firmly. "There's a war on, lad! You'd berra gerron wi' it!"

Bill was filled with trepidation as he walked up the long drive to Moreland Manor. He stood at the entrance and took deep breaths before entering. He found Molly dressing a soldier's wound and waited for her to finish.

"Molly, I know yer busy, but can yer spare me five minutes? I canna wait any longer."

She saw such pleading in his eyes and her heart beat quickly. She wondered why he looked so agitated and asked the Sister if she could take a short break.

Bill waited anxiously for Molly under the shade of a large beech tree. He smiled when he saw her walking towards him and the instant she came close, he could wait no longer.

He took hold of her hands and looked into her anxious face. "I need to say summat to yer. Summat I should've said before!" He had tears in his dark eyes as he said, "I love yer Molly! I love yer wi' all me heart!" and before she could respond, he took her into his arms and kissed her.

Molly responded eagerly to his kiss and when they pulled away, she said, "What took yer so long?"

"I didna' think you'd want an ugly mug like me to kiss yer, that's why," he said with his head bowed.

Molly cupped his face in her hands and looked him in the eyes as she gently said, "You are the most beautiful man I've ever met, Bill Higgins! I dunna see yer injuries, I see YOU!" and at that, she kissed his damaged face to emphasise the point. "I love you fer all that yer are - good and kind and loving!"

When Bill dropped on one knee and asked her to become his wife, she didn't hesitate to respond. "Of course I will! I thought you'd never ask!" Then she laughed.

Bill had two successful operations on his face, and shortly after his recuperation, he married his beloved Molly in a very intimate ceremony at the village church. Their wedding gave both families a sliver of light in the dark days of war. The bride wore a simple, fitted blue dress, which came below the knee and with square shoulders and a slim-fitting waistline. Bill wore his brown army uniform. They married at lunchtime and the families had a light lunch at the farmhouse, followed by cake and afterwards they made their way to their matrimonial home.

Molly loved farm life and whenever she wasn't at work nursing the sick, she would help out on the farm. She was undeterred by the harshness of living in the worker's cottage. The move into the main house had worked well for Violet and Ted. The children loved the fact that there was more space and that they were able to spend more time with their beloved grandparents. Hide and seek remained one of their favourite games and when it was too cold and hazardous to hide around the farm, the house provided many hidey holes. Another favourite game was marbles. There was a dip in the kitchen floor and they would lie on either side of it and roll the brightly coloured glass balls into the dip, but they often missed their target and the marbles would roll across the floor.

Whenever Mary stood on one of the stray marbles, she would shout, "You kids will be the death of me one of these days!" but she would say it with a little smile on her face. She loved to see them playing. She reckoned that they'd be burdened with adult life soon enough.

Jack would chuckle when he saw how Annie always got the upper hand when she played games with John. They would start off with a little bag of marbles each, but by the end of every match, Annie's bag was bulging with marbles. It was the same with board games and cards; she always seemed to win. Jack suspected foul play because Annie outwitted her brother every time. John was steady and hard-working and always ready to lend a helping hand, but Annie seemed to get out of any situation with her guile.

Jack was becoming more despondent week by week. He was by now almost fifty-six and the hard work and harsh conditions were taking their toll on his body. He knew that their family had been relatively unscathed by the war, apart fom their son's catastrophic injuries. Still, although they were able to produce their own food, they had to get permission to kill their own animals for their own consumption, as they were subject to rations like everyone else. The military took thousands of acres of land throughout the country, and Jack called them, "Thieving' bastards!"

The children hadn't witnessed any bombings at first-hand, but they had never forgotten that the two little girls who'd stayed with them, had been killed by a bomb on their return home.

Mary tried to get him to look on the bright side. "Well, let's 'ope that now the Americans have joined the war, it'll soon be over. Besides, we've gorra lovin' family and beautiful grandchildren and another one on the way.Who'd have thought that our Bill could be so 'appy. He's that lookin' forward to becomin' a father. Come on, love, chin up, we've gorra lot to be thankful for."

CHAPTER TWENTY
1942

The preparations for Christmas were in full swing and the children followed their usual routines of picking holly and fir cones and making decorations from them, and they excitedly hung the paperchains from the wooden beams. Violet was busy sewing and Mary in knitting presents while Ted made toys from wood. No-one minded that money and supplies were in short supply, because everyone was in the same situation. Neighbours and friends rallied round each other, pooling their skills and resources.

Christmas saw all the family come together. Everyone was cooing over little Elsie who chuckled at anyone that looked at her; Bill was the proudest of fathers.

Mary noticed Jack and Ted talking in the corner and heard them discussing the war.

"I thought that when the Americans joined, it would soon be over, but it's been a year and we're no nearer to seeing those bloody Germans off now, than we were then," moaned Jack.

"I think if the Japs 'adn't attacked Pearl Harbour, and Winston Churchill 'adn't leaned on Roosevelt, they would never have joined in."

"I told yer that the subject of the war is banned. Now come and join in the celebrations," Mary poked her finger in their direction and warned. "Not one more word about the war or else there'll be trouble."

They kitchen table was extended, so that the whole family could sit around it. Mary and Violet cooked a chicken for Christmas dinner and followed by a Christmas pudding, which in spite of being a wartime special, consisting of grated carrots and potatoes, was surprisingly good.

When they'd finished eating, Frank stood up and banged his spoon against his glass. "I've gorra announcement to make. Me and Clara got wed two days ago. We didna want any fuss, so we got married at the registry office and grabbed two witnesses off the street."

After his announcement, the room fell silent and then everyone was talking over one another. Frank saw the look of shock on his mother's face and took her off into the living room.

"Mum, I know yer upset, but we found out that Clara is expecting and we couldn't wait. Yer know what her dad's like and we didna want him to find out and it would've taken too long to arrange a church wedding. Besides, Clara's very shy and dunna like being the centre of attention."

Mary took him in her arms; she'd forgive her children anything.

They returned to the kitchen and after the pots were washed and cleared out of the way, they made a pot of tea,

Frank called out, "Come on, Mum, read our tea leaves. Tell us how many grandchildren you're going to 'ave."

Mary declined. She was unusually quiet. She'd made her mind up, after reading Violet's tea leaves, to never look into the future again. "Let's play games instead. Who wants to play Happy Families?" she called.

When Annie won two games of Happy Families and three of Snap, Frank protested.

"Come on Annie, play me," Frank chuckled. "I know all the cheats so yer canna beat me."

Everyone laughed when she threw the cards down and refused to play any more. They all sang Christmas carols and then the talk turned to the children's imminent birthdays and John becoming a teenager.

"You'll be finding yerself a girlfriend when yer a teenager," teased Frank.

"I wunna be botherin' wi' girls. I'd rather go out wi' me mates!" he replied, going red in the face.

"You'd berra put on yer running shoes then, or else that Cynthia will catch you," chuckled Bill as he ruffled his hair.

Annie spoke up, "I'm going into double figures this birthday, but I wunna be botherin' wi' boys. They smell!" To which everyone started to laugh. As usual, Annie managed to take the attention away from her brother.

The family gathered again to bring in the New Year and they were full of optimism that 1943 would see the end of the war. They drank to freedom and to a future without fear, to happier times ahead, but little did they know that fate had other ideas.

At the start of the year there were two birthdays to celebrate, first John's and then, two days later, Annie's. For John's birthday, his grandmother had knitted a blue tank top and Violet presented him with his first pair of long trousers which she'd sewn from remnants left after making the blackout curtains. John looked very smart in his new clothes and shyly gave an obligatory twirl. His uncles teased him again about the girls chasing him and John blushed to the tips of his dark hair.

Ted had fixed up the old cart, which had seen better days and John beamed all over his face when he saw it updated and improved. Violet and Mary had saved up their coupons so they could have a nice tea party and made a birthday cake, but that would be postponed until the weekend when they would have a joint celebration. After John had finished opening his presents, everyone sang "Happy Birthday" and then Ted took him outside into the yard where he put a set of keys into his hands.

"Are yer ready for your first lesson on how to drive a tractor?" He laughed at the look on John's face, "When you've mastered how to drive it, yer can only drive it if one of us are there. You'll be an expert by the time yer old enough to drive properly." Ted smiled at the pleasure on his son's face.

John's face went red with excitement and he grinned from ear to ear. He jumped up into the tractor as quick as a flash and was waving furiously to his assembled family as he went off with his dad to practice. It was the best birthday present he could have had!

"It's not fair, just 'cos I'm a girl!" Annie refused to wave to him and remained sullen with her head down.

Mary laughed at her granddaughter. "Why would yer want to ride a tractor when yer dunna like farm work? Just be patient and see what your birthday brings." She knew that asking Annie to be patient was like asking the birds to stop singing.

Two days later it was Annie's birthday. Her grandmother had knitted her a lemon cardigan and Violet had made her a dress in the latest fashion - cream with a dropped waist, little puffed sleeves and a Peter Pan collar. She'd also made a lemon headband to match her cardigan, which kept her long blonde hair off her face. Annie was thrilled with her clothes which fitted a treat and she had no reservations about giving *a twirl* and she sashayed up and down like a model, hand on hip and head held high.

"She'll go far, that one. She's got such confidence and I canna see 'er kowtowing to any one!" observed her grandmother. Never was a truer word spoken.

Annie was then led outside into the barn, where her face wrinkled with puzzlement at the lumpy shape hidden under sacks. She squealed with delight at the sight of a bright red bike. Ted and Jack had found an old bike frame at the back of one of their old sheds. With a lot of elbow grease, they'd got it sorted. They then got a couple of bicycle wheels in exchange for some meat off their farm. There were always people who could get hard to come by items, if you asked in the right places. Ted had painted the frame in pillar box red, but Annie didn't care that the brushstrokes were clearly visible. She loved it! The seat dipped and was like a little saddle, which Violet had buffed up with saddle polish. Annie wasted no time in trying the bike out and they laughed as she wobbled around the yard. Ted put his arm round Violet as they watched on with pride. They still made a handsome couple.

These memories would stand the test of time.

CHAPTER TWENTY-ONE
1943

After a brutally cold and arduous winter, spring finally arrived, bringing with it new life. Fresh leaves were growing on the trees and shoots were peeking through the hard ground, as spring flowers emerged. The sights and sounds of spring brought a feeling of hope that things were about to get better. Lambing season kept them all busy and the menfolk had little sleep whilst they helped the ewes having difficult births.

When Ted brought in a lamb that had been rejected by its mother, to warm by the fire, Annie rushed to hold him. She was smiling as her mother passed a bottle of milk to her and asked her to feed it. She continued to mother the lamb until he was big enough to fend for himself.

"Can we keep 'im as a pet?" she begged her father, "I dunna want 'im to go fer meat!"

Ted tried to put her off but Annie was not someone to be fobbed off easily, and she could wind him round her little finger.

Ted joked with Violet that he'd be bankrupt if Annie got her way with all the lambs she nurtured, but he did allow her to keep the one that she named Woolly. Woolly followed Annie around and she would take him with her wherever she went round the farm. She informed her parents that she was going to be a vegetarian.

"Dunna talk so daft, yer canna 'ave a vegetarian farmer," Ted laughed.

"I'm norra farmer," retorted Annie, "And I never will be!"

Soon spring was over and was followed by a long, hot summer. The weather was perfect for haymaking and Jack, Ted and John spent hours gathering in the hay. Jack loved working alongside his eldest son and grandson, and he was looking less haggard now that he had extra help on the farm. Violet always volunteered to take the refreshments to her menfolk, she loved walking across the fields with the patchwork of colours and feeling the crops tickle her legs as they swayed in the gentle breeze. She couldn't help but smile whenever her beloved husband came into view, with his cap on his head and his blond hair sticking out of it. He made her heart sing, just like he had in the beginning.

August was coming to an end, as was haymaking. Violet looked out of the kitchen window when she heard the tractor chugging as it came into the yard, and saw John jump down from the hay bales on the trailer and run towards the house.

"Here come the workers wi' no time to waste," laughed Mary. "I'd berra hurry up wi' the brew."

Minutes later John rushed into the kitchen, his face flushed and saying, "I'm starving!"

Jack who had followed him in, ruffled his grandson's dark hair and, smiling, said, "You're always hungry, that's cos yer a growin' lad."

"Dad said he wunna be long. I told 'im to wait fer me before unloading them bales." He turned to his granddad and added, "Yer know what he's like so we'd berra hurry otherwise he'll be doing them himself."

The table was laid with homemade bread, cheeses and ham, and homemade pickle. Mary made a pot of tea, reusing the tea leaves from earlier. John ate his lunch so quickly that he hardly chewed it.

Violet laughed and said, "Slow down, you'll get indigestion! Anyway, where's your father got to? His drink's going cold." She peered out of the window and could see the tractor in front of the barn but no sign of Ted. "John, will you please go and see what your father's up to?" She shook her head and said, "What shall we do with him?"

She watched John through the window sauntering over to the barn, hands in his pockets and nodding his head from side to side as he whistled a tuneless whistle. He was quite the young man now and Violet felt such pride for how her son had turned out. He was hard-working and steadfast and had such a happy nature. He was never happier than when he was working alongside his father and grandfather on the farm. She smiled contentedly, but seconds later she froze with fear when John's whistling stopped and was replaced with a blood curdling scream!

They hurried outside towards the sound and saw Ted's feet sticking out from under a load of bales and John frantically throwing them off him. Annie was just coming through the yard on her beloved bike and heard the commotion and set off at breakneck speed. Although Annie didn't know what was happening, she knew it was serious and she was willing Molly to be in.

Molly tried to resuscitate Ted's lifeless body by pressing on his chest and instructing Violet to blow in his mouth. When the ambulance arrived, thanks to Annie cycling to the red phone box in the village, it was confirmed what they already knew. Annie clung to her father's body begging God to help him, reminiscent of a ten year old Violet, all those years ago. John lay on the ground and snuggled into his father, hay clinging to his hair and clothes as silent tears ran down his face. He knew that Annie's prayers were futile.

Mary clung to Jack, tears soaking his shoulder whilst he remained devoid of any emotion, unable to digest the fact that their firstborn son was dead. They all prayed for a miracle that when Ted's still body arrived at the hospital, some sign of life would be detected. Bill and Molly took charge of the situation and helped Violet into the ambulance, assuring her that they would take care of everyone. As the white ambulance drove slowly over the uneven drive out of the farm, Violet held on to Ted's lifeless body, already turning cold. Her violet blue eyes were never more beautiful than now, luminescent with the tears about to fall. The eyes that had mesmerised Ted and made him fall in love with her.

CHAPTER TWENTY-TWO
1944

"It's freezing in 'ere, Mum!" Annie had her arms folded with her hands tucked under her armpits to emphasize the point.

Violet fetched a blanket and said, "Wrap this around you. I'll go and make a hot water bottle."

John declined the offer. "I dunna need a hot water bottle." He glared at his sister. "You should be used to livin' in a cold house, it wanna warm at the farm."

"At least we always had a fire there!" Turning to her mother Annie cried, "I HATE it 'ere, Mum. Why did we have to leave the farm?" She clung to her mother.

"You know why we 'ad to leave the farm!" John replied angrily. "You know that it wanna Mum's decision. She had no choice!" Then more gently he said, "We all wish we were back at the farm and that Dad were still here, but we've just got to get on wi' it the best we can."

John was right. It hadn't been her decision. She'd known that her in-laws had lost all interest in running the farm and had struggled to come to terms with the loss of their eldest son, but their decision had still come as a shock.

Mary had been full of sorrow on the day she'd told Violet that they couldn't carry on. She'd said, "I'm so sorry Violet, but we canna do it any more! We canna keep our heads above water. I knew when we gorra letter telling us they wanted to modernise the farm, that they'd put the rent up."

Jack had stomped about the kitchen calling them "Greedy bastards!" and informed her that they were going to live on a smallholding near to Lillian and Raymond. Violet had felt numb ever since that fateful day when her beloved husband had passed away, but remained strong for everyone else. Then that night she'd finally given way to grief; it had engulfed her. She'd held Ted's pillow to her face and breathed in the smell of him, soaking his pillow with the tears that flowed. She had no idea how she was going to live without him and how she was going to tell the children they had to leave the farm.

The following morning she'd felt tired from lack of sleep, but had walked to the village shop where she'd shared her predicament with Alf. He'd heard of a man called Harold Smith through a friend, who had acquired a village shop and Post Office, aptly named The Village

Store. He was a widower and had recently moved from down south and didn't know anyone. It was twenty-seven miles away, just across the Derbyshire border.

She'd immediately had a good rapport with the shopkeeper and Harold had given her a job straight away. He had a heart-warming smile and a ruddy complexion. He wore his greying hair combed over to the side to hide his balding head and his hazel eyes looked over the top of his dark rimmed spectacles, which were perched on the end of his nose. Violet noticed that he had a habit of taking a pipe out of his pocket and sucking on it unlit, before putting it back in his pocket moments later. He'd told her about a vacant house and had taken a card down off the noticeboard and given it to her, it read THREE-BEDROOMED TERRACED HOUSE FOR RENT. She'd taken the card with her to the phone box and dialled the number on it. The landlord had shown her round and within two weeks she had the keys to number 5 King Street. They'd taken her mother's furniture from storage at the farm and installed it in their new home. It was old-fashioned but it would have to do. It was a very sad day when they said their goodbyes to Ted's family and the farm. However, when they'd first moved to King Street, they kept switching the lights on and off, fascinated at having instant light. The other benefit was that the lean-to housing the outside toilet had corrugated iron roofing so at least they didn't get wet when they used it.

"Annie interrupted her thoughts. "Mum, are you listening? I said, I'm hungry," she looked longingly at her mother.

Violet made some dripping on toast and sprinkled salt on the top and carried it out of the kitchen on a tray with a cup of very weak cocoa.

"We had drippin' last night and the night before!" She didn't attempt to hide her disappointment and when she sipped her drink, she said, "This is disgusting, Mum! It dunna taste like cocoa."

"There's a war on, Annie, in case yer hadn't noticed. Mum's doin' her best. At least we have summat to eat."

Violet noticed that John was becoming increasingly intolerant of Annie's behaviour. He looked so sad. "I get paid tomorrow," she said. "I'll get some coal and then we'll have some fish and chips. How does that sound?"

Annie grinned from ear to ear, but John looked anxious. "Mum, dunna get overspending, you've got rent to pay."

Violet smiled. John was so like his father in his ways. "Don't you get worrying about money; you'll have that to do soon enough."

The bent figure of the coalman was whistling as he climbed down from his cart. He opened up the wooden trap door to the cellar and was tipping a second sack of coal in, when he heard an alarmed voice calling after him.

"Sid, stop! You've made a mistake. I can't afford two!"

"Dunna worry yer pretty little head, I've only purra bit extra in, it's only slack but it'll keep yer goin' a bit longer."

Violet shook her head and tears filled her eyes.

Sid was spellbound by her lovely eyes. "I've gorra daughter about your age and I wudna like her to be cold," Sid kissed her cheek and grinned, "That's from me missus. She said to thank yer fer the pie," he chuckled. "You're a berra cook than she is," he said conspiratorially.

When the children came home from school, they laughed to see a black imprint of a kiss on her cheek.

John said, "I guessed the coalman liked the pie then, Mum," and they all laughed.

That night, they ate fish and chips by a blazing fire and later they filled the tin bath with hot water. Annie went in the bath first, then John and finally Violet. When they were in their pyjamas, they played Monopoly, which seemed never-ending and Annie, as usual, won most of the properties.

"Our Annie will go far," John laughed. "She'll end up rich with her devious ways. She wunna be slummin' it like the rest of us."

Good days like this helped them to get through the bad ones, of which there were many.

Their home was a mid-terraced house, joined by Fred on one side and Audrey on the other.

Fred was an elderly widower, who seemed to live in his flat cap and a pipe in his mouth. He grew vegetables in his garden and encouraged John to grow their own, although John didn't have Fred's green-fingers. He would often give Violet a cabbage or cauliflower and she would make him a pie or some soup as a thank-you.

Audrey was a vivacious, full-figured woman with a mane of red hair and a devil-may-care attitude. She had three children—James, David and Freda—who were of similar ages to John and Annie and they became firm friends, as did Violet and Audrey. Later on, the two women were to seek solace in each other when they shared the same heartbreak, which was to have far-reaching consequences.

CHAPTER TWENTY-THREE
1944

Freda was playing in Annie's bedroom whilst Violet was preparing lunch, when a banging on the door made her jump. She ignored it. She knew who it was. She also knew that they'd be back. They'd have to go out. She needed more time. The persistent knocking brought the two girls downstairs to investigate. Violet managed to grab Annie's arm before she opened the door.

Violet whispered, "Tell him I'm not in."

"Yer mean lie? You always told us that it's wrong to tell lies and that we should always tell the truth," She gave her mother a superior look.

"Just do as you're told for once, Annie, please!"

Annie opened the door to an angry-faced man in a crumpled coat, carrying a bag over his shoulder. Annie stared at the mole on his face. She thought he looked older than Mr Browning from next door and too old to be working.

"You took yer time. I anna got time to stand around all day. Is yer mother in?"

"No, I'm sorry, she's out." She looked him squarely in the face.

From her hiding place, Violet thought, 'She's a good liar, should I be worried?'

"Hmm! A likely story! Your mother's left yer on yer own then?" He eyed her suspiciously.

"Are you sayin' me mum tells lies?"

'Goodness me, she'll convince me that I'm out in a minute,' thought Violet.

Freda came up behind Annie and said, "No she ain't silly. She's just hiding." As soon as Annie gave her the evil eye, Freda knew that she'd said the wrong thing. Her mother was always telling her that she "opened her gob before gerrin' her brain into gear".

Violet emerged from the back of the settee with a duster, "Good afternoon, Mr Anderson, I'm sorry, I didn't hear you, I was just dusting the skirting boards."

"That's a new 'un. I ain't heard that one before. I could write a book called *Excuses, Excuses: Tales from the Rent Collector*. It'd be a best seller and I could retire. I'm sick to death of chasin' round after the people round 'ere." He glared at Violet's red face and added, "Well, have yer got the rent or not?"

Violet emptied her purse and paid him after which he reminded her that she still owed a tanner from last month. When John arrived home from riding his bike with his friends, he saw that his mum was very quiet.

"What's wrong, Mum? Yer look as if you've seen a ghost."

"I'm fine," she lied.

Violet spoke to Audrey. "Jimmy's offered me a part time job at the pub, but I don't want to take it. I don't like leaving the kids by themselves, but I can barely manage with what Harold pays me for working in the shop."

Audrey said bluntly, "Tell 'em that you're goin' because you dunna have any choice."

"They're still struggling with losing their dad. So am I. I need to be here for them and besides, Annie will kick off."

"She'll kick off if yer give her drippin' on toast again. Just tell 'em the truth and if yer don't mind me saying so, your Annie needs to stop being so bloody selfish. She'll soon come round if there's summat in it fer her. Tell her that it will help yer to save up, so they can go to their grandparents. She keeps on about how much she misses riding Sparky."

That was very true. It had broken their hearts to see the animals being sold off at the farm, particularly the horses. She wiped her eyes as she recalled Annie, clinging on to her pony's neck, begging for him not to go. She had knelt in the mud and screamed, tears rolling down her face. Sparky went to the smallholding with her grandparents who had promised to take care of him until such times as they could go and stay.

Bribery always worked wonders with Annie. She was already choosing what she was going to take with her, but John, on the other hand, was as thoughtful as ever.

"Mum, you already work too hard. I'm worried about yer."

"I don't have a choice son," She ruffled his hair.

Violet agreed to work the Friday night shift and Audrey decided she was going to give Violet a make-over, starting with cutting her hair, and Violet's protestations fell on deaf ears. Audrey had a very forceful personality and soon there was a pile of dark locks on the floor as her long hair was cut to collar length and soft curls framed her face.

"Oh my goodness, Vi, you look lovely. Just you wait until I put some make up on yer."

"I only wear lipstick."

"Yer need more than that if yer goin' to work in a pub," stated Audrey.

When her transformation was complete, Audrey shrieked, "Bloody 'ell, Vi. Yer look like a film star!"

John couldn't believe how different his mother looked, and Annie stared at her open-mouthed. Violet wore a blue, long-sleeved blouse that buttoned up to the neck and a straight black skirt as she didn't want to give anyone a false impression. She still needed a lot of reassurance from Audrey to leave Annie and John.

"Gerroff wi' yer, they'll be fine. I anna going anywhere and they only need to knock the wall if they need owt. Anyway, it's only a stone's throw away if we need to fetch yer."

John insisted on walking his mother to the pub and as soon as they'd gone, Annie started pestering Audrey.

"Yer mother wunna like it if she sees you in make-up," Audrey warned, but as usual, Annie got her own way on the condition that she took it off before her mum returned home.

Annie stared at her reflection excitedly. She couldn't believe how grown up she looked. She tried on her mother's clothes and rolled up the sleeves, and pulled a belt tight round the waist and pouted in the mirror as she paraded up and down. That night she had an epiphany. She knew that she had been blessed with the same good looks as her mother, but she wasn't modest like her, and she was going to use them to her advantage. She also made her mind up to learn to speak properly; her mum would be pleased about that. She had no intention of working day and night like her mother.

As they approached the Highway Man Public House, the door flung open and a dishevelled looking man landed on the rain-soaked ground. A tall, balding man, with a cigarette dangling from the corner of his mouth, eyed Violet up and down and followed them in.

Violet screwed up her nose at the unfamiliar smells and the fug of smoke. As they walked towards the bar, the men stared at her and a few wolf whistles were aimed at her. John looked searchingly at his mother, but she squeezed his arm in reassurance.

"Well, me little beauty, me takings will be up wi' you behind the bar." Jimmy leered at her and his eyes lingered on her shapely legs.

John glared at him. Standing upright and tall, he introduced himself. He gripped Jimmy's hand in a tight handshake and noted that Jimmy's hands were sweaty.

"Yer dunna look old enough to 'ave a grown up son!" Jimmy grinned at Violet and with a raised eyebrow he looked her up and down, "You must 'ave started young."

The implication was not lost on either of them and she took a step back. His breath smelt of stale cigarettes and beer and his body odour was overpowering.

"Will yer be okay?" enquired John. "I dunna like him!"

She reassured him that she could look after herself and he begrudgingly left. On his way home, John kicked a stone so hard that it narrowly missed a neighbour's window.

Violet quickly learned how to pull the perfect pint and the men were queuing up for her to serve them. The customers were all men, apart from one woman who held on to her husband's arm and said loudly, "He wunna be comin' here again!" glaring at Violet as she propelled him out the door.

CHAPTER TWENTY-FOUR
1944

People were queuing for their rations and a buxom woman was raising her voice to Harold. He gave Violet a pleading look and she immediately took over serving her.

"Good morning, Mrs Brown. What seems to be the problem?" Violet's voice was reassuring.

"The problem is, the ruddy government ain't givin' me enough food to feed us!" Her double chin shook as she became animated.

"Don't worry, I'll put you an extra slice of bacon and an extra couple of sausages," she whispered conspiratorially behind her hand. "Just don't tell anyone or else we'll start a riot." She stamped the lady's ration book and winked.

Mrs Brown gave Violet a wink as she left the shop, smiling. Harold was keen to hear how she'd put a smile on the face of their most difficult customer.

"She thinks she's had extra rations, but I sliced the bacon just a bit thinner so she had an extra slice. The sausages weren't as fat this time, so she had two more, but she wouldn't have her last ones to compare them with because they'd have been eaten."

Harold chuckled and put his arm round her. "I didn't know yer could be so devious. He kissed her on her cheek and said, "What would I do wi'out you?"

"Well, it doesn't do any harm to let people feel a bit special, does it, Harold? Especially when times are so hard. We all need to feel a bit special now and again."

"Well, you're special to me, but you already know that."

Violet and Audrey followed the news every day. Violet had swapped an old table belonging to her mother in exchange for an old radio and they would sit round it whilst enjoying a cup of tea. Violet would read the headlines on the newspapers at the shop and relay them to her friend. Sometimes, Harold would pass on a newspaper that was left over and they'd study it for any snippets about the war. .

The news was full of D-Day when the biggest invasion by air, land and sea took place and thousands of British, Canadian and American servicemen landed on the beaches of Normandy.

After they'd finished reading the newspaper, Violet would cut it into squares and hang them on a nail net to the toilet

"It's been ages since I gorra letter from Bert, not that he says much. I dunna know if he's gerrin' any leave, or even where he is. He might even be there in Normandy." She looked worried. "He's a miserable old sod, but I miss 'im and so do the kids." She wiped away a tear, but then broke into a smile. "Still I wudna mind meeting some of them Americans. I bet they know how to show a girl a good time. I 'ear they like splashing their cash an' all."

A few weeks later, it was a busy shift at the pub. Violet had been on her feet for hours at the shop, busy serving customers and she'd rather have been at home with her feet up than serving drunken men. It was particularly noisy that night. Men were arguing about the economy and about the war. Opinions got heated, especially when they'd had a few pints and she was straining to hear their orders when, all of sudden, the shouting stopped and all eyes turned to stare at the two American soldiers making their way to the bar.

"Good evening, ma'am. We'd like two pints of yawh best bitter," said one of the soldiers.

"I'm sorry but we're having trouble getting supplies of bitter. Will pale ale do?" Violet gave him a shy smile.

"Awh gee, that's a shame. Guess its two pints of yawh pale ale then." He gave her a pound and told her to keep the change.

The men got belligerent. "Look at them smarmy bastards, splashin' their cash about! Bloody comin' over 'ere and showin' off to our women."

Chuck Garcia politely asked them if they would step aside. He was tall with broad shoulders and had the fitness of a trained military man. The men slowly parted to allow him and his comrade to pass. His friend, Gus, had a one-sided conversation with Chuck, who wasn't listening to a word he said.

"Take mah advice, Chuck, leave the Goddamn dames alone."

Chuck didn't answer. He couldn't take his eyes off Violet all evening; she was stunning. She was wearing a purple jumper and black skirt which showed off her hourglass figure. The purple enhanced her stunning eyes. He waited until closing time, determined to walk her home. As she reached for her coat, Jimmy tried to get too friendly with her and Chuck was immediately on his guard.

"Come on, darlin', give me a kiss." Jimmy stepped towards her, but as she tried to side-step him he grabbed her arm. "Come on, yer know yer want to."

"No Jimmy! I need to get off now. I'll see you next week."

"The lady said No! Get yawh goddamn hand offa her arm now!" Chuck jumped up and strode towards him.

Jimmy swore at him and attempted to punch him, but Chuck moved out the way and Jimmy fell on the floor.

Violet was furious and tried to help him up. "What do you think you're doing? I can look after meself! What is it with you men?" She stormed out the door.

The two friends were having a cup of tea together whilst their children were out on their bikes and Violet confided her worries to Audrey, "Harold keeps dropping hints that he wants to marry me and he keeps offering to give me some of his rations. He's so good to John, in fact he's out delivering with him now, but Jimmy's intentions aren't honourable and he's getting worse. Even though I'm doing two jobs, I still haven't saved enough to send the kids to their grandparents. I don't know how I'm going to tell them."

"Well, they're easy problems to solve," Audrey laughed. "Just use yer good looks to your advantage. If you started to dress a bit more provocative and flirt wi' the customers, they'll be fallin' over themselves to buy yer a drink and every time one of 'em tells yer to get one for yersen, say thank yer very much and put the money in yer pocket. You'll soon have enough money to pay the kids' train fares."

"I can't do that!" She was shocked at her friend's suggestion.

"Of course yer can and as for Harold and Jimmy, well yer 'ave to know how to handle 'em. Just let Harold think that yer might consider gerrin' married later on. I'd snap his hand off if he offered me some of his rations and it ain't an actual lie is it? Yer might think about marrying again - it ain't your fault if he assumes it's him."

Violet clapped her hand over her mouth. "I'm shocked. I didn't know you could be so devious, Audrey."

Audrey chuckled. "Jimmy's an alcoholic and he's always gorra drink on the bar, just keep toppin' it up, he wunna know. Just smile at 'im and act as if yer interested in warr he's sayin' and by the end of the night, he wunna be in a fit state to try it on wi' yer, he'll be too drunk."

"You mean use them! That's wicked! I can't do that!"

"Why not? Men use women so you need to play 'em at their own game. Men think it's alright to take liberties wi' women, so why shouldn't we tek liberties wi' them? Do yer think that Harold's offering to give yer some of his rations out of the goodness of his heart? Course he's not, he's just wants to ingratiate himself wi' yer and Jimmy just wants to get yer in bed. They dunna deserve yer concern. My boss is a creep but I play up to him. He's so bigheaded that he canna see that I wudna fancy him if he were the last man on earth. He meks me skin crawl when he touches me bum and gives me a peck on me lips. I wudna lerr 'im go any further but he don't know that. Anyway, he's good to me and when I can stoke the fire up or give the kids sommat nice fer their tea, it's worth it. The kids are the only thing that matters, Vi. I'd do owt fer 'em, even if they do gerron me nerves sometimes."

A few weeks later, when the children came home they could smell something good cooking in the oven and a fire was roaring in the grate. Violet laid the table with a checked tablecloth and made a pot of tea which she covered with a blue and white tea-cosy that had belonged to her mother.

"This pie's good, Mum. The food has got berra over the past few weeks. How do yer do it Mum?"

"That's because I put bacon and a little more cheese in with the vegetables, thanks to Harold," she could barely look him in the eye.

"He's a kind man, ain't he? He says he can give me more work, but I dunna think he can afford it. He promised to take me off-road and teach me how to drive his van and then I can do the deliveries. It wunna be much different to drivin' a tractor." John's eyes shone with excitement.

Annie, as usual just gobbled the food put in front of her and then wanted to call for Freda, whereas John always showed his appreciation.

"Before you get running off, Annie, I've got something to tell you." Her voice was full of excitement, "I've saved enough money for you to go to your grandparents."

Annie's eyes shone with excitement and she hugged her mother tightly before running up the stairs to repack her case from weeks earlier.

John, as usual, was more reserved and said, "Mum, how 'ave yer managed to save it? You should be stockin' up on coal or spending some on it on yerself."

"You deserve it and your grandparents can't wait to see you. Make the most of it; you'll be a working man next year," she said, and ruffled his hair.

"Harold said I can 'elp him more at weekends. He gave me a shilling just for stackin' the shelves, but I'm sure he canna afford it so I'm goin' to try and gerra job on a farm."

Violet had made very small changes, nothing risqué. Audrey was right; the kids were the only thing that mattered. She was right about Jimmy, too. He didn't notice her topping his drink up and the more he drank the easier it was to keep him at arm's length. The customers were more generous too, but she felt particularly bad about the men spending their money on her, instead of taking it home to their families. She remembered the words of Frederick Smythe: "Having principles won't get you want you want." How right he had been. The only thing she wanted was her beloved Ted and to be in the bosom of his supportive family again.

Audrey came into the pub with a man and Violet followed her into the Ladies and confronted her, "Audrey what are you doing with him? You're a married woman!"

"I know that. It's just a bit of fun and besides it's a free night out. I dunna want to stop in at home when me mum's got the kids fer the night. Dunna look like that, I used to worry all the time about Bert, wondering where he was and if he were alright and it made me feel ill. I had to stop worryin' and try and enjoy mesen. Yer should try it sometime because yer never know what tomorrow may bring."

Violet knew that, only too well and hugged her friend. As they returned to the bar, Audrey's mouth fell open at the sight of the handsome American. She quickly introduced herself and didn't bother to introduce her *friend John*. Chuck brought drinks over to their table but Audrey failed to notice that John had not returned from the toilets. She observed the three stripes on the arm of Chuck's smart olive uniform with the gold buttons. She admired his dark hair and eyes. He still had a hint of a sun tan. She suspected that he'd been fighting somewhere hot like Italy and she wondered if her Bert would come home with a tan. She was fascinated by Chuck's accent and when he spoke, he looked directly at her.

"Is thaht your friend over there?" He nodded towards Violet. "Whaht's her name?"

Audrey quickly realised that he had no interest in her. He could barely take his eyes off her friend and she had to admit that Violet looked stunning now that she was wearing more make–up and her purple blouse suited her beautiful eyes.

As Chuck stood up to leave, he felt in his pocket and took out a small card, which he handed to her.

"Bring yawh friend along," he said, and nodded towards Violet.

Violet didn't want to go to a party, but Audrey was determined. "Yer canna use the kids as an excuse. They wunna be 'ere, it's time we had a bit of fun."

"I've never been to a party before and I don't know how to dance!"

Audrey found it hard to believe that a woman who was nearly thirty-five had never done either of those things. "Well, it's time that yer did. We both deserve some fun and I anna goin' on me own."

CHAPTER TWENTY-FIVE
1944

John and Annie waved excitedly as the train pulled out of the station. Violet looked wistfully at them, perhaps she would go and see Mary and Jack when she felt stronger. She waved until all that was left was the trail of steam puffing out in the air. At least it gave her chance to take on extra shifts.

Audrey popped her head round the door and said, "Bloody Hell, its quiet in 'ere." She didn't give her friend time to start missing her children and wasted no time at all in sorting out clothes and hairstyles for their big night out at the weekend.

They studied themselves in the mirror when they were ready for the party. Audrey had styled Violet's hair into a chignon on the back of her neck with curls on the top of her head. She applied a subtle shade of red to her lips and blue eye shadow which complemented her eyes and finished off with black mascara. Her dress was blue and had a V-neck with little puff sleeves, which had a slight flare and she wore a black patent belt that emphasised her tiny waist. Audrey had her hair in rolls on the top of her head and wore a red dress that showed off her cleavage which bounced when she walked and she wore bright red lipstick to match her hair. Neither of them had silk stockings so they used gravy browning on their legs and drew seams up the backs of each other's legs. Violet wore black shoes with a tiny heel, but Audrey wore high heels and towered over her friend.

Chuck had called in a favour. He sent someone to pick them up in a jeep, but Violet had insisted on being picked up further down the road, away from prying eyes.

Chuck paced up and down and checked his watch again *What if she don't come? What if Awdreey brings another dame, or comes on her own?* His thoughts were running round in his head. *I will kill that Saunders if he's gone off we mayh woman!* He knew that she wasn't his, but she sure would be by the end of the night.

The door opened and in swept Audrey. He held his breath. Had she come on her own? Then he saw her, following behind her friend and his pulse quickened. *She was the most goddamn beautiful dame he had ever seen.*

The two women stood and stared; they had never seen anything like it. There was a table laden with food and drinks and couples were dancing wildly. Women's skirts were swirling and some men were throwing their partners over their shoulders. Within minutes Audrey was on the arm of Gus and being led into the middle of the dancefloor and the Jitterbug was quickly becoming Audrey's favourite dance.

Chuck held a chair out for Violet to sit down. She looked around shyly. She wondered why she'd come. Although she knew Ted was gone, she still felt like a married woman, and that she was betraying Ted's memory by being in close proximity to another man.

Chuck could barely take his eyes off her. She was unlike anyone he'd ever met and he couldn't risk scaring her off. He wasn't used to exercising such restraint and he wondered if he was losing his touch as she didn't seem to be interested in him, or was she playing hard to get? How could a woman have put him on the back foot? "Would yah like a drink, honey?"

He asked her if she would like something putting in her lemonade but Violet declined, she was determined to keep her wits about her. She had never met anyone like Chuck before. Whilst he was getting the drinks, Chuck noticed some of his comrades sitting near her. He spilt his drink in his hurry to get back to her. Audrey came back to the table a couple of times but she quickly returned to the dance floor. Violet smiled at her friend, who was clearly having a good time. Chuck thought she had an amazing smile. In fact he thought everything about her was amazing. The room was noisy so it was difficult to have a conversation, so he asked her to come for a tour of the base. Once outside, he got to know her a little better and she seemed to relax. He noticed her wedding ring and enquired if her husband was in the forces.

She whispered, "He died last year in an accident on our farm."

"I'm sorry for yawh loss, honey," he said insincerely.

He so badly wanted to kiss her, but instead he guided her back inside. The tempo had changed and couples were dancing cheek to cheek. He held his hand out to her and she took it as they walked to the middle of the floor. He held her closely to him. Her hair smelt of lavender, a smell he'd never forget. He wondered if she could hear his heart thudding in his chest. Almost immediately, Audrey and Gus broke them up and Gus whispered in his ear and Audrey enquired if Violet would be okay if she didn't come back with her.

"Let's get outta here. I'll take yah home."

They drove back in silence, both alone with their thoughts. Violet insisted that he drop her off away from the house.

"Yah can't walk back on yawh own. Let me walk yah to yawh door." It was too dark for her to see the pleading in his eyes.

They walked quietly and stood on her doorstep. Chuck looked down at the ground, shuffling his feet. *Goddamn it, Garcia, kiss her.* His thoughts were interrupted by Violet inviting him in for coffee.

"Don't get any ideas, it's just coffee." She led him into the small living room. "Sit down and make yourself at home. I'll just make the coffee," said Violet.

He looked around the neat and tidy room with the old furniture and the beige tiled fireplace. In the hearth stood a shiny brass fire set which held fire tools, which he thought was quaint, like the house. It was small enough to fit in a corner of his house, but it felt homely. He followed the sound of the kettle whistling on the cooker and saw Violet pouring Camp coffee from a bottle and she was about to put powdered milk in it, when he asked for it black. He took it off the worktop and sipped it, and he almost spat it out. Violet took the cup out of his hand and their hands touched and he could not restrain himself any longer.

"Let's forget the cawfee."

They both knew there was no turning back. He pushed her against the cupboard and kissed her with a passion that she reciprocated. They made mad, frantic love there and then on the cold kitchen floor that was covered in red linoleum.

Afterwards, he stared at his hands. "What's this brown stuff all over mah hands?"

"Gravy browning," she laughed. "Stockings are in short supply and even if I could get hold of any, I still couldn't afford them."

She was shivering and trying to cover up her naked body. He helped her to her feet and she quickly put her clothes back on. He placed his jacket round her shoulders and kissed her gently. He admired her honesty. Most people he knew pretended to be someone they weren't and were consumed with appearances, especially women. He knew he didn't deserve her.

"I'll get yah some stockings. Those legs deserve nothing but the best." He took her hand and said, "Yawh shivering, let me get yah up to bed."

He lay next to her on the bed and undressed her, as he lifted her dress above her head and she lay naked in front of him, he knew that he was falling in love with her. He looked into those amazing eyes and kissed the tip of her nose. He took time making love to her; he didn't want it to end. As he tentatively kissed and explored her body, Violet let him lead the way. She had never known a feeling like it.

When Chuck quietly left, she lay in bed thinking about him. She had mixed emotions. Chuck made her pulse race and he aroused feelings in her that were new to her. She thought about her beloved Ted and a tear ran down her face. They'd both been so young when they got married and neither of them had any experience in lovemaking. She had betrayed him by an act of lust! No-one would ever compare to Ted, the love of her life, the father of her children.

The telephone box seemed to close in on her when she dialled the number. Her heart beat quickly and her face flushed when her mother-in-law answered the phone and she felt sure that Mary would hear the betrayal in her voice. They both cried when they spoke to each other.

"It's been a real treat 'aving them stay. Annie seems to be quite the little lady now, but she still likes to be the centre of attention," Mary chuckled. "Burr our John has really grown up. He reminds me so much of our Ted." She cried again when she spoke of him.

After speaking to her children and then to Mary again, Violet agreed to let them stay for longer. Annie was enjoying riding Sparky and John was a great help to Jack. She hadn't heard them so animated since their father died. Annie in particular was excited about going to stay with Aunty Lillian and Uncle Ray and to meet her little cousin, David.

With her children away it not only enabled her to carry on her clandestine affair with Chuck but gave her a chance to earn more money. Jimmy was more than happy to give her more shifts as his takings went up when she was behind the bar. He was infatuated with her and was determined that one day she would be his.

Audrey popped her head round the door. "Bloody hell, you look miserable. I'll stick the kettle on and then yer can tell me all about it."

"I'm really looking forward to them coming back. I've really missed them, but..." She stopped herself from saying it.

"But, you canna see lover boy when they're back. Just tell 'em the truth."

"I can't do that! They'll never forgive me for betraying their father. Anyway I shouldn't be thinking like that. I've always put the children first."

"You ain't betrayed anyone!" She put her arm around her friend's drooping shoulders, "Ted's dead, but you're not. You've had a shit life and it's time you 'ad a bit of happiness and enjoyed yersen a bit."

"I know that he'll get sent home one day and that it will all be over, but I don't want him to leave. I feel so confused, I feel as if I've fallen in love with him, but I still love Ted. How on earth can I love two men at the same time?"

Audrey hugged Violet to her, wishing she could find the right words to say.

CHAPTER TWENTY-SIX
1944

Tom Dawson pulled up outside her house, ready to take her to the train station. Horse and carts were rapidly being replaced with cars, but Violet much preferred this mode of transport and it provided a cheaper service than a taxi. The rhythmical motion of the horses and the smell of the leather seats brought back memories of her mother. She could barely contain her excitement when she heard the train coming and saw the black smoke billowing. Annie ran across the platform and hugged her mother tightly and John kissed her on her cheek, bringly her motherly instincts to the fore again. She listened to Annie's chattering on the way home. John didn't attempt to interrupt and exchanged smiles with his mother.

Within half an hour of coming home, Annie went to play with Freda, John went to ask Harold if he needed any help and life quickly returned to normal as Violet set about the same mundane tasks of housework and working two jobs. In the day, she placated customers that were vexed when they didn't always have the supplies they were expecting and on Friday and Saturday night, she had to keep her wits about her as drunken men leered at her. On week nights she played card games or listened to the radio with John and Annie and on one such night, John interrupted her thoughts.

"Mum, you're not concentrating! You've just let our Annie win. Are yer okay? Yer seem a bit quiet."

"I'm fine, I'm just a bit tired," she lied. She'd been thinking about Chuck. She hadn't seen him for several weeks.

She was clearing the tables in the snug, when someone touched the back of her hair. She spun round and saw Chuck standing there, smiling that big wide grin of his. She spoke politely to him as if he was just another customer, but if anyone had been looking closely, they would have seen the pink flush creep across her face as he whispered in her ear. He couldn't keep his eyes off her. He'd missed her so much. He wished that he'd met Violet before life became complicated. He wanted to take her in his arms and never let her go, but he had to get back to the barracks because he'd used all his passes for the month.

He nodded towards the door and waited for her to follow his lead. Ten minutes later, he was holding her in his arms and nuzzling her hair. The darkness hid the tears that sprung to his eyes. He was scared of losing her. She was the most honest person he had ever known and he knew that she was too good for him. There was a sweet tenderness in their kiss that night and he couldn't hide his feelings any longer.

"Vi, I'm so sorry that I haven't been able to see yah. I've missed yah so much."

"I was worried that I'd never see you again. I thought you'd either met someone else or that you'd been posted somewhere."

"I'm not due to be posted just yet and I need ta tell yah, if I have to go, yah will be the only dame on my mind. I've fallen in love with yah, honey, and that's thah truth."

As she turned the corner to return to the pub, she saw John standing there and froze.

"Who was that man, Mum? Was he an American soldier?"

"Yes, he pops in now and again. I was just putting some empties out when he left," she lied.

"Well, as long as he anna givin' yer any trouble, Mum. I've heard about them Americans."

She ruffled his hair and laughed. "Who've you been listening to? Anyway, he seems like a nice gentleman to me."

It had become serious between them now that they'd declared their love for each other and she would have to tell her children. She'd almost been caught and she couldn't risk them finding out that way. The next morning, Violet approached the subject of Chuck with John.

"You know the American soldier that you saw? Well, he's asked me if he can take me to see a film, but I don't want to upset you." She cast her eyes down as she spoke.

"You mean on a date, or as a friend?" John eyed her suspiciously.

"As a friend," she lied. "You two can come too, if you like." She knew that Chuck would be willing to take them if it meant spending time with her.

"Well, yer deserve a bit of a treat, but be careful. I think it would be berra if me and our Annie come along to keep yer company. He wunna try any funny business if we're with you."

"How did you get so worldly wise?" she chuckled.

"Harold says that yer canna trust men around you and that I need to keep an eye on yer."

"Hmm, I bet he did!" She knew that he didn't want her getting too close to any men, but Harold would never be more than her employer to her.

Annie's eyes grew very round when she saw the big box of chocolates under Chuck's arm; she was easily won over but John was rather more cautious. Annie pushed herself between Chuck and her mother and John sat the other side of him where he could keep an eye on him. It was a George Formby film and they laughed throughout. It had been a long time since they'd done any of that. Afterwards, Chuck came in and had a drink of the coffee which he'd supplied. Annie played cards with him but she was unable to cheat and he beat her three times in a row, which made Violet and John laugh.

"If yawh mother lets me come round again, I will teach yah to play poker, John. The thing yah need ta remember is to keep a poker face," Chuck advised. "Yah must hide your feelings from your opponent."

CHAPTER TWENTY-SEVEN
1944

As usual, Monday morning was fraught, with Annie making excuses not to go to school. Violet knew all too well that she just wanted to listen to the radio that Chuck had acquired for them. It was so much better than their old one. By the time Violet had managed to get Annie out of bed and ready for school, she was running late for work and she made her way to the shop with haste, knowing that Harold would be annoyed. He hated lateness and prided himself on his punctuality.

As Violet rushed into the shop, panting for breath, Harold tapped his watch and said, "I suppose you're going to tell me that your Annie's been playing you up again." He took his pipe out of his pocket and sucked on it.

She nodded, to which Harold tutted loudly. He made no attempt to hide his contempt for her headstrong daughter.

November the twenty-seventh started like any other day, but at eleven minutes past eleven there was a huge explosion and a mushroom-shaped cloud of smoke appeared in the sky.

At the school, the Headmaster took charge. "Come along, children, form a nice, orderly line and follow Miss Perkins. Remember the drill: no pushing and shoving and no running," Mr Peters spoke with a quiet, authoritative air.

Once everyone was in the shelter, children started to cry.

"Is it the Germans, sir?" whimpered Peggy.

George fretted for his cat. "He don't like big bangs, sir."

Winnie cried, "I want me Mam."

Peter said, "It pongs in 'ere, sir."

Annie and John huddled together, each seeking comfort from each other.

"I'm sure the wardens will soon let us know what's happening. Now if you're quiet, I'll read from where we left off."

The children were soon enchanted as their Headmaster read *The Railway Children* using different voices and making train noises.

At the village shop, customers dived for cover and mothers screamed for their children. Violet stood rooted to the spot as she watched the mushroom cloud in the distance. Harold ushered Violet out of the shop. "Get off to the school, I'm sure those kiddies will want their mother. This war is a terrible business."

Anxious parents stormed the school gates and some were hysterical as they clapped eyes on their little ones. Annie pushed past the children at the front and flung herself into her mother's arms.

"I thought the Germans had found us, Mum," she was shaking.

Once they arrived home, Audrey came round with her children, as did Fred. Violet warmed her earthenware teapot and then added used tea leaves to it and stirred. She put a tea cosy over it to keep it warm and turned the radio on. She twiddled the knobs to try and tune into a more local broadcast but to no avail. The BBC merely reported on the events of the war which acted as a morale booster to its listeners, by informing them of victories, however small otherwise broadcasting music and comedy such as *It's That Man Again*.

"Sod it!" Audrey couldn't hide her frustration, "We anna important enough to gerra mention on the news!"

The door swung open and John came rushing in. He could hardly catch his breath. He had news on the events that'd unfolded that morning. "That explosion was the ammunition store at Fauld! People have been killed."

They all sat in silence as John's news sunk in.

The next day, the Derbyshire Times sold out at the shop, it was full of the explosion at Fauld and their local reporter, Gordon Wayne, did an extensive report of the area. He reported that over half of the explosives kept at the ammunition depot had detonated, causing widespread destruction of the area. The local reservoir had been hit causing extensive flooding and a farm on top of the hill was completely obliterated. There was a grainy photograph to accompany the news that the death toll was fifty but expected to rise although it was reported that some bodies might never be found.

The neighbours gathered around the table again, devouring the newspaper and drinking tea. Fred sucked his pipe hard, leaving little puffs of smoke in the kitchen.

John was the first to speak, his voice scarcely more than a whisper. "Mum, that's our old farm. I canna believe it! That would've been us if we were still living there," he whispered.

Annie, ever the optimist said, "Well, at least it weren't the Germans."

John looked at her with contempt and stormed up to his bedroom.

The following day, the shop was alive with customers gossiping about the explosion, with many of them blaming the Americans.

"That wudna have happened if our chaps were in charge of it, the ruddy idiots should've stored them safer," Wilf complained. He took every opportunity to make digs at *them foreigners*.

"I think we should be grateful for their help." Violet rarely got involved with the arguments and kept neutral, but she'd heard enough of the constant mud-slinging towards the Americans.

"Help!? They've been about as much use as a chocolate teapot," Wilf was red in the face.

"There's a war on. We should be kinder to each other. They're miles away from home and separated from their loved ones and have the same worries as any of us." Violet's eyes were sparkling with anger. She thought about Chuck being separated from his *loved ones*. What did she know about them? Had he got a wife or a fiancée, or children? She knew so little about him, but surely he would have told her, wouldn't he?

The conversation quickly changed to the war, which was one of the main things people complained about at the shop and the pub. They berated Hitler, rationing and the Americans coming over here and splashing the cash and catching the eyes of *our women*. The phrase, *overpaid, oversexed, overconfident and over* here was something that was regularly trotted out. Christmas was coming up and families worried about how they were going to provide a Christmas dinner with the lack of supplies. Many didn't feel like celebrating when their loved ones were God knows where. Violet also dreaded Christmas. How could it ever be the same without her beloved Ted? She made a mental note to get in touch with her in-laws. She hadn't seen Chuck for weeks and she missed him. She wondered when she would see him again, if at all. He could quite possibly be dead and she would not be informed as she was not his next of kin, and it made her think again about his family.

CHAPTER TWENTY-EIGHT
1944

In the run-up to Christmas, John spent more hours than usual helping Harold, which caused discord with Annie. John had let her come on a couple of occasions but Harold discouraged it.

"It's a good idea if yer dunna bring yer sister again," he said.

John pleaded her case, "She wunna be any trouble."

"She's too big fer her boots and she's work-shy."

John couldn't argue with Harold's accurate assessment of his sister.

Violet spent what little spare time she had, knitting and sewing her Christmas presents. She didn't have Ted's carpentry skills to help out with the presents, but she was paying for them to go to their grandparents and John, at least, would know the sacrifices she'd made to facilitate that journey but she had no doubt that Annie would complain. They were going to their grandparents to stay immediately after Christmas. Mary had extended that invitation to her too, but she had declined. Violet didn't feel ready to stay with them yet; their grief was still so raw and she felt too guilty to face them. She did however, chat to Mary on the phone and explained to her that it would give her chance to do more shifts at the pub without them. Mary understood the struggle for survival but expressed her concerns.

"I wished you'd come too. I dunna like the thought of yer working in a pub wi' all them men leering at yer."

"I can handle them. I have to take whatever work I can but I will probably come after New Year," she said.

Christmas morning arrived and, although it was cold, the sun was shining. Annie was pleased with the clothes Violet had made for her, and she seemed surprisingly content with what she'd received. John was, as always, easily pleased. Annie had made some crackers, after a fashion - there was no bang, but they helped to make the table look festive. Both neighbours came round for Christmas dinner, Audrey and Violet had saved their coupons as best they could, and clubbed together to provide the food and Fred supplied the vegetables from his garden. They feasted on roast chicken, roast potatoes and brussels and carrots and Violet was particularly pleased to have made stuffing which actually contained onions.

"It's a real treat, Fred. The false promises from suppliers causes such ructions at the shop. Who'd have thought that having no onions would cause so much trouble? Poor Harold, it's not his fault."

Pudding consisted of bread and butter pudding, although there weren't many sultanas in it. There was a lot of laughing and joking, although John didn't join in. It was a very different affair to last year at the farm, when they were still numb from grief even though Ted was still uppermost in their minds and they would never forget him.

Jimmy had given her a bottle of sherry and Violet raised a glass to her beloved Ted. "Still missing you, my darling; gone but not forgotten." A tear slipped down her cheek.

Audrey then raised her glass to Bert. "Keep safe wherever you are, you miserable sod." Then she said, "Come on we're gerrin' maudlin, let's put the radio on and have a sing-song."

John sneaked out the room without anyone noticing and lay on his bed. He covered his ears at the singing. He hated Christmas. He hated this place. He hated life. He quickly wiped away the tears that were running down his face, when his mother tapped on his door.

"I know how much you're missing your dad. We all are."

"It inna just that. I dunna want to work for Harold anymore."

"Why? I thought you liked working for him?"

"I want to work on a farm."

"OK, but be kind when you give him notice. Harold's been good to you."

John pushed past her slamming his bedroom door, "I'm goin' out, Mum!"

"Out where? It's Christmas Day!"

She worried that he wasn't coping as well as she had thought. His father's death was still raw to all of them and John in particular missed the farm. Perhaps if he got a job working on one it might lift his mood, but she had no doubt that it wouldn't compare to working with his father and grandfather, three generations working side by side.

They had a quiet Boxing Day lunch with just the three of them, but John seemed quieter than ever. When Harold arrived for tea, John was in his bedroom and Violet called him down, but after half an hour he still hadn't appeared. When she went upstairs, he told her that had he had a headache and needed to sleep it off.

Harold looked very concerned. "I hope he's OK."

"I think he's missing his Father."

"Would you like me to go up to him? Perhaps he'll talk to me, you know, man to man."

"You're such a kind man Harold, but I think he just needs time to come to terms with it by himself."

They had tinned salmon sandwiches and tinned peaches with evaporated milk for tea. Annie watched Harold dip his bread and butter into the juice and joined in with relish. She agreed with him that it was the best bit. When Harold had gone, Violet went to check on John, who was lying on his bed, staring at the ceiling.

John looked at her imploringly. "Mum, you're not goin' to marry Harold, are yer?"

Violet laughed and said, "Of course not! Whoever put that idea in your head?"

"Harold did. He said that he'd like to be me stepdad."

"Well, I'd like to be well off, but it doesn't mean it will happen," she laughed. "You can get that silly notion out of your head. I promise you that I will NEVER marry Harold. You're going to stay with your grandparents tomorrow, so that might perk you up a bit."

As the train chugged into the station, Annie was jumping up and down excitedly, but John stood passively. He had hardly spoken a word. Annie wriggled free from her mother's embrace, impatient to start their journey, but John returned his mother's tight embrace. As Violet waved them off, she was worried about John's unusual quietness. She went to the telephone box and dialled the number and her heart beat quickly whilst she waited for an answer.

When Mary answered the phone, she listened to Violet's concerns.

"Dunna worry, we'll keep an eye on him. I expect he's missing 'is dad. We all are and it always seems worse at this time of the year. You tek care of yersen, love."

Violet felt her face redden when she put the phone down. Chuck had managed to get a note to her at the shop that he would be attending the New Year dance at the village hall. She shouldn't be going out and having fun with another man, whilst her in-laws and her son were struggling to cope without Ted. She felt a lump in her throat when she thought of him.

CHAPTER TWENTY-NINE
1944-45

New Year loomed and, as Violet sewed the hem of her dress, she could hear the ticking of the clock, but the peace was soon shattered by Audrey.

"Come on, Vi, you need to gerra move on!" She stopped in her tracks, "Bloody hell! Is that real velvet?"

"It's a remnant from an old customer."

"Bloody 'ell Vi, yer goin' to knock 'em dead tonight."

As Chuck watched the door for Violet's arrival, his stomach was doing somersaults; he couldn't bear it if she didn't come. He felt like a school boy waiting for his first date. No other woman had ever made him feel like that. When Violet walked through the doors, his heart skipped a beat and he hurried over and took her hand in his. When he helped her off with her coat, she took his breath away. She wore a dark violet cocktail style dress and her hair had a deep parting on the side and curled softly onto her shoulders.

The village hall was bustling with activity. The majority of the men wore uniform, but Chuck noticed a few young men in civvies glaring belligerently as they leaned against the walls. Audrey was quickly swept away by Gus and she told her friend not to wait for her because Gus would take her home. Chuck took Violet's hand and guided her on to the dance floor and he held her tightly to him.

A soldier interrupted them, "Aren't yah going to introduce us?" He kissed Violet's hand and when the introductions were over, he said, "Yawh a lucky dawg Garcia. You get all the pretty dames!"

"What did he mean?" Violet asked anxiously.

"Take no notice of him, he's drunk. Come on, let's sit down. Let me get yah a drink."

Violet's hands were shaking. She didn't recognise the man beside her. His eyes looked wild and he had a twitch on the side of his face. He squeezed her hand and smiled and the moment of doubt passed. However, the atmosphere soon changed when girls started screaming. Chuck let go of Violet's hand and went over to the two men fighting.

He pulled them apart. "Go and sober up, Hamilton! You're a disgrace!" Then he turned to the other man in civvies and pointed his thumb towards the door "And you, dude, get outta here!"

As the drunken soldier was led away by his mates, he snarled, "Yah think yawh so much better than all of us, Garcia, but you're not!" He turned to Violet and said, "Yah need to be careful of that sonofabitch!"

"I want to go home, Chuck." Violet's eyes were glistening with tears.

When they were alone, Violet let silent tears fall as she said, "I'm just another notch on your bedpost! I want you to leave."

"No yawh not." He stroked her hair, "I've got something to tell yah Honey. We're being moved. I can't tell yah where we're going, but I might not see yah for a long time."

They clung to each other. No words were spoken. They both knew the consequences of war. Chuck then dropped on one knee and took a red velvet box out of his pocket and he opened the box to expose the largest diamond ring she'd ever seen.

"When this goddamn war is over, I will come back for yah. Will yah do me the honour of becoming mah wife?"

They made frantic love before Chuck had to leave.

"Please don't let this be goodbye! I will come and see you off at the station."

"No! I can't bear it if yah saw me off on the train. Let's say our goodbyes now." His voice cracked with emotion. "I'll do mawh best to keep myself safe and I will come back for yah, darling, I promise."

The next morning Audrey came round and saw her friend admiring the huge diamond on her finger.

"Wow! Is that what I think it is? Bloody Hell, it's beautiful. Why are you crying?"

"He's going today but he didn't want me to see him off at the station." She was rocking in her chair.

"Bugger what Chuck wants! Get yersen to the station."

"I won't get there in time. I saw Tom Dawson leave half an hour ago."

"Use John's bike. Quick! Gerra move on!"

Violet could see the plume of steam as the train pulled into the station. Her chest hurt and her legs ached as she abandoned the bike and hurried to the platform. The station was packed with soldiers in brown coats, like a swarm of ants, and women were crying. She

141

pushed her way through the crowds, trying to catch a glimpse of Chuck. She stepped aside for an attractive blonde woman who was surging forward, her face shining with excitement. *She needs to be careful in her condition*, she thought. She was about to give up when she saw the back of a tall, dark-haired man in a russet coat, like so many others, but she knew it was Chuck. She'd recognise those broad shoulders anywhere and the way he walked with a swagger, his coat flapping open over his olive uniform.

"Chuck! Chuck!" she screamed, but her voice got swallowed up in the cacophony of noise. The young blonde woman ran towards him and he dropped his bag and swept her up in his arms. Violet turned away, disappointed that she'd been mistaken. She cycled home deflated and even more depressed than before. She needed her children, who were due home any day.

CHAPTER THIRTY
1945

Violet had been at the shop all morning, getting it ready for business the following day. She did so as a favour to Harold who was staying at his sister's. On her way back home, she saw a black Ford car outside her house and wondered who it could belong to. At that moment, she saw a familiar face poke round the net curtain and the door flew open. She ran towards him with her arms open, Bill hugged her tightly but he was very solemn.

"What's wrong? Where are the children?" Her voice went up an octave.

She could hear pots rattling in the kitchen as Bill advised her to sit down. Frank came in with a tray of tea and put it on the coffee table. He kissed her on the cheek, but he didn't meet her gaze.

"Frank, this is a nice surprise." She looked from one to the other. "Will someone tell me what's going on?"

Frank put his arm around her and guided her to the chair and advised, "I think you'd better do as Bill says. I think you need to sit down."

Bill continued, "I dunna know where to start. It's Harold; he's not what you think he is."

Frank lost his patience, "He's a filthy rotten pervert, that's who he is and when I get hold of him, I'm gonna shove his cock up his arse!"

"That's enough Frank! Violence inna goin' to solve anything. We need to let the police deal wi' it."

Violet sat in stunned silence as the whole sorry affair unfolded. She was unable to speak, until Frank poured her a brandy which he had brought with him.

"I can't believe it! Why didn't John tell me?" she whispered.

"He knew you needed the money and didn't want you to lose your job," Bill's voice cracked as he spoke.

Sobs wracked Violet's body and she rushed to the bathroom and was sick. She wanted to hold her son. She wanted him to know that she was there for him and that she always would be.

"Pack a few things and come back wi' us. Mum said we're not to take no for an answer."

Violet knocked on Audrey's door on the way to the car.

"Please will you tell Harold that I'm not well," his name stuck in her throat.

"You look terrible Vi! You look as if you've seen a ghost. What's wrong? Are the kids OK?"

Frank stepped forward and said, "She's comin' home wi' us for a day or two. Please will yer give HIM the message that she ain't well?"

Audrey nodded and took Violet's hands in hers. They were as cold as ice. "I'll come round for a cuppa when you get back and yer can tell me all about it then."

Violet sat in the back of the car, her mind whirling. She had seen the New Year in with a proposal and had felt optimistic that this was the start of her luck changing but now, only hours later her belief in good fortune was shattered along with her heart. Her pain for John was immeasurable. She willed Bill to drive quicker, her child, her first born, needed her.

When the car drove up the drive, Mary ran out and hugged Violet, tears streaming down her face. "I'm so sorry. I'm so sorry. You'd never have clapped eyes on that beast if we hadn't thrown yer to the wolves!"

"The only person to blame is THAT man!" Violet couldn't say his name.

The two women took solace from their hugs. Jack was a shadow of his former self. He had lost weight and looked gaunt. He kissed her on her cheek and merely said, "He's upstairs."

"Annie's at our Lillian's. We thought it best not to tell her you were coming," Mary was visibly trembling.

When John saw his mother, he buried his head in her shoulder, repeatedly saying that he was sorry.

Violet held him close to her. She felt his pain as if it were her own.

"I thought he were a kind man and I looked up to him. When 'e offered to tek me driving, I were that excited. He took me to a disused airfield to practice and I did really well," John wiped his eyes. "The next time we went 'e changed and 'e became all glassy-eyed and I were scared, Mum!"

"Can you tell me what happened?" Violet enquired gently.

"I can't tell you. I can't tell anyone." He sobbed. "I'm sorry, Mum. I'm so sorry!"

Violet held her son by his shoulders and looked him in the face, "You haven't done *anything* to be sorry about. He's the one that should be sorry! We can't let him get away with it. We need to report him to the police."

"I can't tell them what happened!"

"Look let's not worry about that now. I'll bring you a nice cup of cocoa up."

Bill took the cocoa up and talked with John at length. Mary sat at Violet's side holding her hand, as they sat in silence.

"He's agreed to let me be his chaperone with the police," informed Bill. "He's a strong lad and he knows that Harold needs stopping. He says that he wants to come home wi' you Vi. Me and Molly can come back wi' yer, if yer like. I'm sure Elsie can stay wi' either of her grandparents if need be, but first I think we should speak to the police whilst yer here.

Bill drove to the police station and reported Harold Smith. The next day, a plain-clothed policeman came to the small holding. Annie had stayed at her Aunt Lillian's, and Bill and Frank insisted on staying to give their support.

Violet agreed for Bill to be the appropriate adult, being as he was the one John had confided in. She waited in the kitchen with her in-laws and Frank whilst Detective Connor sat in the lounge with John and Bill. Afterwards the detective spoke to the assembled family.

"Just to let you know, Mr Smith has been arrested by your local police. We need to do some background checks, but I expect we'll find that he's done this before. Someone from your local constabulary will be in touch in the next few days. In the meantime, it's best not to discuss this wi' anyone." He shook hands with everyone and then he was gone.

"Well, at least they've arrested him, so you won't have to face him just yet," reassured Bill.

"I hope the police beat the shit out of him! I wish I could be alone wi' that bastard for five minutes; he'd get what's comin' to him." Frank balled both hands into tight fists.

"Violence wunna solve anything. Let the law tek care of him." Bill reasoned.

Mary raised her eyebrows at Frank but she did not chastise him for his bad language.

CHAPTER THIRTY-ONE
1945

Bill and Frank took Violet and her children back home. They drove in silence, apart from Annie asking questions.

"Why aren't you talking? Have you had an argument? When me and Freda fall out, we stop speaking to each other, but it doesn't last for long."

"No, sweetheart, we're all just tired." Violet squeezed her daughter's hand.

"Besides, you talk enough fer all on us, we canna get a word in," joked Frank but his laugh was hollow.

John paled as they drove past the shop, which was locked up. A small group of people were reading the notice on the door: CLOSED UNTIL FURTHER NOTICE. Violet wondered what they were going to do about their rations. What was she going to do for money? She'd have to take more shifts on at the pub but she didn't like leaving John. Not for the first time, she wished they were still at the farm with her beloved Ted and his extended family.

Violet peeped round Annie's door and saw that she was sleeping soundly. She tapped on John's door but got no response so she opened it gently and crossed over to his bed. She sat next to him and stroked his hair, like she'd done when he was a baby and watched his chest rise and fall. The events of the day had been exhausting for him. She knew how difficult it had been for him to reveal his experience to the police.

Audrey came round and she looked pale, had no make-up on and her eyes were puffy from crying. "The police have been round and informed us that an allegation of a sexual nature, had been reported by a minor. They asked James if Harold 'ad ever been inappropriate to him and stuff like that. James went really pale and he wuddna look that policeman in the eye. It was as if he'd turned into stone, but he left 'is card in case James remembered anything or wanted to talk, " She grabbed Violet's hands tightly, "Please tell me that it inna your John! Is that why you went away?"

Violet nodded her head.

Audrey looked stricken and said, "When he'd gone, I cornered James and he admitted that's why he stopped workin' fer Harold. I reported it to the police straight away, but he said that he still wuddna tell 'em. Why didn't they tell us? Why couldn't we see? What sort of mothers are we?" She wiped her eyes, "Well, me: I'm too busy havin' a good time to notice the change in me own son."

"Can you imagine the gossip mongers if this gets out? Everyone will be pointing their fingers at us," Violet's voice was barely a whisper.

"We ain't done anything wrong. We're both having to be mother and father to our kids and tryin' to keep a roof over our heads. He was a really nice policeman. He said that they would try and contact Bert for me. He'll bloody kill 'im if he gets his hands on 'im!"

Violet had no choice but to take on extra shifts at the pub to supplement her loss of wages and soon after, she served a man she hadn't seen before.

"Good evening. It's Mrs Higgins, isn't it?"

"Who's asking?"

He gave her his card and introduced himself as Gordon Wayne, reporter for the Derbyshire Times. "There's a rumour going round about our friendly shopkeeper. He was seen being escorted away by the police. I understand that you work for him, so perhaps you can shed some light on the matter. It's of local interest. People are getting anxious about their rations and wondering if they are going to get food at all."

Violet refused to be drawn into passing on any information, so he finished his drink and left. The following day, she went to the phone box and dialled the number on the card that had been put through her letter box. She asked to speak to Detective John Carmichael. He had been assigned to the case, but he was out the office so a message was left for him to get in touch with her.

Harold's arrest was briefly mentioned in The Derbyshire Times. No details of note were published but that didn't stop folk from speculating. One of the rumours circulating was that Harold was a spy, another that he had been thieving the rations. Women could well believe the latter, because they had been promised food many times and it hadn't materialised.

A few days later, Detective Carmichael visited Violet and brought her up to date with their investigation. "Harold Smith is an alias, one of many that he used. His real name is actually Harold Cavendish. That news article in the paper brought forward a witness, another boy. We expect there will be more, but people are very reluctant to come forward about these sort of things."

Violet saw him to the door and thanked him for coming and watched as he visited Audrey. When she saw the car leave, she went next door and noticed the net curtains twitch across the road.

"I had no idea that he was so evil! I don't know how we're going to get through it!" cried Violet.

"Our James says he cuddna face goin' to court, I've tried everything but he canna face it. I asked him why he hadn't warned John about Harold and he said that he thought it were just him, and that it was 'is own fault." She put her head in her hands and sobbed, "That manipulative bastard made him feel like he'd asked fer it! If I clap eyes on him, I will kill 'im with me own hands!"

A day or two later, a smartly dressed stranger knocked on Violet's door, and asked for her by name. He was short in stature and was smartly dressed in a navy overcoat and wore a trilby hat.

"Yes, who's asking?" Violet was guarded.

"Malcolm Gibson." He shook Violet's hand. "I've been asked by Mrs Greensmith to manage the shop in her brother's absence. I canna manage the post office and run the shop by meself. I was hoping that you'd consider coming back to work. She has given me a letter for yer." He took a crumpled envelope out of his pocket and handed it to her.

Dear Mrs Higgins,

I would be obliged if you would continue working in the shop until further notice. If there was any other way, I would not be asking you. I will ensure that your wages are backdated and you are paid in full for the time you work there. I trust this arrangement will be mutually beneficial. I cannot allow my brother's business to suffer whilst he is temporarily indisposed.

I must make this clear that once my brother is cleared of these ludicrous charges, your services will no longer be required.

From

Mrs Florence Greensmith

Violet took a cursory glance at the contents, before asking him in for a cup of tea. She scrutinised the letter and her hands shook as she looked up at Mr Gibson.

"My dear, I can assure you that I would be very grateful for your assistance. I know this must have come as a surprise, but I'm sure that yer need the money. We all do. Times are 'ard. I know her husband very well. We go for the occasional drink together and I can tell yer that brother and sister aren't close. My friend despises his brother-in-law, although he has not divulged the reasons he was arrested, but I'm sure it will all come out in the wash. The only reason Florence wants Harold's business to carry on is because she can't afford to keep him for nowt. He's been bailed to her address and it's causing friction at home."

"Well, Mr Gibson I will have a think about it and I will let you know, but I must say that the people from the village are missing the shop."

Customers were asking questions about Harold. The rumours were rife, but Violet was thankful that the nature of his arrest and John's involvement were not in the public domain. She was fortunate that her son was sensible and had been able to see past helping Harold. He knew that the villagers needed the shop and that they needed the income and John preferred her working in the shop rather than working at the pub with drunken men leering at her.

Violet had seen her children off to school and was getting ready for work when she saw a ginger-haired man in uniform, walking up the street. He looked weary, as if he was carrying the troubles of the world in his kit bag. Audrey screamed and ran outside when she saw Bert walking up to their house. Violet felt a pang of loneliness when she saw them hugging and kissing. She could hear raised voices and sobbing coming from next door. She was glad to be going to work as the noise intensified and she could hear them thudding up the stairs and the bed squeaking.

The pub was quite busy, with it being a Friday night and Violet was serving a customer when she saw the lone figure of Bert leaning against the bar, quietly supping his ale when Alf Smith, who was worse for wear, slapped him on the back.

"Yer not got yer missus wi' yer tonight, Bert?" When he got no response, he said, "She's a bobby dazzler that's fer sure. If she were my missus, I'd keep her on a tight leash."

"Perhaps you should mind yer own business, Alf! I've just come in fer a quiet drink."

"I might take a pop at her mesen. I've heard that she's fair game, especially wi' the Americans."

Bert slammed his drink on the bar and grabbed Alf by his grubby collar. He pushed him against the wall and punched him in his belly. When Alf doubled over on the floor, he kicked him. He unleashed his frustration and anger on him.

Jimmy quickly intervened and threw them both out. "Yer barred! Both of yer!"

Another row exploded when Bert confronted his wife.

"What sort of example are yer setting yer kids, Bert?" She soothed the situation by saying that Alf was just a drunkard. "I've been out a few times. I'm entitled to have a bit of fun, but I have never been unfaithful. You have always been the love of my life. Let's make the most of our time together."

Bert's leave soon ended and there were tears all round. "When's this bloody war goin' to end Vi? I canna stand it much more!" Audrey sobbed.

The two friends were a source of comfort over the coming weeks and when they were asked to go to the police station, they went together. Detective John Carmichael was a middle-aged man who had a gentle manner about him and his experience enabled him to put people at ease.

He shook their hands and said, "It's better for you if the neighbours don't see us coming to your houses. I know what village gossips are like. It's good that you are both supporting each other, as both your sons have fallen prey to Mr Cavendish, but I shall still have to speak to you separately and I'm sure that I don't need to remind you how important it is to keep anything we discuss to yourselves."

Violet sat in the waiting room whilst Audrey sat with Detective Carmichael in his office. She shook her head as she came out of the interview room. She was very pale and her make-up had smeared on her face. As the detective asked Violet to join him, Audrey whispered

"Bloody Hell, Vi. We'll need summat stronger than a cuppa when we're done here."

The detective smiled at Violet. He rarely got emotionally involved with his cases, but he had sons that were a similar age to the two boys, and he could only imagine how they and their mothers were feeling. He also knew how quickly people pointed the finger of blame at mothers who were doing their best in these difficult times. He felt great sympathy for them both.

"We've been contacted by a Mr Smith, the brother of the late Mrs Cavendish. He'd seen the article in the Gazette and put two and two together. Apparently he'd always had suspicions about his sister's husband. He felt that he hid his true colours and that his gentle demeanor was merely a facade. He claims that he noticed a change in his sister a few months before she died, but he didn't get chance to speak to her alone because her husband didn't leave them alone together. Anyway, the coroner found nothing suspicious about her death and the verdict was suicide. Apparently, she'd become depressed because she couldn't have children. However, Mr Smith did not believe that she would ever take her own life."

"Are you saying that it wasn't a suicide?" Violet's voice trembled.

"Well, we are going to attempt to find out. She gave her friend a letter and asked her to keep it safe and only to open it if anything happened to her. Unfortunately, her friend's house was bombed and she lost her life. The few possessions that were saved were given to her sons and the letter only recently came to light when they were sorting through their mother's belongings. Apparently, Mrs Cavendish had started to suspect her husband as being up to no good. She got fed up of constantly moving, which seemed to be precipitated by visits from the police, and whenever she asked what those visits were about, he would tell her that it was about burglaries, or come up with similar excuses. Mr Cavendish moved to this area after his wife's death, but by then his wife had already written the letter. She wrote that a woman had accosted her and had called Harold a pervert and that she needed to open her eyes. Obviously she had been very shaken by the turn of events and thought the woman was mad, but when she relayed this to her husband, he apparently became very aggressive towards her."

Detective Carmichael asked for refreshments to be sent through. As they were drinking their tea Violet's hands trembled and she held on tightly to her mug as the magnitude of the situation sunk in. Harold was a cold and callous man, who only thought about himself and he had used her to get access to John. She expressed this to the kind gentleman sitting before her.

"Don't you worry, Mrs Higgins, we'll get him. He's only got away with it for so long because parents don't want their childrens' reputation sullied. It takes courage to go to court, but it's the only way we can get it on his record. Your son is a very brave young man. Mr Cavendish has escaped prosecution for years but not anymore, not if I have anything to do with it." He stood up signalling the end of their conversation. "We are going to trace all the people who have complained in the past and we've applied to have Mrs Cavendish's body exhumed. Mark my words; he won't get away with it this time."

In the post, Violet got a letter from Chuck, stating that he was missing her and that he loved her. He couldn't say exactly where he was but that, so far, he was safe. He signed off with *From your loving fiancé Chuck. PS I can't wait to marry you xxxx*

She wished he were here. She felt so alone. She remembered that one night in April when she was able to steal a few hours alone with him. She'd been unable to fathom out why he could only spent a short time with her, when he had a week's leave before being posted to the Far East. He told her that he had a few things to sort out before he went away and to trust him and that the only thing that mattered was their future. She hadn't told him about Harold, she didn't want to worry him.

Violet had been sick two mornings in a row and she couldn't face food, but she assumed that it was her body reacting to all the stress. Ted was uppermost in her thoughts. John needed him more than ever.

CHAPTER THIRTY-TWO
1945

On the evening of May 7th the BBC broadcast a speech by the Prime Minister, Winston Churchill, who announced that Germany had surrendered and that it would be official one minute after midnight; that day would became known as VE Day.

Joy swept the nation, street parties sprung up and families were reunited with loved ones. However, allied forces were still fighting in the Far East and Japan and they didn't return home until World War II officially ended on the 2nd of September 1945.

Violet couldn't wait for Chuck to come back from America. He'd promised her that he would return as soon as he could. She hadn't told him her news yet and she hoped he'd be back for the court case against Harold Cavendish, which would most likely be early next year.

Although the war had finished, rations were still in force and would be for several years. Violet faced the daily moans from women who still couldn't get the items they wanted, but generally everyone's mood was brighter now that the Germans had surrendered. John had left school in the summer and now that he was working on a farm, he seemed happier than he'd been for months. Annie was doing well at school, but in spite of life having become calmer, she was filled with dread. How was she going to break the news to her children that they were to have a brother or sister next January?

Audrey was a source of great comfort to Violet, but their lives changed when Bert came home from the war. Many men expected their wives to give up their jobs and Bert was no exception, while women were reluctant to return to a life of domesticity. Violet heard many arguments coming from next door. Bert was also initially suspicious of her friendship with Violet. He knew that her good looks attracted men.

One morning there was a loud knock at the door and she was surprised to see a young policeman standing on her doorstep. She wondered why John Carmichael hadn't come, but he quickly assured her that his call had nothing to do with any previous case.

"Do you know a gentleman called Charles Garcia?" he asked.

"Chuck?" She was puzzled. She invited the police constable in. "Has he been hurt?" Her body shook with fear.

He took his helmet off and sat down, and placed it on the floor next to the chair. "It's nothing like that. There have been some allegations made against him and my sergeant wants yer to come down to the station."

"What sort of allegations?" Violet's mind was racing.

"It's best if we discuss it at the station."

She agreed to go after work. Audrey was concerned for her friend as she'd had more than her fair share of bad luck. She reassured her that Annie could go round for her tea as John was working until late. Malcolm Gibson was a godsend, he was the most considerate of men and he always enquired about her welfare and supported her throughout their working days together. He knew that she was worried about something and insisted that she went home early.

There were two policemen in the stuffy room. One she recognised as the young constable who had been to her house, and an older one who had three stripes on his arm. He introduced himself as Sergeant Willis and his sidekick as Constable Peters.

"Could yer tell me what your relationship is with Mr Charles Garcia?" Sergeant Willis asked.

"He's my fiancé. Why?"

"Well, well, well. He has been a busy boy. Were you aware that he has already got a fiancée with a child on the way?" He grinned as he saw her pale. "She has accused him of theft." He waited a moment for his statement to sink in. "In fact, Mr Garcia is actually married to a Mrs Cynthia Garcia. It seems as if he has a penchant for rich women." He grinned. "The army will take a very dim view of his behaviour and will no doubt kick him out."

"I'm not a rich woman. In fact, I'm the complete opposite!" She held her head high. She would not show this man how upset she was.

"Hmm, well, I can imagine what he saw in you." He looked her up and down, "Has he ever given you any of these items?" He showed her some photographs of jewellery and a gold watch. "These are items that Miss Dawson claims he has stolen from her and given to you."

She felt sick when she saw the large diamond ring and it was all she could do to stop her herself from checking if it was still on the chain under her jumper. She shook her head.

"Well, I'm not sure that I can believe you. It may be necessary to come and search your home."

"Feel free to come any time. You won't find anything!" she retorted.

Sergeant Willis sneered, "Well, you know what they say? Hell hath no fury like a woman scorned. I bet she was very annoyed when she found out about you," he chuckled.

"I find your attitude rather disturbing, Sergeant Willis. You seem to find this all very amusing." She glared at him.

"Well, what do you ladies expect when you get mixed up wi' American soldiers?" He stood up and walked to the door. He put his hand out to shake her hand, but she declined. He winked, "I'll be in touch."

Violet glared at him. He reminded her of Frederick Smythe. She walked unsteadily as she made her way to the Ladies, where she splashed her face with cold water. How could he do this to her? Why had she been so stupid? She took the chain from round her neck and stared at the beautiful diamond, the prisms of light were blurring through her tears. Her conscience said that she should return it, but her heart said, "NO." How did she know if that woman was telling the truth? The only thing she was sure of was Chuck's love for her.

CHAPTER THIRTY-THREE
1945

Malcolm broke the news to Violet that Harold wouldn't be coming back. The lease was up for renewal and he'd decided not to renew it.

"It's a pity that you canna afford it, Violet. It's a little goldmine. You'd know exactly what to do; you've been practically running this place yourself."

"I couldn't do that, Malcolm! I'd never raise the money. I've got kids to think of and what if it didn't work?"

"What if no-one takes on the lease? Or what if someone does lease it, but don't want yer services? You'd end up working more shifts at the pub and yer berra than that."

Violet thought about the day on the station when she couldn't find Chuck. She remembered seeing a pregnant lady, dressed in expensive clothes, running towards a man who looked like Chuck. The realisation suddenly hit her. No wonder he didn't want her to see him off at the station. She thought about the belligerent man at the dance who made the remark about not trusting him and the drunk who had said, "You get all the pretty dames, Garcia." She saw everything clearly now. Her engagement ring meant nothing! His words meant nothing. She should return it to its rightful owner.

Audrey made a cup of tea and said, "Here, get that down yer. Bloody Hell, Vi, I canna believe it! You have to take on that lease. You've gorra child on the way and a family to support and you're not going to be able to work with a baby. It's your birthday soon and it's fast approaching Christmas. Then it will be the kids' birthdays and you'll have nowt."

"But if I take over the lease, I'd have to find £150 for a year's rent upfront and £20 bond. How am I supposed to do that?"

"You'll have to sell that ring." She put her hand up as her friend started to protest. "Dunna worry about that woman, it sounds like she's not short of money, but you are! You've got to survive. Never mind all yer bloody principles, think of the kids."

"But where would I sell it? It's on the police wanted list."

"Jimmy knows how to get rid of knocked-off stuff. You'll have to ask him."

"I can't! It's stealing! It's wrong!"

"I'll tell you what's wrong! It's you having a raw deal! You've gorra think of the kids, Vi. You could let someone 'ave that little flat cheap and they could look after yer little one whilst yer in the shop."

The police knocked loudly on her door and she noticed the neighbours' curtains twitching. There were just the two of them—the same two policemen she'd seen at the station. She allowed them to look around. She didn't want them to get a search warrant, as if she was a criminal. *But I am a criminal*, she thought.

Sergeant Willis held up a pair of nylons. "My goodness, what did yer do to get them? My missus would kill to gerra pair of these."

She snatched them out of his hand. "I wonder what your wife would think if she knew how much you've relished going through my underwear drawer."

He held up a pair of silk knickers and she went to grab them, but he threw them to Constable Peters, who threw them back, laughing.

"I think you have seen enough, so unless you've found any incriminating evidence, I'd like you to leave. Your behaviour is disgusting!"

He looked her up and down and said, "I'll tell yer what's disgusting! It's those bloody Americans, coming over here and flashing their cash around and taking our women!"

"Oh Sergeant Willis, anyone would think you were jealous," she said sarcastically.

He looked at her with contempt and slammed the front door on his way out. It took her an hour to clean up the mess from their search. She felt violated. She'd just cleared up the unnecessary mess with minutes to spare when Annie came in from school.

Violet went to the police station at the request of Detective Sergeant Carmichael. He had news for her.

"We've got some good news to tell you. We've tracked down Mr Cavendish's past accusers and one of them is willing to give evidence. We've also exhumed his wife's body but we're still waiting for the post mortem results."

She told him about her treatment at the hands of Sergeant Willis, but she declined to make an official complaint.

He thought that she'd had a raw deal in life and seemed like a very nice woman. He despised men like Sergeant Willis, calling him *a misogynist in a uniform*. He would be keeping an eye on him. He shook her hand. "Rest assured, Mrs Higgins, we will get Mr Cavendish this time."

Violet waited until the end of the evening to speak to Jimmy. She hadn't topped up his drink. She needed him alert.

"What's up wi' yer face, Vi? Yer look troubled."

Violet told him about her predicament. She hadn't told him that she was pregnant; it wasn't obvious yet. She was careful to edit her version of events. She knew that Jimmy would be jealous of Chuck.

Jimmy said, "Leave it wi' me. I'll see what I can do." He thought, *I could punch that smarmy bastard in the face!* He also thought about Violet with her *little girl lost look. Well, it will cost her, she's played me for a fool for long enough.*

Jimmy's mate put his loupe to his eye and whistled, "Very nice. Top quality. It's a two carat, exquisitely cut diamond. Bloody Hell, where did you get it, Jimmy?"

Jimmy told him about Violet and the American, but mentioned no names.

"I think you're a bit smitten with that young lady, Jimmy," he grinned. "Leave it with me. I'll see what I can do and, for the record, I canna stand them flash Americans either."

Violet waited until she saw the lights go out at the pub. Her hands were shaking as she knocked on the back door.

"Well, Lover Boy must've had a lorra money. That ring was worth three hundred pounds, at least! Of course, because it was hot, we couldn't get its full worth."

"How much did you get, Jimmy?"

"One hundred and eighty quid!" He wafted it under her nose, but as she went to take it, he pulled it out of reach. "Not so fast, sweetheart! What do I gerrout of it?"

"Tell me how much you want and you can have it Jimmy. I'm so grateful to you."

"It ain't money I'm after," he leered at her. "I need yer to be nice to me, if yer get my drift."

She turned to go, but he barred her way. "I know yer need this money, but I'm not goin' to just hand it over like that! I've had to take all the risks." He smirked, "You can take it or leave it. It's a win-win

158

for me. Either I keep the money or I get to spend time wi' yer, just the two of us."

"I'll, I'll tell the..."

"Tell who, the police?" He laughed. "*I don't know owt about a ring officer*," he mocked. "You'd be the one gerrin into trouble. You'd end up wi' a criminal record." He grabbed her hands and stroked them. "All yer have to do is be nice to me for an hour or two and then I will give yer all this lovely money and the ring will never be mentioned again."

She snatched her hands away from him. "That's blackmail!"

"I know darlin', it's a harsh world innit? You've got till tomorrow to give me yer answer."

Violet tossed and turned all night, her thoughts going round and round in her mind. She had naively given Jimmy an expensive ring and now he had the upper hand. She couldn't go to the police because she'd lied to them, but she couldn't let him keep the money. Why had she been so stupid to trust a man? She didn't know how she was going to support her family. She couldn't work with a baby. She gave up trying to sleep and got up to make a cup of tea. The thought of Jimmy made her feel sick.

Daylight was a relief after such a long night and she was pleased when Audrey popped round.

"Bloody Hell, you look as if you've been up all night."

"I've been awake for most of it, thinking about Jimmy. He's blackmailing me into sleeping with him before he hands over the money," Violet put her head in her hands.

"The devious old buggar! He's been after you since day one. He's jealous because of Chuck and he's making yer pay fer it!"

"I need that money, Audrey. I'll soon have another mouth to feed. The only chance I've got is to take over the shop and how can I do that unless Jimmy gives me my money?" Tears ran down her cheeks. "He wants me to prostitute myself to get that money. I just can't!"

"Yer can't let him gerraway wi' it! That's theft! He's tricked you, so you've gorra do the same to him. I'll talk to Bert when he gets home, he hates Jimmy."

"Do you think he'll come with me? I think he's a bit wary of Bert."

"I think we need to be a bit more devious than that. We need to play him at his own game. Leave it wi' me. Me and Bert will come up with a plan."

Jimmy reeked of cheap aftershave. He was wearing a smart blue jumper and his hair shone with Brylcreem. Violet was not the only one who noticed that Jimmy was spruced up.

"Bloody Hell, 'ave yer got a date or sommat?" asked Bill, one of the regulars.

"Yer never know. I've gorra feeling that tonight's me lucky night."

Violet caught Audrey's eye; she felt sick. Jimmy clearly intended to carry out his vindictive plan. Violet hoped that their own plan would work. Audrey ordered half a pint of pale ale and asked Jimmy to have one with her. He poured himself a whisky and she engaged him in conversation whilst Violet slipped one of Bert's sleeping pills into it. Both women looked at each other anxiously; Jimmy didn't touch the drink.

Jimmy was keen to get rid of the stragglers. "Come on gentlemen. Haven't yer got homes to go to?" After he locked the door, he strode over to Violet and pinned her against the wall. He pushed her skirt up.

"Stop it Jimmy! You know you've got the upper hand, there's no need to be so rough."

"Do yer think that I don't know what you've been up to? Coming over as all sweet and innocent, when all this time you've been gerrin' me drunk and robbing me blind!"

Violet protested her innocence, but he wasn't listening. "Did yer think I'd fall for that stunt pulled by yer mate? I'm a man of me word, darlin'. I'll keep my end of the bargain if you keep yours. You've just got to be nice to me and I'll hand over the money."

"You expect me to prostitute myself to get the money that's mine. That's not right, Jimmy!"

"Well, that ain't strictly true is it? Technically that diamond ring dunna belong to you. You handed it over to me. Yer know what they say, possession is nine tenths of the law. What did yer have to do to gerrit?"

"It seems as if I don't have a choice, but please don't rush me. Let's just sit and talk first. I'll make us a cup of coffee."

160

"No yer won't, I'll do it. I've waited this long, I suppose I can savour the moment a bit longer." Jimmy brought in two cups of coffee and put them on a coffee table next to the settee.

She took a sip and spluttered, "There's no sugar in it."

"You told me that you didn't take sugar!"

"I do in coffee, Jimmy." She held her cup up and said, "Do you mind?"

Jimmy went back into the kitchen. She needed to be quick. She took a plastic spoon out of her bag and quickly stirred his coffee. When he brought her coffee to her, he sat so close to her, that she could feel the heat coming off his leg.

"Well, what do yer want to talk about?"

"Tell me about yourself. Have you ever been married? Do you have any children?"

"I dunna want to talk about it. She was a cheating bitch! I'm berra off without her!"

She watched whilst Jimmy sipped his coffee. He stood up and said, "Come on, it's time we went upstairs."

"How do I know I can trust you? You haven't shown me the money."

"Do yer think I'm that stupid? I'm not going to show yer where I keep it, you might run off wi' it."

"There's got to be trust on both sides, Jimmy. You're expecting me to trust you, but you won't trust me!"

"That's life. Come on, Vi."

She reluctantly followed him upstairs, wondering how she was going to stall him. As she entered the bedroom, Jimmy was lying on the grimy bed. On the bedside locker was an ashtray overflowing with nub ends and a whisky bottle lay on the floor which was almost empty, and next to it magazines showing bare-breasted women.

"I'm just popping into the bathroom, I won't be long." Violet quickly locked the door behind her and gagged at the overpowering smell of body odour. The bathroom was grimy and had dirty washing strewn across the floor.

"Hurry up, Vi, or else I'm goin' to come in there!"

"I'll be out in a minute. I'm just freshening up."

She could hear him thudding across the room and jumped as he hammered on the door.

His speech was starting to slur. "Well hurry up about it!"

Her heart was beating quickly. She muttered to herself, "How did I end up in this situation?" She wished she was back on the farm in the safe arms of Ted. She took a deep breath and thought, *Pull yourself together, think of the children.*

Jimmy stopped calling out and she gingerly opened the door, and breathed a sigh of relief. Jimmy lying face down on the bed with his arm hanging over the side, snoring loudly. Bert poked his head round the door, he'd managed to sneak through to the back earlier whilst Audrey had engaged Jimmy in conversation, and hidden behind the settee.

They started their search downstairs and gradually worked their way through the furniture emptying the drawers, including the kitchen cupboards and the sideboard. They felt in his jacket pocket hanging on the back of a chair, but there was just some loose change in there. When they got upstairs, Jimmy was still snoring and Bert rolled him over and she felt under the mattress.

"Can yer feel owt, Vi?"

She shook her head, so Bert rolled him the other way.

She got excited. "I can feel a fat envelope but I can't quite grip it, Bert."

Bert shoved Jimmy off the bed and he landed on the floor with a bang. He groaned, but carried on sleeping.

"Grab the money and run!" ordered Bert.

Back at home, Bert poured them a glass of brandy. "He wunna miss it," he grinned.

"What if the police come?" fretted Violet.

"He ain't goin' to involve The Old Bill. He canna prove anything. I put him back on the bed and we left everything as we found it." Burt cracked his fingers. "I dunna know how I didn't punch his face in!"

There was a stunned silence when Violet counted the money.

"He was goin' to give you one hundred and eighty quid!" Audrey was incensed. "The robbin' swine! There's three hundred and fifty quid there! Yer can set up shop now, Vi and never go back to that bloody pub again!" She hugged her friend to her ample bosom.

"I'm scared. Jimmy isn't going to let me get away with it, is he?"

"What can he do? He canna prove anything. He's a blackmailer and a bully. Yer need to tell him that yer not going back. Don't worry, Vi, I will come wi' yer to the pub and make sure you get yer wages," said Bert.

Violet's hands were shaking when she walked into the pub at closing time. Jimmy was belligerent and pointed his finger in her face.

"You thieving bitch! I know it was you!"

She looked him in the eyes. "That's right. I took it. You were robbing me! That ring was mine. You know that I needed that money and you took advantage of me! Did you really think that I would sleep with you? What sort of a woman do you think I am?"

Jimmy raised his hand but Bert quickly came from behind the door. He grabbed Jimmy by his collar.

"I can't stand men that hit women! She ain't comin' back and yer can give her, her wages. I always thought you were a waste of space, but blackmailing a woman that's tryin' to do the best for her kids!" He shook his head.

Violet walked out with her head held high and her wages in her pocket. She hooked arms with Bert, thankful for his friendship.

CHAPTER THIRTY-FOUR
1945

The shop thrived under Violet's management. Her children were happy that she wasn't working at the pub anymore, particularly John.

"It's goin' well for yer Mum, I'm glad that you dunna work at that pub anymore, but I still dunna understand how yer got the deposit."

"I just put a bit aside when I did extra shifts and I sold a ring that Chuck bought me."

"What sort of ring?" He looked at her suspiciously, "Do yer mean an engagement ring?"

"No, silly," she lied. "I couldn't have got engaged to Chuck - he was married, but it was worth quite a bit of money."

"He was married and he was givin' yer expensive jewellery? Why would 'e do that?"

"People do all sorts of things in wartime and behave in a way they wouldn't normally do, more spontaneous, living for today as your time could be up at any moment." She could see that John was willing to accept her explanation. "And talking about being spontaneous, there's something I need to tell you. I hope you won't hate me for it."

"I could never hate you. Just tell me," he said anxiously.

"You're going to have a little brother or sister," she scrutinized John's face.

"You're having a baby?" he queried.

"I'm so sorry. I've let you down. I still love your father, I always will. I just got swept away with the excitement." Tears rolled down her face.

"You could never let me down, Mum." He wrapped his arms around her. "Let's hope that I have a brother. I dunna want another sister like Annie," he laughed. "But how are yer going to work and look after a baby?"

"Audrey is going to help out at the shop."

"Dunna feel bad, Mum. I like Chuck, but there's not much 'e can do about it now he's had to go back to America."

Violet didn't tell him that he'd been accused of theft by a woman who was having his baby, and that the ring Chuck gave her was actually stolen and that she had absolutely no right to sell it. "How am I going to tell your grandparents?" she fretted.

"They'll understand. Grandma told me that yer would meet someone else one day. Annie told her about Chuck and she took it surprisingly well. She was just concerned that you were going to get hurt. She said you were vulnerable."

When Annie was told the news, she said, "I thought you were getting a bit fat, Mum." She typically thought about herself when she added, "It isn't going to share my room is it?"

They'd had to get rid of all traces of Harold at the shop before they could work there and Audrey had helped Violet to change things round and decorate. They'd put a woman's touch to the shop making it more inviting, particularly for women.

Rationing was still in place and Violet needed to have patience with irate customers, who expected things to change straight after the war ended. Her pregnancy was becoming obvious, which made her the subject of village gossip.

"She's widowed, yer know," said Ida Watson.

"I heard she were knockin' about wi' an American soldier," said a scandalised Betty James.

Ada Brown came to her defence. "Ain't yer got anythin' better to do wi' yer time?" She'd always appreciated Violet's kindness.

Audrey was a great help in the shop and a quick learner. The customers enjoyed sharing banter with her. No-one could have guessed that her smiling face was a mask and that soon, she and her friend would be attending a harrowing court case.

Detective Carmichael had informed Violet that the case against Harold Cavendish was due in court the first week in December, earlier than expected, and a solicitor had prepped John for his time in court.

"I'm scared, Mum. I dunna want to see him. I feel sick!" John confided.

"I'm so proud of you!" She ruffled his hair. "Detective Carmichael told me that Harold has been charged with killing his wife. He's still on bail. He'll be going to court at a later date for that. It just goes to show that you never really know anyone. The good thing is that it's all being heard at Derby assizes, so hopefully the village gossips won't get to hear about it." She kept her anxieties to herself. She was dreading seeing Harold and she wondered if Gordon Wayne would be there, ready to expose their secret.

Bert drove Audrey, Violet and John to court, where they were meeting Bill and Frank. John sat in the front next to Bert and the two women sat in the back, clutching each other's hands. Not a word was spoken during the journey.

Bert squeezed John's shoulder before they ascended the stone steps into court. "You've got this Lad, chin up."

Bill and Frank were waiting outside for them to arrive, Frank pacing up and down chain smoking, leaving a fug of smoke in his wake, and Bill standing passively by the steps. Detective John Carmichael and Detective David Wiley were waiting for them in the foyer and the senior detective shook their hands and offered John reassurance.

Whilst they were waiting to be called into the courtroom, John sat mute between his Uncle Bill and his mother looking at his feet. Audrey chatted with the two policemen but Bert sat quietly by her side, his fists clenched into tight balls.

The foyer was busy with groups of people either huddled together in small groups or milling about talking which gave Harold the opportunity to enter by a side door. He was accompanied by a tall young man and they stayed out of sight at the back.

The court usher called, "Will all people connected with the case of Regina v Cavendish please enter Court Three?"

The group entered the courtroom to find Harold sitting with his lawyer and looking at the floor. Bill had to restrain Frank from running over to *bash his brains out*.

A voice called out, "All rise for The Honourable Judge Johns."

Violet paled as the rotund figure with rubbery lips walked in wearing his official robes. He scoured the court room before sitting down. Violet felt as if she was going to faint and kept her head down, unable to look at him.

A young man called Charles Whitmore was called to the stand. He was a little older than John, but his testimony was shaky and he broke down under questioning. The court was adjourned for a short break, during which time it had become apparent that the young man was unable to carry on. His evidence was dismissed.

Detective John Carmichael, represented the police and put forward a strong argument, that Harold Cavendish had used various aliases for the sole purpose of escaping detection and that he had moved around the country to escape his accusers. The court adjourned for lunch after he had given his testimony and during that time, John surprised everyone. His demeanour changed and he sat upright and declared, "I'm not goin' to let him gerr away wi' it! He'll only do it to another kid." He looked determinedly at his mother. "I dunna want yer to come in. Please, Mum, stay out here wi' Audrey. I'm goin' to tell that judge everything and I don't want yer to know all the details."

Violet held him close. She had to respect his wishes and although she wanted to support her son, part of her was relieved not to have to face Henry Johns again. She hoped that he wouldn't put two and two together and realise that John was her son. Although it was a long time ago, she suspected that he was the type of man to hold a grudge. She didn't want her son to pay the price for what she and her mother had done, all those years ago. Audrey sat close to her and held her hand as the men returned to the courtroom.

Bill, Frank and Bert supported John throughout. He stood in the witness box and spoke in a clear voice. He looked directly at Harold, who didn't look up as John, prompted by the prosecutor, revealed the sordid details. After John left the witness box, Judge Johns adjourned the session. Apparently he wanted to look into Harold's background in fine detail. Harold Cavendish was led out through a side door by his lawyer, to avoid any hostile reception from others.

There was a sense of relief that John didn't have to go to court again. They hoped that justice would be done. However the calm didn't last for long. The Gazette had a photograph of Harold against salacious headlines: LOCAL MAN IN COURT ACCUSED OF MOLESTING YOUNG BOYS. It caused a stir in the shop and all the newspapers sold out very quickly. People devoured the news. They had more customers than ever, all wanting to pass on titbits and gossip. Audrey and Violet kept their nerve and feigned disbelief, sticking to the mantra, "We don't know anything."

Malcolm Gibson proved a supportive friend. He had put two and two together, but he never let on. He would make them *a nice cuppa* and ask about their welfare. He was the kindest of men.

Jimmy was also the subject of village gossip. His drinking had spiralled out of control. He'd become a belligerent drunk and his customers were going elsewhere for their beer.

Violet was on her way home from working at the shop when she heard footsteps behind her. She knew who it was by the smell of alcohol and stale cigarettes. The stench of his body odour made her gag.

"Yer think that yer someone special wi' yer shop, don't yer? Well, I know what yer are - yer a whore!" He pushed her against the wall and put his hand round her throat. "You owe me for gerrin that money for yer. You thought I wanna good enough for yer,but your nowt but a whore!"

An unlikely source intervened and when a large handbag hit him across the back of his head, it stopped him in his tracks. "Leave her alone! You should be ashamed of yoursen, Jimmy Greensmith! Yer a disgrace! Now clear off before I start shoutin' blue murder and everyone will come out to see what the rumpus is and set about yer!"

Jimmy scuttled back to the pub and Ada accompanied Violet home and set about making her a cup of tea. A bit later Audrey came round when Ada left to get her husband's tea. "If Jimmy keeps this up, you're goin' to have to tell the police," she advised.

Violet was anxious. "He'll tell them about the ring."

"What ring? They canna prove anything and besides he would implicate himself."

"What if they ask how I got the money to put down on the shop? They're sure to find out it was from the ring." Violet paced up and down, pressing her hands against her back.

"They canna prove anything. Stop worrying, or else that baby will come early."

Although the shop was doing well and they had a better standard of living, something was missing in her life. She often reminisced about life with Ted and she refused to believe that Chuck's words were false. He'd told her that he was in love with her, and she longed to hear those words again. Her children were growing up quickly, John spent long hours at work and Annie was turning into quite the little lady. She'd spent many hours watching film stars and improving her speech. Violet worried about her because she was too beautiful for her own good.

A few weeks later, when Violet came home she found a calling card on the mat which had two words on the back. *Call me*. She decided that she would go in person to the police station. She was able to leave the shop in the capable hands of Audrey and Malcolm. The rhythmical motion of the horse and cart and the clip clop of the horses hooves made her feel sleepy. She thought about her mother again and how they'd taken revenge on Henry Johns. It seemed so long ago and she had not expected to come across him again! Tom Dawson dropped her outside the police station. He was the soul of discretion and never asked questions.

Detective Carmichael asked her to sit down. "We've had two more complaints against Mr Cavendish and therefore, Judge Johns has agreed to delay his sentencing until the other complaints have been heard. He is due to appear on a murder charge in the next few months and he will be going to prison for a very long time. Although he's out on bail, he has very strict conditions."

As she left his office, Constable Peters called after her, asking if he could have a word with her. Violet was thankful that Sergeant Willis was off duty. The constable took out some paperwork and informed her that the charges against Chuck had been dropped.

"You mean she made it all up?" Violet shook her head in disbelief.

"There was insufficient evidence. We only had her word for it. Sergeant Willis thinks she must have found the ring in his pocket and wrongly assumed that the ring was for her and when she realised the truth, she wanted to pay him back. She obviously thought that by getting theft charges brought against him, it would affect his military career!" He chuckled. "It's strange that you haven't seen that ring, though. Perhaps it was for someone else." He winked.

Violet's eyes flashed. "It's just a game to you, isn't it? I don't care what you think!"

As she slammed the door behind her, Constable Peters grinned. *She has beautiful eyes and a lovely arse,* he thought.

CHAPTER THIRTY-FIVE
1946

Late into the night, after hours of labour, James Charles Higgins was born. He weighed in at 8lbs 2ozs and had a full head of dark hair. When she'd given birth to her other children, she'd had a loving husband and family by her side. Now there was just Audrey to hold her hand. As her tears spilled onto her baby's head, the midwife squeezed her fingers; she'd seen this situation all too often since the war.

Audrey cried to Bert, "I'm goin' to try and find that bloody American if it kills me. He needs to know he's gorra son."

"Don't talk daft, woman! Have yer any idea how big America is? It's like lookin' fer a needle in a haystack. There's bloody hundreds of babies bein' born to them Americans and they wunna give them gals a minute's thought. Take my advice and stay out of it. Vi wunna thank yer for interfering," advised Bert.

"He loves her. He'd come back if he knew," Audrey insisted.

"He's married! He's just like them other bloody randy Americans. Just keep yer nose out!"

Audrey had an idea. She rummaged in her wardrobe and found the handbag that she'd used to go out partying. There was a little hole in the lining where she'd hidden Gus' address. She thought about him and how prejudice stopped him being with James, *the love of his life*. She had been an effective and knowing ruse for him.

Two months after the baby was born, Harold Cavendish appeared at court for sentencing. John took the afternoon off work to look after his little brother, and to be there for Annie when she came home from school. Audrey and Bert accompanied Violet and they met Bill and Frank at the court.

Judge Johns solemnly read out his indictment. "Harold George Cavendish, you were charged with molestation and attempted rape against minors." He addressed the foreman of the jury. "Have you reached a verdict in which you were all agreed?"

"Yes Your Honour. We have."

The jury found Harold guilty so Judge Johns addressed Harold directly. "Harold George Cavendish you have been found guilty of the most heinous of crimes against young boys. I have no doubt that this is just the tip of the iceberg. You have shown no remorse for your crimes and I believe you continue to be a danger to children; therefore I have no choice but to give you a custodial sentence of four years. Officer, take him down!"

Frank shouted, "Four years for what he did! He wants locking up for good and the key throwing away! I hope you die in prison. You bloody pervert!"

Harold didn't look up. Judge Johns banged his gavel and shouted, "Order in court! Please refrain from shouting in the gallery, or else I will hold you in contempt of court." He looked up at the gallery and Violet thought she was going to be sick. They locked eyes for a second and she had to grip the handrail. "Officer, take him down."

A voice called out, "All rise for the Honourable Judge Johns." He stood and disappeared in his red and black finery.

Later, when James was almost seven months old, Audrey confided in Violet. "My Bert's about to lose his job. He's that depressed and 'is mother's in poor health and he wunna be able to afford to go and see her every week. I dunna know what we're goin' to do and they're purrin our rent up."

The following day, Violet went round to see Bert whilst Audrey was at the shop.

"You'd do that for me Vi?" Bert was overwhelmed.

"It's the least I can do for you. I wouldn't be in the position I'm in, if it hadn't been for you."

"There's an empty shop near me Mother's, that's up for rent. I'll look into it and see 'ow much they want upfront and fer the bond." He hugged Violet tightly and said, "Yer a good friend, Vi."

A few weeks later, a large van came next door and when the last stick of furniture was in it, the two friends said their goodbyes.

"I dunna want to leave yer, Vi. I will miss yer, but thanks to you, Bert can follow 'is dream." She cried on her friend's shoulder. "How are yer goin' to manage wi' James?"

"Don't you worry about me. I'll manage."

"I'll pay yer back every penny, Vi," promised Bert.

"I don't want you to worry about that. You know that I would have given you half that money if I hadn't needed it for taking over the shop." She kissed him on the cheek. "If it hadn't been for you, I wouldn't have any of that money back. You and Audrey have been true friends and I'm going to miss you."

Fred passed away a few weeks later and had a small funeral with just villagers attending - he had no living relatives. A family of six moved into Fred's and within no time, his well maintained garden became a weed-ridden dumping ground for a stained mattress, and an old rusty pram as well as littered empty bottles and cigarette ends.

Another family of five moved into Audrey's house and they could be heard arguing and fighting late into the night.

"We canna go on like this Mum, I can hardly keep me eyes open at work and I need to have me wits about me. A farm can be a dangerous place and our Annie canna concentrate at school."

"I don't know what to do. They don't look like the sort of people I could complain to."

"Mr Winterson is relying on me more and more. He's struggling wi' his health, so if I moved in it would help 'im and you could move into the flat above the shop."

"No, John, NO!" Violet sobbed.

"Mum, I've gorra grow up sometime. You're trapped between two rough families and it makes sense for yer to move into the flat above the shop. You'd be able to look after James berra. I know it's small but it's berra than livin' next to these lot."

"How did you get to be so grown-up? I must admit, it makes sense. The people that rented it weren't reliable and are moving next week. Besides they're putting up my rent on this house again and it's not the same without Audrey."

Customers were intolerant of the continued rationing and arguments frequently broke out such as the two women fighting over the last slice of bacon.

"That belongs to me!"

"No it doesn't! I was 'ere first."

Ada Brown stood between the women and warned, "I will chuck yer both out if yer don't calm down."

Violet was grateful to Ada. She had proved to be a reliable, hard-working woman, although she missed Audrey's wit and humour.

Malcolm beckoned her over. "Your neighbour brought this over." He held out the letter in his hand. "It was sent to their house and she asked me to send it back."

Violet's hands shook as she took the letter out of his hands. "It's addressed to Audrey." She turned it over in her hand. "It's got a military stamp on it!" Her heart was beating quickly. "Why would they be writing to Audrey?"

"Go and take a break, love. Yer look as if you've seen a ghost," coaxed Malcolm.

Her hands shook as she drank her tea. She took the letter out of her pocket and examined it. She held it up to the steam from the kettle, but stopped when she heard Malcolm's voice.

He held out his hand. "Yer need to give me the letter, Vi."

"Please Malcolm; let me speak to Audrey before you send it on to her."

"That's highly irregular, but I suppose it won't hurt to leave it another day." He patted her on her shoulder and took the letter out of her hand.

A deep voice answered the phone, "Good afternoon, Bert's Butchers. How can I help yer?"

"Hello Bert. It's Violet. How are you doing?"

"Vi, it's lovely to hear your voice. Business is good. How are yer all?"

"We're not too bad. Is Audrey about?"

"No, but I'll gerr' her to ring yer tonight."

Violet sat by the phone willing it to ring, and when it did, her hands trembled as she lifted the receiver. "Why has a letter come for you franked with the United States army?"

"It'll be from Gus. I wanted to ask about Chuck."

"Why would you want to find out about Chuck? You know how he let me down. Why would you do that? I thought you were my friend? Why would you go behind my back?"

"I *am* your friend. Gus gave me his forces address. I thought he would speak to Chuck and that if he knew about James he would help yer. I dunna think you've had the full story, Vi."

"He's married, Audrey! How could he marry me if he was already married? He got engaged to another woman and got her pregnant!

173

Why would I want anything to do with him? I could never trust him again. I was a fool to think he ever loved me. I don't need a man. I can manage on me own."

"I still think there's more to it. Perhaps he'd have gorra divorce and you know that woman was a liar, so you canna believe anything she says. I was only trying to help, Vi. Why don't yer wait and see what it says?"

Audrey phoned Malcolm the next day, but her pleading fell on deaf ears. When Malcolm had finished his phone call, he put his arm around Violet's shoulders and spoke softly to her. "I know yer want to know what's in it and Audrey's given me permission to give it yer, but if the post office found out, I'd lose me job. I'm sorry, love, but I will have to forward it to Audrey. I would give it yer if I could."

A week later, Audrey phoned the shop, "Vi, I don't know how to say this. I—I canna find the words."

Violet's knuckles were white as she gripped the receiver and as she listened to Audrey's words, she struggled to breathe. The phone dangled against the wall as she slid to the floor. The customers stared as Ada put her arm around Violet's shoulders and led her to the back room.

"Come on, love, I'll put the kettle on. This lot can wait for a few minutes."

When the kettle whistled, Ada warmed the brown earthenware pot, put fresh tea leaves in it and poured Violet a strong, sweet tea to help her get over her shock.

The rumour mill was working overtime as the village gossips watched the unfolding drama. Violet held James close to her kissing the top of his head—the dark hair, just like his father's. She whispered over and over again, "Your Daddy's dead, your Daddy's dead." She relived Audrey's words; "He died in a car accident." She couldn't get over the irony of it. He'd been in the war without so much as a scratch and then got hit by a drunk driver when he went home. She had so many questions running through her mind; questions that would now remain unanswered.

CHAPTER THIRTY-SIX
1947

The murder trial of Harold Cavendish attracted a lot of media attention. A photograph of Harold, his head bowed and being led into court in handcuffs, was splashed across the front page of The Derbyshire Times; The headlines read: PERVERT SHOPKEEPER ACCUSED OF KILLING HIS WIFE. The case of the mild-mannered shopkeeper was also covered by some of the national newspapers and carried headlines such as SILENCED TO KEEP HIS SECRET and PURE EVIL.They all contained the salacious details of the case and Violet was thankful that at least the boys' names were kept out the newspapers.

The shop was besieged by reporters, all wanting to find out any titbits that they could publish. Violet kept up her pretence that she knew nothing, but some of the customers were only too willing to talk to the press, despite not knowing anything. Janet Cooper was reported as saying that she never trusted him, and Sandra Mason accused him of being shifty. Alongside their interviews was a photograph of them in their rollers and headscarves, dressed in their wrap-around aprons. The press didn't care if the two women knew anything or not, as long as it sold newspapers. Violet was horrified when they filmed her opening the shop and her image was in the newspaper. She felt sick whenever any reports of the case came out. The newspapers in the shop sold out immediately as people formed a queue to buy one. Arguments and a tug of war would break out when the last newspaper was sold. She despised the people who devoured the newspapers, searching for new little titbits to pass on, and yet she was guilty of the same thing. She couldn't drag herself away; it was like picking at a scab and preventing it from healing.

Annie had the newspaper open and was reading the news about Harold. "I can't believe it! I didn't like him, he was horrible to me and he didn't want me to go to the shop with John," she stopped in her tracks. "Oh my God, Mum! Do you think it was because he wanted John to be there by himself? Did John say anything?"

"I don't think you should be reading this stuff, Annie. It's not healthy. Pass me that paper now."

Annie was not willing to let the subject drop. "Oh my God, I knew there was something wrong when we came back from me

Grandparents that day. You all treated me like a child, but I knew there was something wrong when you were all quiet in the car. It was about him wasn't it? John was one of the boys in the paper, wasn't he?"

"Annie, will you stop saying *Oh my God* and will you stop going on? Please drop it. I don't want to hear that man's name mentioned in this house again!"

Annie folded her arms and scowled. Her mum couldn't look her in the face. She would ask John the next time she saw him, but she knew the answer.

Harold pleaded not guilty to murdering his wife and when the quiet spoken shopkeeper took to the stand, a hush descended on the packed courtroom. He held the Bible in his right hand and said in a clear voice, "I, Harold George Cavendish swear by almighty God that I shall tell the truth, the whole truth and nothing but the truth."

When questioned by his defence barrister about his relationship with his wife, Harold bowed his head and wiped his eyes. "We had a good relationship, but my dear Gwennie was suffering from severe depression on account of being childless. She became delusional…" He cried into his handkerchief, blew his nose, and cleaned his spectacles, before adding, "I loved my wife. I would never have hurt her."

"How did it make you feel when your wife questioned you about the rumours of your inappropriate behaviour with minors? Did it make you angry towards her?"

"I could never have got angry with my dear wife. I felt sad that her delusional thoughts caused her to suffer."

When it was the prosecutor's turn to question, Harold he took a firmer stance. "But they weren't rumours, were they Mr Cavendish? You were in fact found guilty of those crimes."

"It doesn't mean that I was actually guilty. It means that the jury were duped into believing those lies. I was much maligned."

"Are you saying that the jury got it wrong? That your accusers got it wrong?" That they misunderstood your actions?" He paused for effect. "You would also have us believe that your poor, delusional wife also got it wrong. What an unfortunate man you are!" said the prosecutor sarcastically.

Harold nodded his head and dabbed his eyes.

"Well, Mr Cavendish, answer me this; why would your wife have given a letter to her friend to only read if something happened to her, if she were not of sound mind? That doesn't sound like a woman who was mentally ill. It sounds like a very rational woman scared for her life. A woman setting plans in motion to prevent you doing harm to anyone else. Would you agree? Or have I got that wrong as well?" The prosecutor was relentless.

"You're twisting things!" Harold's eyes burned with anger for a few seconds. Then he bowed his head and wiped his eyes again. He spoke in a whisper. "Like I said, she was suffering from a mental illness."

"Why didn't you seek medical help for her?"

"Well, people are funny about mental illness aren't they? I thought that I could take care of her meself." Harold continued to speak quietly.

"I put it to you Mr Cavendish that these are all lies and that you are quite willing to put all the blame on your late wife in order to protect yourself."

Dr Hargreaves was called and he relayed the last time he saw Gwendoline Cavendish. "She came to see me just a few weeks before her demise. She'd been suffering from abdominal cramps, nausea and diarrhoea. I advised her to eat a bland diet and I gave her supplements."

"Did Mrs Cavendish show any signs of suffering from a mental disorder?"

"No, she did not. I found her to be the same bright and intelligent lady she usually was. In fact she was only concerned about being well enough to attend her god-daughter's wedding."

"So, in your professional opinion, Dr Hargreaves, Mrs Cavendish did not express any suicidal thoughts."

"That's correct."

Throughout the murder trial, various professionals and friends were called upon to give evidence, including the pathologist who carried out the post mortem on the exhumed body. He stated that he had found traces of arsenic in her body. He also confirmed that she would have been unable to administer the last few doses of arsenic herself, because she would have been too weak.

The defence team called Harold's brother-in-law who had been subpoenaed to give evidence.

"Tell the court how long you have known the defendant?"

"Twenty years."

"And in all that time, has your sister ever confided in you that she felt threatened by her husband? In fact, am I right in saying that Mr Cavendish provided well for your sister."

"Yes, materially he did."

"And am I right in saying that the letter your sister wrote was during the time she was suffering from depression?"

"Yes, but—"

"Thank you, Mr Smith, no further questions."

It was the time for the prosecuting barrister to speak. "Was your sister a private sort of person, Mr Smith?"

"Yes, my sister was a very private person."

"Then would you agree that it is unlikely that she would have talked about her marriage to friends or relations?"

"Yes, I think that's quite likely."

"Then would you also agree that you had a close bond with your sister, and if she was going to confide in anyone, it would have most likely have been you?"

"Yes, we were very close."

"Did she ever speak to you about her relationship with the defendant?

"No, she never had the opportunity. He never left us on our own. He was always there, hoverin' around like a fly round meat."

"Could you please tell the court if you noticed a change in her demeanour the last few times you saw her? Did she behave differently? For instance, did she appear to be depressed to you? Or show any fear towards her husband?"

"She seemed unusually quiet and timid, but like I said, I never had the chance to find out how she was feeling because He..." he looked pointedly at Harold, "...never left her side."

At the summing up, the defence barrister argued that Harold Cavendish had been a devoted husband who had provided well for his wife. He had looked after her when she was depressed, and in fact, their friends and acquaintances had spoken about his devotion to his wife. The prosecution portrayed the defendant as a manipulative bully who would stop at nothing to prevent his wife finding out about his perverted behaviour towards children.

The jury were sent out to reach a verdict but after several hours, they had failed to do so, resulting in the court being adjourned until the following day when it was hoped that they would reach a verdict and indeed, after several more hours of deliberation, the jury did return a unanimous verdict. They found Harold Cavendish guilty of murder.

The seasoned presiding judge solemnly delivered the appropriate sentence. "Harold George Cavendish, you have been found guilty of the murder of Gwendoline Margaret Cavendish, by poisoning. She was a loyal and loving wife and when she discovered your perversion towards young children, and in particular pubescent boys, you set about ending her life in order to silence her. Therefore, I have no choice but to sentence you to the most severe of punishments as set out by the law." He then placed a black cap on his head and said, "Harold George Cavendish, you will hang by the neck until you are dead. May God have mercy on your soul." Then turning away from the convicted man, he said, "Officer take him down."

Harold almost collapsed on the spot and needed the support of two officers to leave the dock.

CHAPTER THIRTY-SEVEN
1947

When the Victorian prison came into view, Harold's stomach churned and his body visibly shook. Strangeways was a foreboding building with red brick turrets and an imposing chimney which was over two hundred feet high. The prison was dark and dingy and there was a smell of human excrement, body odour and disinfectant. The noise of prisoners shouting and banging on bars, echoed round the building and filled him with dread.

Harold had enjoyed a quiet life and he wondered how he was going to endure prison. The food was disgusting slop, he wouldn't even have fed it to the pigs, and at night whenever he was dropping off to sleep, he was wakened by shouting. There was no respite. Even the most hardened criminals hated crimes against children, especially ones of a sexual nature and they made no secret of their hatred for him. They rattled the bars and shouted names at him. He was afraid for his life. He believed that the prison officers would turn a blind eye if any of them meted out their own punishment. He was prescribed painkillers for an alleged bad back, and after a mental health assessment, was put on suicide watch with a prison officer checking on him at regular intervals. He made a mental note of the staff who were vigilant and took their responsibilities seriously, and those that couldn't give a damn about the men's welfare. Although the tablets made him drowsy and took the edge off his anxiety, Harold quickly realised that if his plan to avoid the death sentence, was to work, he would need his wits about him. He was not prepared to hang by a rope.

He thought about Gwen and muttered to himself, "You stupid bitch, Gwen! Why couldn't you mind yer own business? This is your fault! And as for those stupid boys, well they enjoyed my affection. How could they do this to me? Attention seekers, the lot of 'em."

Whenever the pills were administered Harold held them at the side of his mouth. Most of the staff didn't bother to check properly if he'd swallowed them or not.They were lazy sods in his opinion. He knew that his hanging would bring the crowd out baying for his blood. Well fuck 'em! He had other plans.

Harold noticed that the officer on the night shift had failed to do his checks after midnight and guessed rightly that he had nodded off. He'd be in trouble in the morning. Harold poked his finger into the small hole in the side of his mattress and pulled out a sock. Smiling with relief he shook it out on the bed and swallowed his stash in two goes with the drink he'd saved from earlier.

Starting to drift into a dreamlike state, he felt relaxed as his mind drifted. He was surely floating to Heaven and Gwen would already be there. Good, he would get a chance to have his say and he'd let her know how vexed he was with her.

Three weeks after the conclusion of his trial, the headlines read DEAD and another said GOOD RIDDANCE, whilst another said HE HAD THE LAST WORD.

Harold Cavendish had committed suicide and many felt cheated, especially Gwen's family.

CHAPTER THIRTY-EIGHT
1950

They were having their tea, when Violet approached the subject of James being too big to keep sharing her room. Annie jumped up from the table.

"He's not sharing my room!" She stood with her hands on her hips.

"Well, he can't carry on sleeping in my room any longer. He'll get teased when he goes to school."

"Well, he doesn't need to tell anyone," reasoned Annie.

When Annie came home from school, Violet's bed was in the lounge. Malcolm was a Godsend. He'd heard her dragging furniture around and had come to her aid.

"You're sleeping in here and he's got your room? That's not fair! He's got the biggest room. I'm the eldest."

"Well, we can swap if you like but you will have to put up with me coming in and out to use my wardrobes and dressing table. I can hardly put them in here, can I? There's barely enough room for my bed as it is."

Violet chuckled to herself as Annie rushed into her bedroom, muttering that she would stay where she was.

John visited as often as he could and he was getting more restless as the weeks went by. "I'm doin' more work and I'm still gerrin' the same money," complained John.

"Why don't you look for another job? I'm sure there are other farmers that would appreciate your skills."

"I'm sure yer right, but I canna do that to 'im, he's gerrin old and he canna work like he used to."

Annie and James always vied for their brother's attention whenever he visited and if James sat next to him, Annie always tried to push her youngest brother out, but he never gave in to her. Violet was often reminded by how much he was like Chuck, with his determined ways and his dark hair and eyes.

The shop was all-consuming and left Violet too tired to socialise and make new friends. She missed Audrey so much. Her days started very early and ended well after the closed sign hung on the door. Her life was all work and bed. In fact she couldn't even go to bed, even when she was exhausted, because Annie, who insisted on bringing her friends round and watching television or playing music.

Annie was also getting increasingly frustrated and one night it all came to a head.

"I'm fed up of living here, Mum. It's too small! I don't want to keep helping in the shop and listening to the customers moaning. I want me own life. I want to be a secretary to someone important. I'm going to get out of this dump as soon as I can!"

Violet rolled her eyes. "Not this again, Annie. I'm doing me best."

Annie stomped down the stairs and slammed the door behind her and moments later, James peeped round the door, bleary-eyed. She took him back to bed and read him a story. She knew that things had to change.

Annie successfully applied to go to evening classes to learn shorthand and typing. In the meantime, John had moved to a farm twenty miles away, after his employer put the farm up for sale, which meant that she saw even less of him. However, one evening John made a surprise visit. He was talking quickly, like he always did when he was excited.

"Mum, you have to take it. It's a great big house. Tristleworth is a beautiful little hamlet, it's like time's stood still. You'll love it."

"It sounds lovely, but I'm me own boss now. I don't know if I can work for someone else. I'll be a skivvy and at their beck and call!"

"You're at everyone's beck and call now, including our Annie's. The customers give yer a 'ard time even though it inna your fault that rations are still in place. Think about it, Mum - James will have a big room to himself, we all will. We'll all be able to live together again, and our Annie will still be able to go to night school. Things canna go on as they are. It's time fer a change, Mum."

Over the next few weeks, Violet became increasingly depressed. John was right. She was tired of working at the shop and listening to the customers' moans, and the paperwork seemed never-ending. Annie was becoming more selfish and continued to bring her friends round and stay up till later and later, with no thought for anyone else. On one such night, Violet was tired and needed to go to bed.

"It's time to go now, girls." Violet's tone sent them scurrying down the stairs.

Annie was incandescent with rage. "Mum, what did you do that for? That was embarrassing!"

"I've had enough of your selfish behaviour, Annie. I work my fingers to the bone to keep a roof over your head and food in your belly, but you don't give anyone else a thought. The only person you care about is yourself! This flat isn't big enough for the three of us and it's time I did something about it!"

Annie was taken aback. Her mother was always the most placid of people. "It's not my fault that you moved in here Mum and that you're old and want to go to bed early. It's not fair that you begrudge me bringing me mates round. I think you're the one who's selfish, Mother!" She stormed down the stairs still shouting about her *miserable life* but she would not let her mother see her tears.

James had only been in bed for a couple of hours when Annie had her outburst and he came out of the bedroom, rubbing his eyes again. Violet knew she had to do something about their intolerable situation. Perhaps John was right and it was time for a change; time to leave the painful memories behind.

Mrs Thorne-Herbert was very impressed with Violet's interview. Not only was she immaculately dressed but she had a gentle speaking voice. She did, however, wonder if Violet was up to the hard work expected of her, but the position had remained vacant for almost a year.

She was not the only one having misgivings. Violet too had doubts about her prospective new employer. She reminded her of Lady Fitzroy. She also worried that she would have to rely on the grocer's van for her shopping, which only came round every fortnight. She knew that she would be paying over the odds for food. However when she saw the house, any doubts she had disappeared, but she understood all too well that there was no such thing as *free accommodation*.

CHAPTER THIRTY-NINE
1950-1951

Violet looked at the half-empty van and thought how little she had to show for forty years. John borrowed his boss's car, a grey Ford Anglia, and drove them round the winding roads to Tristleworth. The roads looked so different to the last time she'd come, when the sun had been shining.

Annie ran from room to room. She thundered up the two flights of stairs with James in her wake. She wanted the attic bedroom which was the largest of the five bedrooms and, as usual, got her own way. However, her excitement soon disappeared when she realised that she had to cycle four miles to the bus stop, in order to get to night school, especially now that the weather was turning cold. She was also unhappy about having to babysit her young brother whilst her mother was at work. On the nights that Annie went to night school, a girl from the village came to babysit for a few hours and James much preferred it as Linda was much kinder to him than his sister. Ocassionally, depending on his farming tasks, John would come home in the evening, especially when Linda came to look after James, and he would do his utmost to get back whilst she was still there.

When Annie was complaining about babysitting, Violet tried to pacify her. "James will be at school soon. We have to work together Annie and at least we're back together as a family."

Annie's response was to stamp up the stairs and bang her bedroom door, but only a few minutes later, she came down again and sat huddled round the range in the kitchen. "It's freezing here, Mum! I wished we'd never moved!"

Mrs Thorne-Herbert was a hard task master, but her husband was a real gentleman. Mary Jones, the housekeeper and cook, was standoffish with Violet, but her husband Michael who maintained the garden was welcoming. The Joneses lived in a suite at the Manor House. Bill Edwards lived in a tied cottage next to the woods which was in the shadow of Tristleworth Manor. He did maintenance on the house and also acted as chauffer and occasionally as a butler.

One day, Violet was sure that she was being gossiped about and stopped to listen outside the kitchen door.

"She draws welfare benefits, Michael," Mary tutted.

"Now, now, Mary, you don't know that for sure. Leave the poor woman alone."

"I do know that, because she goes to the post office a few miles away. Mrs Smith saw her in there. She rides her bike up there every Thursday. Trust you to stick up for her! You can't resist a pretty face, can ya?"

"I don't know what you're talking about, woman! Anyone would think you're jealous."

"Jealous? Don't talk so ruddy daft! There's something about her. I don't trust her! How can she afford to dress like that, when she hasn't got a husband? More to the point, why does she want to dress like that? She's only a skivvy!"

The kitchen door burst open and Michael Jones rushed out, his face red. He looked embarrassed when he saw Violet standing there, but his wife just smiled at her, a smile that was as false as she was.

"I didn't see you there, Mrs Higgins. Can I do something for you?"

"I was just looking for some scouring powder, Mrs Jones." She held her head high, but shut the door behind her with a bang.

A voice called behind. "Hello, Mrs Higgins. What's up with ya?"

"It's Violet. Nothing I can't handle, Bill."

"Well, you know you can tell me anything, don't ya?"

Violet noticed how his smile went up to his eyes which had crow's feet around them. Eyes that were cornflower blue, he also had a soothing baritone voice.

"I bet that Mary's been her usual charming self. She's a vindictive witch. I honestly don't know how Michael puts up with her."

Violet smiled as she walked home. She wished Audrey were here, she'd soon put Mary in her place. In a strange way, she even missed the customers at the shop, but it was all worth it to have her family together again. She had no time for self-pity or, indeed, a rest. She had to get on with her own work and prepare the meal for her family, before going back to the Manor to serve the Thorne-Herberts their evening meal. In no time at all, it was time to meet James. Her legs ached as she walked down the road to wait for the school bus, which was late.

Twenty minutes later, she saw the old yellow bus, coming down the hill. James was the first to get off the bus and ran towards her smiling. "The bus broke down. You should've heard Bert swearing, Mum! He said *bugger*!"

186

Violet turned away from him with a smile on her face. "Thank you, young man, but there's no need for you to say it."

It was nine o'clock and the Thorne-Herberts still hadn't had their dessert. Violet looked anxiously at the clock. She hated leaving James with Annie but her employers were impervious to her anxious looks. Why would they notice? Or even care? She was only there to be at their beck and call.

As soon as Violet arrived home, Annie practically launched herself at her mother. "You're late! Thank God you're home. He's been a little brat!"

"No I haven't! It's you, you're mean!" James glared at his sister.

"Anyway, you should be asleep by now young man," Violet couldn't keep the tiredness out of her voice.

"You said you'd be back in time to read me a bedtime story!"

Three stories later, Violet flopped on the settee. The fire had turned to ash and she shivered. "Couldn't you have put a log on the fire, Annie?"

Annie complained, "So you want me to keep an eye on the fire as well as that spoilt brat? I can't wait to get out of here, and as soon as I get a job, I'm off. I'll be finished my course soon and I should be able to get a good job with my qualifications. You won't catch me skivvying for other people like you!"

The sneer in her daughter's voice hurt her, "Well. I hope you never have to struggle to make ends meet like I have. I really hope that your life will be easier than mine."

Annie was instantly contrite and offered to make her mum a mug of Horlicks.

Over the weeks, Bill proved a good friend. He was always there to lend an ear when she needed one and their friendship fuelled the village gossips.

"There's no fool like an old fool," said Mary to Joan, the market gardener's wife.

"Well, she hasn't got a husband has she? She probably thinks he's a good catch, but what can he offer her? He's older than her and single and nowt to show for it. If she's after his money, I think she's going to be disappointed," said Joan.

"Well, I think he's a bit of a dark horse. I mean what do we actually know about him? He's worked here for years and we still don't know owt about him."

"We dunna know much about her either, do we? It's a bit of a funny set-up if you ask me. She must have been very young to have children that old and then she's got that little 'un and no husband and I'd still like to know how she can afford to dress like that." Joan mused.

"She seems to get all the men dancing to her tune. I wouldn't trust her wi' my husband, or anyone's for that matter. Even Mr Thorne-Herbert seems to treat her like she's sommat special." Mary pulled a disgusted face.

The village hall held whist drives and Old Time Dancing classes and, once a week, a youth club. Some of the youngsters came from surrounding areas on motorbikes and the occasional car, but mostly they cycled. John was wearing a blue sweater and had his hair cut short with a side parting, but Annie was still in her bathrobe.

"Aren't you coming to youth club, Annie?" John asked.

"It's boring. I can't be bothered."

"Linda will be expecting you."

"She won't even notice if I'm there or not. She's too wrapped up in you to notice," Annie said.

John blushed but couldn't keep the smile off his face.

Annie turned up at the youth club half an hour before it was due to close. She stopped to admire a two-door Hillman Coupe, which was an improvement on what the lads usually turned up in. As she pushed the door open, she took a backward look at the car and carried on walking, resulting in her not paying attention to what was in front of her.

"Look where you're going!" she snapped as someone almost knocked her over on their way out. Two strong arms prevented her from falling and she looked up into the most amazing green eyes!

"Well, hello there. I was just about to leave this dump." Pete Smithson grinned at Annie.

She held her head at an angle. "Well don't let me stop you!"

"Perhaps you can show me a good reason not to leave."

She flounced off, calling over her shoulder, "You should be so lucky!"

He let out a slow wolf whistle. He liked a girl with spirit.

Annie played hard to get for three months. Pete turned up in different cars to impress her and he tried to make her jealous by flirting with other girls, but she was a tough nut to crack. As a last resort he stopped coming to the youth club for a few weeks.

"I dunna know what yer playing at, Annie." queried John. It's obvious that you both like each other. He's probably not going to come back now."

"Who are you to give me advice? It took you ages to ask Linda to be your girlfriend."

"That's because I was shy! We canna say that about you. Per'aps you're better off wi'out him anyway. He looks a bit of a Jack-the-Lad to me."

"How would you know?" Her eyes were flashing.

She ran up the stairs and slammed her bedroom door. Her brother knew her too well.

Annie cursed, "This is a bloody joke," as she pushed her bicycle up a steep hill.

The car drove slowly alongside her and the driver called out of the open window, "I thought you were a lady," and chuckled adding, "Would you like a lift?"

She turned her face away from him and surreptitiously wiped the smudged mascara from under her eyes. Pete's persistence paid off and he put her bicycle in the back of the estate car.

A few weeks later, he presented her with a ring. She didn't care that it only had a diamond chip in it. She let him put it on her finger and when they kissed he put his hand under her blouse, but she batted it away with a warning; "Don't you take liberties with me, Peter Smithson!"

"I'm not taking liberties. We're engaged now! Come on, I can't wait any longer!"

"You'll have to wait until we're married!"

Violet and John both tried to get her to slow down and to get to know Pete better before making such a commitment, but her mind was made up. She was determined to have a Christmas wedding. They'd found a little terraced house for rent and she couldn't wait to move into it. On a bitterly cold winter's day, a few weeks later they were married in a register office, just weeks away from her nineteenth birthday. Annie wore a simple cream dress which had a cinched waist and a full skirt with a short jacket to match, and Pete wore jeans and a jumper.

CHAPTER FORTY
1953

When Violet had to leave for work in the evenings she frequently asked herself if she had done the right thing. If only she'd known that Annie was going to leave home so soon, she would not have needed to leave her poky flat. She worried about Annie marrying a man she hardly knew, but she'd done the same thing herself. Although Violet hardly heard from Annie, she was reassured by the fact that her daughter wouldn't put up with any nonsense from a man. One of the good things about needing a babysitter was that Linda and John fell in love with each other and became engaged and they were determined to do things properly. They were not going to have a rushed affair like Annie. Linda started collecting things for her bottom drawer and all manner of lists were drawn up.

One morning Violet was carrying out her cleaning duties and as she set about dusting the drawing room the deep, cultured voice of her boss spoke behind her. "Good morning, Higgy. How are you today? Has my wife spoken to you about the dinner party yet?" He looked at her blank face, "Well, no doubt she will. We're having some rather important guests to stay."

Later, Bill caught up with Violet on her way home from work, "They must be very important guests, to want me dressed up like a dog's dinner," he exclaimed. He smiled at Violet's worried face, "Don't look so worried, when I've plied them with enough plonk, they won't notice if you serve them from the left or the right. You do this every night; this is just on a larger scale. You'll be fine, I'll look after you."

Linda styled Violet's hair into a French plait, with a bouffant at the front. Her hair was still dark, but was beginning to show the odd strand of grey. She wore pearl earrings, a bargain off the market, and some coral lipstick, to match her nail varnish and she used a touch of mascara and blue eyeshadow and coloured in her arched eyebrows with a dark eyebrow pencil. Her new uniform was a white overall that was buttoned down the front and had pleats at the bottom. She wore a pair of white loafers, which Annie had left behind.

"You look great, Mum! You still manage to look like a lady even in your overall," John said proudly.

"Well, they've got some important guests coming tonight, so I have to look smart. It's really good of you both to watch this little one again."

"Who are you calling little? I'll soon be seven." James drew himself up as tall as he could and came up to John's waist.

The guests, all seven of them, were having pre-dinner drinks in the drawing room. Violet could hear laughter and inane conversations as they all talked at the same time.

"Are you sure your husband will make it, Isabella? He's awfully late." Mrs Thorne-Herbert wondered why her husband had invited the odious pair.

"He wouldn't miss it for the world! He's been looking forward to it for weeks, in fact we both have."

Bill banged the gong, announcing that dinner was being served. Ladies bedecked in jewels and evening gowns were escorted by husbands in tuxedos and thin bow ties. Ten places were set; nine of them were occupied.

Violet was clearing away the first course when there was a commotion in the hallway and Bill announced the arrival of their late guest.

Mary banged the pots and pans about. "The beef will be dried out! I've never heard of such a thing! It's just plain bad manners to turn up late!"

Bill held out his arms for the serving dish. "Here let me take that, Vi. It's heavy."

Mary was muttering under her breath, "It's not his job to go running around after the likes of her! No-one helps me and I'm older than her! Any road, he shouldn't be addressing her in that familiar manner."

Violet brought out the vegetables and stopped in her tracks. She'd recognise that voice anywhere!

"Come on Higgie, we're starving! Here, let me take that off you," Charles stood up and took the dish off her. He was oblivious to the icy stare from his wife. He was also unaware that one of his guests couldn't take his eyes off her.

Violet's hands were shaking as she served the guests. She spoke in a quiet voice to the latecomer, "Would you like carrots, sir?"

"I can't hear you. Come closer."

She could feel his warm breath on her face and the spittle from his rubbery lips. He smelt of brandy and stale cigars. She felt bile coming up into her mouth. Bill noticed how pale she'd turned and took the dish from her.

"Oh dear, Higgie, you don't look at all well. Get cook to give you some water," suggested Mr Thorne-Herbert.

Violet was sick in the toilet afterwards and splashed her face in cold water. She went to the kitchen and had a drink of cold water and accepted a mint from Mrs Jones.

"Thank you. I think it was the heat and I haven't eaten."

She looked at her reflection in the opulent mirror in the hallway and took a lipstick from her pocket and applied it to her lips. She touched her hair and walked back to the dinning room with her head held high. He wasn't going to get the better of her. She wasn't a naive girl anymore, and anyway what could he do to her with a room full of people?

As Charles looked anxiously towards Violet, Ursula leaned into him and discreetly said, "Stop fussing about the servants!"

Bill blended into the background but he was on high alert. The guests thinned out as they retired to bed and Violet carried the last of the dirty pots into the kitchen. Just as she reached over to the tap to get some water, she felt a sweaty hand on her shoulder. Alarmed she turned round.

"Well, we meet again! Once a skivvy, always a skivvy," he sneered. He was a belligerant drunk. "No wonder your son got himself into a bit of bother. A bit of a prick-teaser like his mother! Still what do you expect from low breeds like yourselves?" She was trapped against the sink. "You haven't got your mother to protect you now!"

"I think you've lost your bearings, sir. This is the servants' domain," Bill stood in the doorway. "Let me show you to your bedroom. Mrs Johns has already gone up."

"I don't need showing! I can make my own way." He turned to Violet and said, "No doubt I will bump into you again, before we go home."

Bill helped Violet on with her coat and noted that she was trembling. He escorted her up the path and as they looked up at the light in the window they saw a portly figure staring out of the window in their direction. Bill accepted Violet's offer of a cup of tea and as he sat quietly in the fireside chair, sipping his tea he asked no questions.

Something was shining by the light of the fire and he discreetly picked it up and put it in his pocket.

As Bill left, he tapped the side of his nose, "You just leave him to me."

Bill smiled when he saw that Isabella Johns was taking breakfast alone. He went into the kitchen where Mary Jones was still in a bad mood.

"Some people 'ave no manners," she fumed. "He was late arriving and now they'll be late leaving. It mucks up me schedule."

"I tell you what, if you put his breakfast on a tray, I'll take it up for you."

"Well that's very kind of you, Mr Edwards, but I don't know why we should wait on the likes of 'im. But perhaps it will speed up their departure."

Bill knocked on the bedroom door to the Blue Room and got a gruff reply. He rested the tray on the bedside table and opened the curtains to let the sun shine through. As Henry Johns sat up in bed, Bill placed the tray with two boiled eggs, toast and coffee on his lap and passed him a copy of *The Daily Herald*.

"I will be up later to take your tray and see if there is anything else you require, sir." Bill bowed his head subserviently and smiled as he felt in his pocket.

It was late morning and the guests had started to depart, except for Judge and Mrs Johns.

Mrs Thorne-Herbert, was agitated, "Oh Charles, I will be glad when they've gone. It's awfully bad mannered to arrive late and to overstay one's welcome."

"I couldn't agree more my dear, but I'm afraid I can't hang about waiting for them. I've got things to do." He strode off up the drive swinging his cane as he went to the market gardens. He loved nothing better than visiting his farms and took an active interest in all things related to the estate. He knew all the extended families and enjoyed hearing about their lives.

Ursula Thorne-Herbert took Isabella Johns for a tour of the gardens. She was relieved to hear that they had engagements the following day and would be leaving shortly. Michael Jones was talking about the roses when they heard a crash. They all hurried towards the noise to find Henry Johns lying prostrate at the bottom of the stairs and a blood stain on the blue and black carpet. Bill hurried from upstairs and Mary from the kitchen.

"Oh my poor darling, what happened?"

"I—I—I don't know, Izzie," he stammered. "I was just walking down the stairs and I slipped! I think I've broken my ankle and my back is killing me!"

Isabella wiped the tears off his face. "His head is bleeding! What are we going to do?"

In no time at all, Bill had taken charge of the situation and quickly returned with the first aid kit, cleansed the cut on his head and stuck a plaster on it. He then rushed into the garden and returned with a wheelbarrow, which helped him to get the injured man into the car. It was decided that it would be quicker if Bill drove him to hospital.

"I'll come with you, darling."

"It's best if you stay here, Madam. I'll take him. You're too distraught. He needs someone calm with him. You can rest assured that I will take very good care of him."

"Argh! Can't you drive more carefully, you oaf!"

"I'm so sorry, sir, but these roads are very bumpy. Oops, sorry Sir. I didn't see that hole," Bill smiled as he looked in the mirror and saw his passenger writhing in pain on the backseat.

Hours later, Henry Johns was tucked up in bed with six stitches to his head, a plaster cast on his leg and an ice pack on his back. Isabella was distraught when she had to return home on her own, but Bill reassured her that he would take good care of her husband.

Bill took a tray of food up to the house guest and as he knocked on the bedroom door, he took a small bottle out of his pocket.

"There you are, sir. Fillet of fish just as you like it." Bill stood outside the bedroom door and waited.

"Argh!! Edwards, where are you? Come and take this bloody food away!"

"Is it not to your satisfaction, sir?" He could barely keep his face straight.

"I hate chilli! My lips are on fire!"

"I'll get you some ice cream, sir."

Mary Jones threw the meal into the bin, "The cheek of the man! I've never 'ad a complaint about my cooking before. Take this up to him and I hope it ruddy chokes him!" She passed Bill a tray with toast and two boiled eggs.

After two weeks of convalescence, Henry Johns was well enough to be going home. Charles was only too happy to let Bill drive his car and husband and wife smiled broadly as they waved until the car was a speck in the distance.

Bill looked in the mirror. "You've certainly had a run of bad luck, sir. I expect you will be glad to get home. Your experience at Tristleworth will be one you're unlikely to forget."

"I think you're enjoying this, Edwards!"

Bill's face was solemn. "I can't imagine why you would think that, sir."

"I don't trust you, Edwards!"

Violet invited Bill to have a cup of tea with her. "You're very cheerful Bill. Anyway, you deserve more than a cup of tea; you deserve a medal!"

"Well, he's gone now, Vi, and I don't think he will be invited back. He was too much trouble." He handed his tea cup back to her and smiled.

At breakfast the next morning, James called excitedly, "Mum, Mum, I've found it!" In his hand was a blue and black marble, "It's my favourite."

"Where was it? I've searched everywhere!"

He pointed next to the hearth and said, "There."

CHAPTER FORTY-ONE
1953-1954

Annie worked in a typing pool at a nearby factory and Pete carried on working as a mechanic and would come home in various cars he'd been working on. As she walked up the road, she could see a Ford Zephyr parked outside their house. Pete was home early for once. However, the usual argument ensued as soon as Annie walked throught he door and saw him sitting with his feet up, reading the paper.

"What time did you get back?"

"About an hour ago," he answered.

"Oooh, the tea smells good," she said sarcastically.

"Don't start the minute you gerrin', Annie!"

"Well, I'm sick of this. We both go to work, but you do sod-all when you get home. I do everything and it's not fair!"

"You can't expect me to do women's work. Besides, mine is a more tiring job than yours. You only sit on your arse all day, yapping away while you tap the typewriter." He threw the newspaper on the floor and strode towards the door. "I'm off to the pub."

Their arguments were becoming more frequent. Annie resented that he came home from work and expected his meal on the table, and then would sit with his feet up, either reading the newspaper, or watching the television whilst she washed up. She became increasingly resentful that he didn't lift a finger. And she would call him a "Lazy Sod!" After any such arguments, Pete always stormed off to the pub and would come back late expecting his conjugal rights.

By the time they reached their third wedding anniversary, things were improving and the arguments were getting less frequent. Even so Annie wondered how they'd got through the first years of their marriage. Then as their anniversary approached, once again the subject of children cropped up.

"Don't you think it's time we started trying for a baby?"

"Not this again, Pete. We're still young yet. There's plenty of time for that. Don't let's us get into this now, let's just enjoy tonight. I can't believe that you're taking me to a posh restaurant to celebrate our anniversary."

Annie had worked overtime, along with Betty who was a few years older than her and before she left work, she changed into a black woollen dress that showed off her curves. She backcombed her hair and applied red lipstick to complete the look. Pete was waiting in the carpark in another borrowed car and he wolf-whistled when Annie walked towards him.

Annie leaned through the open window and asked, "Can we drop Betty off, Pete? It's so cold to walk home and it's on our way."

After introducing them to each another, Violet detected some tension between them. Pete chivalrously opened the door for Betty, but instead of thanking him, she gave him a withering look. Undeterred, Pete was his usual chatty self, but Betty remained sullen in the back of the car.

The restaurant was a noisy place to eat. Wooden tables covered in checked tablecloths were crammed closely together and and each one had a centrepiece consisting of a few plastic flowers in a small jar. The waiter managed to find them a place by the window in the corner which offered the salubrious view of rundown shops, some boarded up and others in need of a lick of paint. During their meal - fish and chips which Pete smothered in ketchup - Annie brought up the subject of Betty.

"Have you met her before, Pete?"

"No, but she looks like a right old battle-axe," he chuckled. "She needs a man to purra smile on her face."

"You mean like you?" Annie said sarcastically.

Pete ordered a bottle of wine and winked at Annie. "Come on get that down yer."

"Are you trying to get me drunk, Pete Smithson?" Annie laughed.

Throughout the evening he gave Annie his undivided attention. Her heart fluttered as he looked lovingly at her, his green eyes devouring her. She had to admit that he was a very handsome man.

The following morning, Annie couldn't keep the smile off her face. Their night of passion gave her a little frisson of excitement whenever she thought about it. She chatted away to Betty, although it was a one-sided conversation. She couldn't imagine what she'd said or done to upset her.

"You're very quiet today, Betty. Is something bothering you?"

Betty just shrugged and didn't look up from her typing. The atmosphere stayed like that for the next two days, and she had no choice but to tackle Betty head-on.

"Have I done something to upset you?"

Betty just shook her head. "You've been funny ever since you met my husband and you were quite hostile towards him. Why? He said that he'd never met you so it can't be something he's done."

"He says a lot of things. Don't mean it's true," Betty muttered under her breath.

"If you've got something to say, Betty, just spit it out!" She stopped listening after she heard her say, "I've seen him at the pub with a tarty looking woman..." The following words - "They were all over each other and I didn't know he was your husband" - were nothing but distant echoes and Annie felt numbly as if the room was closing in on her.

Annie made excuses not to be intimate with her husband and he in return, made excuses for coming home late. "The car took a long time to fix," or "It was one of the lad's birthday so we went for a drink," and so on, but still she kept quiet although the first time he was late home, after their romantic evening together, she put his meal in the bin and stopped cooking for him after that.

Whenever Pete staggered in from the pub, which was most nights, Annie waited up for him and it always ended in an argument, with her being vexed at him spending her housekeeping money on booze, followed by their neighbour thumping the wall. She knew that things had to change, so she decided not to get mad, but to get even, and get even she would! There was not a person on earth that would get the better of her, especially a man. Hell would freeze over before that would happen. From then on she pretended to be asleep and peeped through slanted eyes as he struggled to take off his clothes before falling into bed. When he was snoring, she picked his jeans up off the floor and rummaged in his pockets, taking a handful of money out, but not enough to arouse suspicion. Once she'd saved enough money, she set the scene.

When Pete came home from work on time, he could smell something good from the kitchen - roast chicken. The table was laid, Annie's make-up was applied to perfection and she wore a tight-fitting skirt with black stockings and stilettos.

Pete couldn't take his eyes off her. "You look beautiful Annie," he drooled. However when he to attempted to kiss her, she side-stepped him. She was so beautiful, but her calm demeanour scared him. He knew that she was at her most deadly when she was calm.

When they had finished eating their meal, Annie poured them a glass of wine each and raised her glass, "Let's propose a toast."

"What are we drinking to?" Pete asked gingerly.

"The end of our marriage," she said icily.

"No, Annie, you can't mean that. We love each other," he begged.

"You love the pub more."

"I'll give the booze up. I will do anything. Just don't give up on us." Tears ran down his face and he gripped her hands tightly. When his pleading fell on deaf ears, he let go of her hands and warned her, "I'm not going to walk away empty-handed!"

"It's a good job that I saved then, isn't it?" She looked him in the eye and pointed to the suitcase by the side of the armchair. "Everything's in there," she said coldly.

"You scheming, little bitch! How long 'ave you been planning this?"

"Long enough." She handed him the rent book and wafted a wad of notes. "Now sign this over to me."

He signed a letter saying that he wanted taking off the rent book and snatched the money out of her hands, not querying where it had come from. She had given him the sum of ninety pounds, the equivalent of three months' wages.

She couldn't keep the smile off her face when she watched him swagger up the street with his suitcase. "The fool didn't even know that I paid him off with his own money," she muttered. She took a twenty pound note from inside her bra and laughed out loud.

Two days later Pete turned up with his mate in a van. She could barely contain her joy at seeing their hideous sideboard and the ugly mustard lamps loaded into the van. The last thing to go was the garish rug. She had always hated them; his family had no taste. She did however, feel a stab of pain when they looked at each other for the last time and he said, "I never wanted this, Annie."

Annie gave a month's notice at work and informed their landlord that she was vacating the property. The furniture that was left was sold off, which provided her with enough money to take the train to

London and to pay for a rented room. Annie hated sharing a house with three other women and was determined that it would only be a temporary situation.

She quickly found a typing job, where she came to the attention of Sir Rupert Fairfax. Within weeks of meeting her, he interviewed her for the position of his personal assistant.

Annie had spent many hours listening to newscasters who spoke the King's English and perfected their diction. She made good use of her looks by modelling herself on film stars like Jean Simmons and Grace Kelly and she knew that it had paid off when Sir Rupert offered her the job without even looking at her credentials, which were few in truth. Although, she was aware that she'd only got the job by beguiling him, she was nevertheless determined to prove her worth and in no time at all she had become Sir Rupert's right-hand woman, always both efficient and discreet. She travelled to places she could only ever have dreamed of and her work, and the monetary awards it offered, became all consuming. She was able to rent a small flat on the outskirts of London and her visits to her family grew less and less.

Anyway, she hated the countryside.

CHAPTER FORTY-TWO
1955

In 1955, John and Linda were married. John was twenty-five years old and his bride, twenty-three. They'd saved hard and insisted on paying for everything themselves, but Violet contributed by making Linda's wedding dress, which had a round neckline and was covered in lace at the top, pinched in at the waist and hung into an A-line. She wore it with a lace veil that hung to her waist. John wore a single-breasted suit with a blue tie. In spite of a cool autumnal breeze, the sun was shining.

Violet had stared in amazement at Annie, when she sashayed up to the front of the church in a blue silk dress with a lacy collar and sat in one of the front pews.

"You look beautiful, Annie. Every inch a lady. I wish your father could see how well you've both done. I'm so happy that you could make it, and I can't wait to hear all about your job."

"Thanks Mum. You're looking lovely yourself, I love your hair shorter and purple really suits you, but I'm sorry, I can't stay. I've got to go straight to the airport after they've taken their vows."

"Where are you off to this time?" Violet turned her head away. She didn't want Annie to see the tears in her eyes.

"Brussels."

After the ceremony, they all stood outside the church to have photographs taken. When Violet and her children and partners smiled for the camera, Violet felt the hole left by Ted but, as they waved Annie off, Bill stood by her side, a calming influence as usual. He squeezed her hand and she squeezed his.

The village hall had been transformed. It was bedecked with yellow chrysanthemums and white lilies and white and gold balloons. The tables were set out for sixty people with name plates and small posies of flowers on the tables.

Frank interrupted her thoughts, "Penny for 'em, Vi."

"I was thinking about Ted. I wished he was here; he'd be so proud."

"Yes, he would have been." He took hold of her hands and leaned in closer. "You're not too old to find love again Vi. I think yer should give him a chance."

Violet looked puzzled. "Give who a chance?"

"Oh. Vi open yer eyes. Anyone can see that he's mad about yer an he seems like a decent man." Frank turned and smiled, "Speak of the devil."

"Can you jive, Vi?" Bill offered her his hand.

"I'm not very good at it," she said shyly.

Her brothers-in-law slow handclapped her, aided and abetted by their wives, until she got up to dance. She was laughing as Bill twirled her round the dance floor. She was surprised that he was such a good dancer. She hadn't danced with anyone since Chuck. As the tempo changed, Bill held her gently as they waltzed. He had surprisingly muscular arms.

After the wedding, James sat at the kitchen table with his head in his hands and said, "I wish John still lived here. It feels lonely with just you and me, Mum."

"I know, the house is too big for just us, especially since Annie left." She hugged James tightly. "Anyway, being as it's a nice day and I've still got a day left of my holiday, why don't we get our bikes out and go off for a ride. I can make us a picnic, if you like."

James jumped up and down excitedly. "We haven't been out on our bikes for ages!"

They cycled to the post office and Violet cashed her postal order. Thank goodness for Bert; he never let her down. She bought some biscuits and a few sweets and set off to find the perfect place for their picnic. An hour later they found just the spot by a brook and Violet laid the blanket down and spread the food out. It was a mild day for autumn and they spent the afternoon looking for wildlife. James used an empty jam jar to catch minnows, and when he caught one he wanted to take it home until his mother persuaded him to leave it where he'd found it. The talk then turned to Chuck.

"What was my dad like Mum? You never talk about him."

"What's brought this on, James?"

"I haven't dared to ask you before, because I didn't want to upset you."

Violet went all misty-eyed when she thought about him. "He was wonderful. You look a lot like him; you're like him in your ways to."

"How did you meet him?"

"One night, when I was working in the pub he came in for a drink. He walked in as large as life." She smiled at the memory, "And he swept me off my feet and then he was sent back to America, all too soon. He was supposed to come back and marry me, but I never saw him again."

"Didn't he want to meet me?"

"He never knew about you. If he had, I know that he'd have come back." She choked back her tears. "When the war ended for our servicemen, the Americans were still fighting abroad and your dad wasn't allowed to tell me where he'd been sent. When the Japanese finally surrendered, they were all sent home. He hadn't been home long when he was killed in a car accident." She couldn't hold back the tears any longer. She took James in her arms and said softly, "I think we would have been so happy together, but we'll never know. The only thing I know for sure is that we really loved each other."

That night they both had an early night and slept soundly, but all too soon, the alarm clock woke her up from a deep slumber. Violet groaned. It was Monday morning; school. She opened the curtains to a grey morning and quickly got dressed and made her way to James' bedroom. He was still snuggled up in bed.

She shook him awake. "Come on, or else you'll be late for school."

"Do I have to go, Mum? Can't I stay here?"

"You know the answer to that, James. I don't want to go to work, but I have to. I can't leave you here as you're not old enough to be left on your own."

"I'll be good. I won't get into trouble."

She sat on the side of his bed. "You'd tell me if there was anything wrong, James, wouldn't you?"

He turned away from his mother's gaze and said, "I'm fine, Mum. I'll get ready in a minute."

Violet was polishing the brass doorknob on the drawing room door, a position in which she could hear voices coming from the adjacent library. Mary Jones was gossiping with Janet Cauldwell, the woman who did the washing and ironing.

"Like I've said before, Janet, there's no fool like an old fool!" Mary said in hushed tones.

"Her was cavortin' about like a teenager and he was makin' cow eyes at her! I said to my Gordon, 'I've never seen the likes of it!'"

"Did you see how high her skirt went up?" Mary's voice was rising. "You could almost see her knickers."

"Well, they were clean and paid for." Violet's voice had a hard edge to it as she stood in the open doorway.

The two women turned quickly. "We didna see you there, Mrs Higgins." Janet averted her eyes but Mary Jones held her head high and brazenly stared at her without saying a word.

Violet walked slowly past them and as she left the room, she looked over her shoulder and said, "Tell your Gordon, I'll get him a photo." She smirked as they stood with their mouths open. She mused that John shouldn't have invited everyone to the evening reception.

As she opened her front door, she picked up two red bills, one for electricity and one from the water board. There had been a few times when she regretted moving here, and today was one of them. The house was cold and the electric bar heaters she'd bought did little to heat the rooms and were expensive to run. She made herself a cup of tea and sat in the fireside chair thinking about that fateful morning when she'd found her mother's tiny body in this very chair, cold and lifeless by the dying embers of the fire.

Violet jumped as the wall clock chimed. She took the vegetables out of the cold larder and prepared tea. James would be home soon and desperate for food.

Later, when John and Linda came to look after James, John couldn't keep the smirk off his face when he asked, "Is that your warpaint, Mum? I still canna believe you said that to 'em."

"Well, I wished I hadn't but I'm tired of being judged, especially by the likes of them. I'm dreading tonight though, but I can't let that Mary see that."

Violet took a deep breath as she walked into the kitchen. Mary glared at her. "Here, take these vegetables through." She thrust the hot dish in Violet's direction, but held on to the cloth.

Michael saw what his wife was doing and snatched a tea towel up and offered it to Violet. He refrained from shaking his head at his wife, whose face was burning with indignation.

The exchanges remained formal throughout the evening between the two women. When Violet walked home, she heard a familiar voice behind her.

"Are you OK, Vi?" asked Bill. "You look to be in a hurry."

"I am. I can't wait to get away from there." She nodded her head towards the Manor and told him about the events of the day.

He laughed out loud. "I would have loved to have been a fly on the wall. I bet your name was mud, both Gordon and now Michael will cop it."

Bill walked her home and sat by the fire whilst she made them a cup of cocoa. When Violet went to check on James, Bill noticed the two red bills unopened on the table.

When she came downstairs he said, "Vi, there's something I want to say." He put his empty mug on the table and took her cup out of her hands. "You must know how I feel about you. I have never met anyone like you before. You're an amazing woman."

She put her hand up to stop him and softly said, "Bill, don't."

"I know that you don't feel the same way about me, but I would cherish you and care for you for the rest of my life, if you'd let me."

She noticed that his cornflower blue eyes were glistening in the glow of the fire. He was an attractive man and was steadfast and sincere - like Ted.

"I don't expect you to answer me now, but please will you think about it?" He took her hand and kissed it as he left.

Violet tossed and turned all night. She had dreams involving Ted and Chuck and when she woke at five o'clock, she lay in bed considering the pros and cons.

CHAPTER FORTY-THREE
1955

James was complaining of bellyache again. She went through the now familiar saga of persuading him to go to school and the guilt she felt at having to go to work. As he pressed his pale face against the bus window, she felt a stab of guilt.

At work, Violet cleaned the brasses with vigour and scrubbed the stone steps. Lunchtime came round very quickly, but instead of getting herself lunch, she took her bicycle out of the shed and cycled to Brookfields Farm. She followed the path round to the cottage in the grounds and spotted the blue and white curtains she'd made for them, blowing in the open window.

Linda was surprised to see her. She noticed how tired Violet looked and commented on it. "Come and sit yersen down and I'll make us a cup of tea. John will be back for his lunch in a bit."

When John walked into the kitchen in his overalls, he reminded her so much of Ted, apart from being dark-haired. He walked like him, talked like him, had the same mannerism, and had the same huge smile.

"This is a nice surprise. Have yer got some time off work?"

"No such luck. It's James, there's something wrong with him. I'm having trouble getting him to school. I've asked him what's troubling him but he won't talk to me about it. Please will you see if he'll talk to you?"

"I anna sure if he will, but we'll be seeing 'im tonight and I will try."

The discussion then turned to Bill.

"He's asked me to marry him."

"I'm surprised thar he took so long. Anyone can see he's mad about yer. What did you tell him, Mum?"

"I didn't give him an answer, John. To be honest, he took me by surprise."

"He's a good man, Mum. I like 'im."

"But how can I bring a man into my son's life? I'd have to leave him on his own with James."

"Mum, he's not Harold!" He spoke softly to her.

"Well, I hadn't thought about that. I just don't want him to get let down. I like Bill very much and I love his company. He's so mischievous but I find it hard to trust men."

"I know thar our James likes him and Bill really teks an interest in 'im. You wouldn't have to worry about the bills and your house is too big for just you two. Dunna just dismiss him, Mum."

Violet stood on the corner, waiting for the school bus to come. The weather had turned cold and it was already spotting with rain. This was her least favourite time of the year, when the countryside had lost all of its vibrancy. She stood underneath a large oak tree which was almost barren, apart from a few brown crinkled leaves, unwilling to let go of the last vestiges of life, but it provided very little shelter from the rain that was getting heavier by the minute. The bus was late, which was nothing unusual; it had a habit of breaking down. She knew that James wouldn't like her meeting him off the bus. He was after all, almost ten years of age, but she was worried about him. Twenty minutes late, the yellow school bus finally came into view and she watched it as it crawled down the hill. When James got off the bus she could see that he had a black eye and his coat was ripped.

Violet rushed towards him, "What's happened to you?"

"Don't fuss Mum, I fell over. Anyway, I've told you before that I don't need meeting off the bus. I'm not a baby!"

"I know you're not, but I'm worried about you. Come on, let's hurry home. We're getting soaked."

Violet made several attempts to find out what had happened to him, but James refused to change his version of events. She could only hope that he would open up to Linda and John. She was reluctant to leave him but she had no choice but to go to work. Not for the first time, she wondered if she had done the right thing coming here and being at the beck and call of people who had a pampered lifestyle.

Violet found it hard to concentrate at work and Mary Jones was particularly snappy that evening. It took all of her willpower not to throw something at her. The evening seemed never-ending and the idle chit-chat at the table delayed her clearing the table. It was nine o'clock before she could clear the dining room table and set up for breakfast.

When Violet returned home, half an hour later than usual, she was anxious to know if James had confided in John.

"He's bein' bullied by a new boy because he anna gorra dad. He called him a bastard, so James hit him and got a black eye as a result. I will run yer up to school tomorrow and see his teacher. Try not to worry, Mum, we'll sort it."

"I don't understand. There must be other children who lost their dad in the war."

"It's probably because he's smarter than the other kid, Mum."

"More likely it's because James is so good looking. He's probably secretly envious of 'im," suggested Linda.

During the lunchtime play time, James was avoiding Smithy by hanging round the toilets at the back of the playground. They stank of stale urine and it was a place that most of the kids avoided. He was deep in thought, when Janet came running towards him.

"Come quick James. Yer mum and yer brother are here."

James' face turned red when he saw the kids move to the side, to let them through. Soon after, he was summoned to the Headmaster's office. He waited outside on a chair until the door opened and Mr Turner called him through. James only half listened to what he was saying. "This is unacceptable behaviour. I won't tolerate this sort of thing in my school!" He droned on but his ears pricked up when his brother spoke.

"I'd like to know what yer going to do about it. If you dunna sort this Mathew Smith out, then we will be taking it up wi' the Education Authorities."

"Now there's no need for any of that. I have sent for the young man in question and I will deal with him, but I must reiterate, I will not stand for fighting in my school, regardless of who started it. Now run along to class now, James. I think we're finished here." He stood up and said, "Good day to you all."

Mathew Smith was sitting in a chair outside the headmaster's office. He stood up when Mr Turner called his name. He was a head and shoulders taller than James and twice as wide. John bashed his shoulder into him as he walked past him and issued a threat under his breath.

"Next time you'll 'ave me to deal wi' and I hit a lot 'arder than me brother!"

Bill had been avoiding Violet, but he literally walked straight into her as he entered the Manor by the side door, as she was leaving for home. She looked down shyly.

"Vi, I'm so sorry if I embarrassed you."

"It's not that. It's James." She wiped her eyes.

"Come home with me, Vi. Tell me all about it over a cuppa."

She stood open-mouthed when she stepped into Bill's cottage, which was warm and cosy. In the kitchen was a black range with a fire glowing in the grate. She sat in the fireside chair and watched Bill as he busied himself in the kitchen. She relaxed as she supped her tea and told him about James.

"Would you like me to talk to him?" Before she could answer, he asked softly, "Have you thought any more about what I said?"

"Bill, you're a lovely man but I'm scared. I've been let down before and I have a son to think of."

"I would never let you down. I love you and if you'd only let me, I could be a father figure to James. You could live here with me; you wouldn't have to worry about paying the bills. That house is too big for two of you and its cold and eats electricity."

"Well, that sounds very tempting, but I really have to think of James. Perhaps you could try to spend more time with him."

Violet noticed that since Bill had been spending more time with him, James seemed happier and more self-assured. There had been no more excuses about going to school. In fact he was ready and out on time to get the bus, and on his return was cheerful.

On one such afternoon, James came home from school in a particularly good mood. "Smithy's mum has invited me for tea. Can I go, Mum?"

"I thought you were sworn enemies?"

"We're friends now. Smithy said that he'd rather be my friend than my enemy," he laughed.

"How did that happen?"

"Bill's been teaching me self-defence and I'm really good at it. He also told me to keep my friends close, but to keep my enemies closer, so I have."

"You kept that quiet," she laughed. "They are very wise words."

CHAPTER FORTY-FOUR
1955

Bill tapped on the study door. "Can I speak to you, sir?"

"Yes, of course, Edwards. What can I do for you?" He gestured to Bill to take a seat. He listened with a smile on his face and then said, "I think this calls for a sherry."

As Bill left his study, Charles Thorne-Herbert shook his hand and patted him on the back. This did not go unnoticed by Mary Jones.

"I'm telling you that something's going on. Don't you roll your eyes at me, Michael! They were drinking sherry. I saw their glasses and he patted 'im on the back."

"For God's sake, woman, why don't you mind your own business for once in your life?"

She stood with her mouth open as her husband stormed out the door.

Violet looked anxiously out of her bedroom window. There'd been a smattering of snow. She'd invited Bill for Christmas dinner and was looking forward to the whole family being together, including Annie. Violet listened to the weather report, which forecast more snow.

"Dunna worry Mum. I'll pick her up in the tractor, if I have to," laughed John.

"That would be a sight worth seeing." The thought brought a smile to her face.

James helped his mother to make paperchains and then he put shoe whitener on the fir cones before adding glitter, just as his siblings had done when they were young. On Christmas Eve, the presents were put under the tree and the decorations were up. There was excitement in the air. James was beginning to question the existence of Father Christmas, but he still had enough uncertainty to become excited by the prospect of this magical being granting the wishes on his Christmas list.

The smell of cloves and cinnamon permeated the air. Violet took two glasses out of the cupboard and smiled. Bill brought the smell of Old Spice aftershave with him. He wore a pair of flannel trousers and an open-necked shirt and Violet thought that he was a fine figure of a man; a man who made her feel safe. James was allowed to stay up to watch a fantasy play called *Where the Rainbow Ends* and Bill helped him to make his favourite drink of Creamola Foam and chuckled as James was undecided on the flavour. He watched him open the tins and spoon the powder in from Strawberry and Raspberry and watched the water turn a fizzy red. He reminded him of his Eric and his heart ached when he thought of him.

When James had finally settled in bed and gone to sleep, Violet came downstairs and they enjoyed a relaxed evening, drinking mulled wine and eating mincepies. Before he left for home, Bill got down on one knee and took Violet's hand in his. "Please will you do me the honour of becoming my wife?" He pulled a red velvet box out of his pocket and held out the diamond solitaire and she allowed him to put the ring on her left finger.

"Do I take that as a 'Yes'?"

She nodded and he kissed her shyly for the first time. Her beautiful, eyes glistened with tears. He was a perfect gentleman and said, "I want to do things properly. I don't want to take advantage of you."

"Bill, you don't really know me. I'm not the perfect woman you seem to think I am. I've done things that I'm not proud of."

"Vi, we've both got a past. The only thing that matters is the future and the life we can have together."

John waited on the platform for his sister's train to arrive. He was stunned when he saw her rushing towards him in a long red coat with a fur trimmed collar and a felt hat in the same colour, and wearing red lipstick to match.

"Trust you, Annie, to wear stiletto heels in this weather. You'll break yer neck if yer anna careful," he chuckled.

Annie enjoyed being the centre of attention when she arrived home and she was only too eager to talk about her adventures as she travelled round the world, but she informed them that her boss was not a nice man.

During Christmas dinner, John led a toast. "To Mum and Bill, may you have many happy years together." He laughed and added, "It's about time." Even Annie looked happy.

Heads turned as Bill accompanied Violet and James to church and sat together on the back pew. There was a collective gasp from the village gossips, and heads turned to look at them when the vicar read out their banns. The happy couple could barely contain their laughter.

Mary Jones, elbowed her husband in the ribs and declared, "See, I told you sommatt was going on."

One month later, Violet and Bill had a quiet wedding in the church with just family and two special friends attending. The reunion with Audrey and Bert was a joyous occasion. Audrey had changed very little and still had a mass of red hair, albeit from a bottle. The bride wore a suit with a pencil skirt in a delicate shade of purple and the bridegroom a dark blue suit. Bill's Aunty Hetty and Uncle Fred had arrived two days before the wedding and were delighted to be sharing their big day.

After the ceremony, James questioned, "Can I call you Dad now?"

"I'd be honoured if you did. You know I love you like you were my own, don't you?"

Hetty cried at their exchange. "I'm so happy for you, Bill. It's about time you found happiness. June wouldn't have wanted you to be alone for the rest of your life." She hugged him tightly and added, "He's such a nice boy; he reminds me of our Eric."

Bill carried his bride over the threshold. "Put me down Bill, you'll pull your back."

"Hey, I might be seven years older than you but I'm not past it yet. I'm in the prime of my life," he laughed.

The only piece of furniture that Violet kept was the fireside chair that her mother had loved so much, but she made new curtains and cushions and brought a woman's touch to their home. She heard the barbed comments from the village gossips, "It didn't take her long to gerr' her hooks into him," or "They're acting like a couple of teenagers. It's disgusting at their age! She's middle aged and he has got to be in his fifties."

She laughed to herself. She had no complaints. Bill had put a spring in her step. Violet still had to carry out her waitressing duties in the evening, but would smile at the thought of returning to their snug little cottage. The thought of Bill waiting to walk her back home after work gave her butterflies in her stomach.

The smooth, rich tones of Bing Crosby played on their gramophone as they danced round their kitchen to *The Anniversary Waltz*.

"Oh no, you're not dancing again!" James laughed. "Still, I suppose it makes a change to you jiving." He gave them a card. Inside it read, *Happy first anniversary to Mum and Dad* and was signed, *James Edwards*.

CHAPTER FORTY-FIVE
1968

The letter came at lunchtime, one month before Bill was due to retire. "It says they have a ground floor flat in supported accommodation that has become vacant and we need to arrange to get the keys for the viewing. I will ring the council straight away." Then Bill hesitated, "But what about you? Will you be able to cope, living in supported accommodation?"

"I'd live in a tent as long as you're by my side and we can't go on as we are. Ever since our boss passed away, it's been unbearable. His son has no manners. We always felt valued when his father was alive, but these younger ones treat us like skivvies and that Mary Jones is getting worse. Ever since she retired and was allowed to stay on in their grace and favour quarters, she's spied on me and breaks her neck to tell tales about me." She kissed the top of his head. "Anyway, your arthritis is getting worse and it's time that you took it easy. In fact, it's time we both did."

Violet thought back to how she'd struggled to make ends meet before marrying Bill, when her savings had to top up her meagre wages just to eat and keep warm. Bill had saved her from all that and she'd never been happier than when she moved into his home, but now it was time to move on.

They viewed the flat. It had a double bedroom, a small lounge, a kitchen that was just big enough for a small table and chairs, and a bathroom with a shower. There was a large community room where the residents got together to socialise. It had woods at the back and she noticed that the communal garden had lots of birds feeding from the bird table and feeders. There were more flats to the front and sides of them and it was called Cherry Tree Lodge, on account of a large tree dominating the front lawn.

"It's not the peaceful countryside we're used to, is it?"

"Don't worry Bill, I've lived in far worse places, believe me. We'll be fine."

They looked around their home for the last time. It was where they'd started their married life and where they'd spent thirteen happy years, but they weren't getting any younger. It was time to slow down;

they'd both worked too hard all their lives. At least the flat would be easy to keep neat and tidy and it would be much easier to keep warm.

They soon settled into their new surroundings, but there was one thing they hadn't bargained on and that was the pettiness of some of their fellow neighbours.

One evening, they were having a social gathering and a young man came with a guitar and sang and everyone contributed to the buffet.

Violet wore a blue dress that came to her knee, and Bill whispered in her ear, "You knock spots off these women. No wonder you're getting dirty looks."

"Well, I'm a lot younger than them and I wouldn't have qualified for a place like this if I weren't married to you, but I'm just as entitled to be here as they are."

He smiled. She'd become much tougher with age.

"Hey you can't sit there. That's Betty's and Clive's seats." Elsie looked Violet up and down and tutted.

There was a jigsaw on the table and Bill put a couple of pieces in and was told not to touch it. Bill whispered in Violet's ear, "This place wants livening up a bit." He took her hand and they started jiving to the music. They found it very amusing that they were being gossiped about.

Bill was in a lot of pain after dancing, but he wouldn't show it.

"Dunna worry about them miserable buggers," said a man who introduced himself as Paul and his wife as Janice. "You're just what this place needs."

From then on, they became the best of friends. Janice was the first really good friend she'd had since Audrey and it made her realise how much she'd missed the friendship of another woman. Audrey had been a constant source of comfort though some very difficult times and she would have more time to go and see her now that she wasn't working.

The barbed comments and the whispers continued. Betty Granger seemed to be the ringleader. She was younger than the others and, at the age of sixty three just five years older than Violet. She had been the youngest until Violet arrived. Betty often made snide remarks and looked at her as if she could kill her. She reminded Violet of Mary Jones. Her husband Clive was older than her and wore a hearing aid.

"I reckon he turns it off so he can't hear her," Bill chuckled. "I know I would if she were my wife."

One evening her husband was reading a book in the community room. He looked up and smiled when they approached.

"What have you done with her, Clive?" asked Bill.

"Oh Betty's gone to see her sister. She won't be back till late. Once that pair get nattering there's no stopping 'em." He smiled and returned to his book.

Violet and Bill saw the bus pull away before they got to the bus stop, so they decided to take a steady walk. As they passed The Hare and Hounds, they discussed popping in for a quick drink before getting another bus. The pub was noisy and filled with smoke, so they took their drinks into the snug, but stopped in their tracks as they saw a couple cosied up in the corner. The man had his hand on the woman's thigh and they jumped apart when they saw Bill and Violet. They both looked like rabbits caught in the headlights of a car and the woman blushed to her roots.

"Hello Betty, I thought you were at your sister's." Bill couldn't keep the mischievous twinkle out of his eyes.

Betty stammered and for once was lost for words. James, Elsie's husband seemed equally lost for words. They hurriedly drank up and left the pub, leaving Violet and Bill in fits of laughter.

"Blimey, I've never seen old James move so fast," Bill laughed. "Perhaps there's life in the old dog yet."

Violet felt sorry for their partners, but they wouldn't find out from them. Betty didn't show her face in the community room for a week. When they did see James, who was being particularly helpful to his wife, Bill couldn't help but comment.

"You've got a good un there, Elsie." He couldn't keep the mischief out of his voice.

Betty never troubled them again and always greeted them like long-lost friends whenever she saw them.

Bill called it Karma.

Over the years, they settled into a comfortable way of life. John and James and their families were regular visitors, but Annie's visits were few and far between. Violet and Bill became committee members and helped to organise different activities and trips. Violet taught sewing and she had about half a dozen regulars who came for lessons.

One of the trips they organised was to Blackpool and it turned out to be a very wet day after which Bill caught a cold. His cough became increasingly worse and due to his suppressed immune system, it developed into pneumonia. Violet, John and James and their partners were very supportive and took turns to sit with Bill, but Violet never left his side. Annie was abroad and was unable to get back. He was admitted to hospital as his condition deteriorated and Violet helped the nurses by sponging him with cool water to bring his temperature down, and trying to give him sips of water. However, just a few hours later, as her head was on his chest, she heard the beating of his heart stop as his life slipped away. Her cries echoed round the ward as if from a disembodied soul. She clung onto Bill's body, soaking his pyjamas as she wept. She cried until her tears were spent, and as she stood up her legs gave way and her two sons helped her into a chair. She felt empty, numb. She had lost her beloved husband, her best friend and her knight in shining armour, gone at just seventy-two years of age.

After a local funeral, Bill was laid to rest with his late wife June and their eight year old son in a country churchyard in Kent. Violet refused to stay with any of her children. She felt closest to her beloved Bill in the home they had shared for the past seven years.

CHAPTER FORTY-SIX
1983

The telephone was incessant and Annie cursed, "I wished you'd go away, I'm busy."

Her diary was full and her in-tray was overflowing. She hadn't got time to keep answering the phone. Whoever was on the other end of the phone was very persistant and Annie sighed as she put her Dictaphone down.

She snatched up the phone and spoke. "Good morning, Annie Smithson speaking." Her voice had an icy tone to it but her face took on the pallor of the dead as she held the phone to her ear. She sat in stunned silence, trying to gather her thoughts, before she put the phone down and galvanised herself into action. She needed to put plans in place; their trip to Geneva was only two days away. Annie was used to getting her own way, especially with men, but getting her own way with her boss was a different matter entirely - he was a stubborn old goat. However, if her womanly charms didn't work, she could always resort to blackmail.

She tapped on Sir Rupert's door and he called, "Enter." He looked up from his desk and smiled at her. She shuddered at the way he undressed her with his eyes. "Yes, Annie, what can I do for you?" His eyes lingered on her chest.

"I need leave, sir."

"Leave? We're at our busiest time. It will have to wait until we get back from Geneva," he said dismissively.

"No, Sir, I need it now!"

"Don't be so ridiculous! You're my right-hand woman. I need you with me." His belly dragged on the table as he stood from his chair and looked up at her.

"All the arrangements are made. I've booked your favourite hotel, *The Soho*." She handed him a piece of paper. "Here's the itinerary, the dates and times are highlighted. Your chauffeur will take you and fetch you back from the airport and I've been in touch with the agency and they have found a replacement for me."

"A temp! I don't want a ruddy temp!"

"The agency assured me that Miss Braithwaite is very competent. She has impeccable references, sir."

"I don't care! You can't leave me in the lurch!" His face turned red.

"My mother needs me. I need to be with her."

"Well, I need you. I'm sure three weeks isn't going to make any difference."

Annie straightened her back and drew herself up to her full height. She was a head and shoulders taller than him, especially when she wore stiletto heels. She gave him what her brother called her *beady-eyed stare*. "I need my leave now. Its way overdue, Sir!"

She watched in disdain as the portly figure of Sir Rupert Fairfax stomped up and down his office, his grey beard waggling as he roared. "Well you can't have it just like that. I won't allow it. You're coming with me and that's the end of it!"

How he likes the sound of his own voice. She stood with her hands on her shapely hips. A stray blonde curl escaped her neat chignon as she squared up to him. "No, it's not the end of it!" she said boldly. "I've shown you nothing but respect and loyalty for years. I've stayed late many times, given up my weekends, put up with your tantrums and not had a life of my own ever since I became your PA. I don't think it's asking too much to put my mother's needs before your own!"

"How dare you? You get paid very good money. You've been all over the world and seen and done things that you could only have dreamed of, if it weren't for me."

"I've also experienced things that have left a bad taste in my mouth!"

He started to protest, "Who do you think you're talking to?"

"I know exactly who I'm talking to! I know all your sordid little secrets. I'm sure Lady Fairfax would be very interested in reading my diary, Sir."

Sir Rupert slumped in his chair. His face took on a grey tinge and his tight, thin lips turned blue. He tugged at his collar as he tried to breathe.

"Like I said, I need my leave with immediate effect."

"I'd be very careful if I were you. That sounds very much like blackmail!"

"Blackmail's an ugly word, sir, but then so is fraud. I think you get my drift." She leaned over his desk. "Let's just say that we're doing each other a favour. I will keep your secrets and you can give me paid leave."

Her hands shook when she left the office, but she had been determined to get her own way. She tittered as she realised that she was more like her mother than she had known. She smiled at the thought of going home. If only I'd known then, what I know now, she mused.

CHAPTER FORTY-SEVEN
1983

Annie held her mother tightly. She had lost a lot of weight and her hair had gone very thin, but she was still a stunning woman. She wore trousers and a blue jumper which accentuated her eyes, but her clothes hung off her tiny frame.

"I'm so sorry, Mum. How could I have put that slimy toad before you; before everyone?

'It seems as if you put him before yourself, Annie, but you're here now. Let's make the most of it before you have to go back."

"I'm not going back. I'm staying here with you." She felt relief when she spoke those words out loud. 'I'd been so thrilled when I got that job. When I was young, all I wanted was a job like that. How could I have been so stupid? Look at me now! I'm fifty years old and what have I got to show for it? I've got a few bob in the bank and a nice car, but no husband and no children. I envy John and James; they have so much more than money."

"Well you know what they say? Be careful what you wish for." Violet noticed her daughter's beautiful, manicured finger nails as she took hold of her hand; she never wanted to let it go.

"Mum, did you ever wear the watch or the jewellery I sent you?"

"Well, they were certainly expensive and beautiful but I never really went anywhere to wear them. I would often get them out my jewellery box and hold them in my hands and it would make me feel closer to you, but it also made me feel sad."

After becoming Sir Rupert's PA, Annie had travelled all over the world, staying in five-star hotels and eating in top restaurants. She could afford expensive gifts and sent them to her mother, believing that they would bring her joy. It had never occurred to her, until now, that she was showing how successful she was by sending her family such gifts. She should have known that her family and, in particular, her mum and John did not measure success in monetary terms. How could she have been so shallow? All her mother had ever wanted was to spend time with her. She'd missed out on so many family occasions—like her brother's wedding, when she rushed off immediately after the ceremony to the airport. She remembered the look of disappointment on their faces, particularly her mother's. She had thought that, at twenty-five, John was too young to get married and didn't want him making the same mistake that she had. She was glad that she'd been proved wrong because, nearly twenty-eight years on and four children later, they were still happily married.

When her young brother, James got a lucrative job in advertising, Annie had sent him an expensive watch. She hadn't known that it was little compensation for her absence at the party that John had thrown at his farm. Then she was in Japan when James got married ten years ago.

Annie now embraced her new-found freedom and spent as much time as possible with her family. She became a favourite Aunty to her nieces and nephews. She'd saved enough money to live on for the next year, and she had got her deposit back when she vacated her flat. However, she signed up with a temping agency and worked a few hours a week to keep some money coming in. The hours she spent reminiscing with her mother were the happiest and yet the saddest of times of her life. Her mother loved to hear about her globetrotting adventures and she laughed out loud when she told her about getting the upper hand on "Sir Almighty" and also on her ex-husband, Pete.

"You should have seen his face, Mum. His double chin swung like a hammock and his desk was wet with spittle," she giggled. "As for Pete, it was easy to get the better of him. He was all looks and no brains."

"He didn't know you very well if he thought he could get the better of you." She laughed, but grew serious and said, "You were too young to get married but you wouldn't listen."

"Well you got married young and I bet you didn't listen to your mum."

"Well things were very different in my day and your father was a good man; he was a different kettle of fish entirely to Pete. I never regretted marrying him, not for one single day. Besides my mother never really cared, but she needed me in the end." She spoke in a whisper. "You have no idea what it was like back then. Women had few choices and life was gruelling; long hours and back-breaking work with little reward. When I look back, I'm not proud of some of the things I did, but a mother will do anything to feed her children. You children have always been the most important people in my life. I wished I could have given you more, but to be honest, there were many times when I wondered how I was going to feed you."

"There was nothing better that you could have given us, Mum. We always felt loved. You've been a better mother than I've been a daughter."

Annie gently coaxed her mother into telling her about her life, a life that she rarely spoke about. It took days for her to tell her tale; she was becoming weaker now. She saw her mother in a new light and felt ashamed at how selfish and shallow she'd been. She had never once given a thought to how her mother had felt and how tough life had been for her. She made a promise to herself that from then on she would change her behaviour. If she could have one wish granted, it would be to turn back the hands of time.

Violet's hair had gone thin in spite of refusing chemotherapy, so she had it dyed blond and cut short like Annie Lennox. Her rebellious streak was always there, bursting to come out and when the women in the community room made remarks like, "Look at her, mutton dressed as lamb!" or, "Watch out girls, here she comes, the merry widow," her answer to that had been to wear her skirts even shorter. She had plenty of experience of being gossiped about and had developed a thick skin.

Violet lived for another two years, longer than expected, and Annie had no doubt that it was down to her strong will, and her refusal to leave her beloved family. She was in awe of her mother's strength. Not only had she survived a life of hardship, but she had borne her illness without complaint and with dignity. When she finally succumbed to the cancer that ravaged her body, her family were by her side. The two men cried silent tears and held their wives close. Annie howled with pain as she lay next to her mother on the bed, with her head on her shoulder willing her lifeless body to take one last breath. The family stayed at John and Linda's farmhouse and took comfort from being together, but when Annie retired to bed she was alone. She wished she'd done things differently, but as John had reminded her earlier, their mother didn't believe in regrets.

When Violet had moved to John's, just two weeks before she died, Annie had the unenviable task of emptying her mother's flat which was neat and tidy and very on trend. She'd made chintz curtains to match her settee, which had plumped-up cushions in pastel shades. She had to smile; on the glass coffee table were strategically placed magazines: *House Beautiful*, *Woman's Own* and even a *Smash Hits* with the Eurythmics on the front. She sat in her mother's favourite chair and her grandmother's before her, and thought back to that fateful day, when she lost the person she loved most in all the world: the day she looked into her mother's beautiful eyes for the last time: the day she thought her heart would break.

The sun shone on the mourners as they followed the flower laden-coffin into the church where Violet had married her beloved Ted and where Annie and John had spent their happiest years as children. Annie wondered how the sun could shine so brightly on one of the darkest days. Ted's brothers and sister, partners and children attended as did their friends Audrey and Bert and their three children and Janice and Paul from Cherry Tree Lodge.

Violet was laid to rest in the church graveyard next to her beloved first husband, Ted, and near her parents; together again.

CHAPTER FORTY-EIGHT
1986

When Annie had walked out of her job as his PA three years before, Sir Rupert had been shaken to the core by her confrontation, but his mood had quickly turned to anger and he'd been furious at her audacity.

His club was a place where men could vent about politics and women, especially women, without fear of recrimination and it was where he first vented his feelings towards that *scheming bitch*!

"I swear that if I ever clap eyes on that woman again, I won't be responsible for my actions." Sir Rupert swilled his brandy round his glass as he spoke.

"You have to show these fillies that you're the boss," said Roger Thorndike.

"Does that apply to Lady Sophia?" laughed a ruddy-faced man. "I'm sure you show your dear, lady wife, who the boss is." A ripple of laughter followed.

"She even had the nerve to ring me and ask for a reference! I couldn't believe it when I heard her voice on the telephone; I could barely get my words out."

"I hope you told her where to go, old fellow," said Roger.

"Well, I let her sweat for a day or two, but then I decided that it was better to get rid of her for good." Besides, Emma was shaping up nicely. She was a sweet little thing and never complained when his hand accidently touched her pert little bottom, but he kept those thoughts to himself. "If truth were told, I'm glad to see the back of her, the bloody Ice Queen. No wonder she was divorced and had no children, the frigid bitch! Good riddance, that's what I say. Let's drink to that."

He frequently praised her successor and how he had moulded her into the model PA. Emma was the exact opposite of her predecessor, quiet and subservient, but she was also very astute. However, she had a strong belief in God and she'd been brought up with a moral code and Sir Rupert's behaviour went against everything that she believed in. After three years, she could no longer turn a blind eye, unlike Annie, who had only cared about the perks she had for being his PA.

After a trip to Thailand, Emma failed to turn up for work and her mother phoned to inform Sir Rupert that she was off sick. Later he

226

heard a commotion outside in the corridor and went to investigate and found two men trying to get past security, one had a recording device with a microphone and the other a flash camera.

"Are the allegations about you true, Sir Rupert? Wouldn't you like to put your side of the story, sir?" The man was persistent. The camera flashed as they were led away by the burly security men.

He wondered what on earth was going on. He flopped in his chair and reached for the brandy in his desk drawer, his hands trembled as he twisted the top and poured himself a stiff drink. He lit a cigar and calmed himself and ordered his chauffeur to drive to the back of the building, but as he sneaked out the back he was accosted by the two men who had been removed earlier.

"Would you like to give us your side of the story, Sir Rupert?" He looked up puzzled and the flash went off. He shielded his face as the press confronted him. "Is it true that you have been misappropriating funds? Is it also true that you visit S&M clubs when you are away? Wouldn't you say that the tax payer has a right to know how you spent parliamentary funds? Does Lady Fairfax know about your secret trysts in houses of ill repute?"

They bombarded him with more questions, and the camera continued to flash in his face as his chauffeur hurriedly opened the car door for him and drove the car away at speed. Sir Rupert reached in the drinks cabinet and took out the brandy and gulped a mouthful of the soothing nectar. When he arrived home, the press were there too, swarming round the wrought iron gates of his large Georgian home. Lady Fairfax had called the police, who prevented the mob from following his car up the sweeping driveway when the gates swung open.

"What is going on?" demanded Cybil Fairfax, as she towered over her husband.

"I—I don't know," he stammered but he had a good idea. *I bet it's that conniving bitch. She threatened me with her diary.* Then he had another thought. *No-one's going to believe her. Dear, sweet Emma will back me up. She hasn't got a malicious bone in her body. Besides she's too timid to speak against me. Oh, yes, I can rely on Emma.*

The phone rang incessantly until he took it off the hook. Later that night Lady Cybil packed her suitcase and left for their place in the country, and he was summoned to meet with the Prime Minister. He was terrified of a confrontation with his boss. Margaret Thatcher could turn a man to stone with her glare. He thought, *still, they don't have a shred of evidence against me. Things will soon return to normal.* He had not bargained on Emma's meticulous notes and her tenacity. He had been caught on the back-foot by a mere youngster; a girl who looked as if butter wouldn't melt in her mouth.

Annie popped out in her lunch break to buy the dress she'd seen in the boutique window, earlier in the week. She was hurrying back to work, when she heard the monotonous tone of the news-seller shouting, "Read all about it. MP accused of lewd behaviour. Get yer copy here. Read all about it!"

She picked up a newspaper and saw a photo of Sir Rupert Fairfax looking like a rabbit caught in a headlight. She skimmed the article and the words FRAUD and S&M stood out. She bought a copy and tucked it under her arm, she would have to read it later.

Working, she listened to the tape twice and still made typing errors. Mr Foreman wanted the letter ready for posting that afternoon but she turned the tape off, unable to concentrate. She picked the newspaper up from her desk and scrutinised it. Sir Rupert had underestimated young Emma's strength of character and moral fibre. Her cheeks flushed at the thought of her own shallowness and how convenient it had been for her to turn a blind eye. Every sordid little detail was laid bare for all to see. He had been suspended by the Prime Minister and his wife had gone to their country home in Cheshire. She remembered her mother's words: "He'll get his comeuppance one day." Well, that time had finally arrived.

CHAPTER FORTY-NINE
1986

Annie was swept along by a sea of people all making their way to the tube. She did not want to miss the train. James had rung her earlier, but had refused to tell her his exciting news over the phone and she couldn't wait to find out; he could be so annoying at times. She heard the nasal voice on the tannoy, "The train arriving on platform three is the 19.00 hours train to Oxford, calling at..." She didn't hear the end of the announcement. She only had three minutes to get to the waiting train. The carriages were full and she looked alluringly at a young man in a suit, who immediately offered her his seat and was rewarded by Annie's disarming smile.

James met her off the train in his car. She swore that he looked more handsome than ever. He ran over to meet her and hugged her tightly.

"You look great, Sis. You look more like Mum every time I see you, except that you're about a foot taller than she was."

Her sister-in-law, Sandra, stood at the door when she heard the car pull onto the drive. Annie immediately looked around for her niece, Ruth.

"She tried to stay awake for you, but you'll see her tomorrow," said Sandra.

"You've got this place looking lovely. Your job must be going well, James."

He nodded and thanked her as he poured out three glasses of wine, "I've had a visitor."

Annie tapped her fingers against her glass, "Well come on, tell me! Don't keep me in suspense any longer."

"I have a brother." His voice was a whisper.

"I know you've got a brother and you've got a sister," She pointed to herself and said, "Moi," and laughed.

James turned his dark head away and picked up a letter off the sideboard and handed it to her. She looked at the American address on the back and started to read it. The date on it was 25th October 1945.

My darling Vi,
I have been home for a month now and I can't bear to be so far away from you. I'm longing to see you again. As you may know by now, I haven't been entirely honest with you. I have a wife but I have asked her for a divorce. I

have never loved anyone like you; in fact I had never been in love until I met you. I married for money and I stayed with her because I have a young son. I haven't been a good husband. I always had an eye for the women, and for the finer things in life, but I swear, with you it's different. I had an affair before I met you, but please don't believe her lies. She had many affairs before me, but she held me to ransom with threats directed at you. Some would say that I asked for this misery and perhaps they're right. My life is empty without you and as soon as I can, I will be back for you. I miss you, Honey and love you with all my heart. I can't wait for the day we can be together.

I have put Gus's address on the back. Please write back to me. You will break my heart if you don't,

Your ever-loving Chuck

xxxxx

"Apparently he'd asked one of the servants to post it for him, but his wife intercepted it. David, his son—my brother—said that his uncle told him about Mum and he was heartbroken when she didn't reply. He said that his mother was a cold woman and didn't think she'd ever loved his father. He found the letter in her bedroom drawer after she died."

"How did he find you?"

"Well, he tried the US Army to start with, but they were obstructive. They said that the files were confidential, so he came to England to find Mum. He said he owed it to his dad to let her know the truth. His father's friend, Gus, had Audrey's address, so he visited her and she told him that Mum had passed away and told him about me."

"How do you feel about that?"

"Weird. He seems a nice man, but I've already got a brother. David is ten years older than me. He's invited Sandra, Ruth and me to visit him and his family in America, which was nice of him, but as far as I'm concerned, Bill was my dad in every way that mattered. He made us happy and he loved us up until the day he died. I don't know how Mum carried on after he'd gone."

"Well, she didn't last too long after, did she? I still remember Chuck, he was a bit flash but he was a handsome devil. Actually you look a lot like him. He swept Mum off her feet and it's so sad that she never received that letter. She must have felt that he'd gone home and forgotten all about her. Still, the love she had for Bill was solid; they were the best of friends."

Annie told him about Sir Rupert Fairfax. "I'm dreading getting a call. I'm sure they will want my testimony. I don't know how that young woman had the bravery to out him. It makes me feel awful! I feel as if anyone who questions me about it will think I've only looked out for myself."

John could barely look at his wife, who was struggling not to laugh. Annie had never spoken a truer word.

On Monday morning, Annie received a phone call from Roger Thurvaston. He was investigating the allegations against Sir Rupert and he asked her if she would come to his office in Whitehall. She was unusually tongue-tied on the phone.

Her heart was pounding as she stepped out the lift on the fourth floor. She wore her blonde hair loose on her shoulders and she'd paid particular attention to her make-up. She wore a dress that she'd just bought from a boutique. She knew that the Mary Quant shift dress would show her legs off to their best advantage and she paired the black and white dress with a pair of white boots. Roger Thurvaston was taken aback when he saw her. He offered her a seat, but he found it difficult to focus on asking her questions, when she crossed her legs. He smiled at her when she took her diary out of her shoulder bag with dates and assignations in it.

"Thank you, Ms Smithson, this will be very useful." He stood to shake her hand and noted that they were more or less the same height. "I will most likely be in touch with you again. Thank you so much for coming. Perhaps next time we can meet somewhere less formal, somewhere a little closer for you." He saw her to the door and as she turned to smile at him, a flush crept across his face. He hoped she hadn't noticed.

He put a call through to his secretary and asked her to get him a strong coffee.

Annie couldn't keep the smile off her face. As she travelled back on the train, she closed her eyes but all she could see were a pair of hypnotic brown eyes.

Two days later, she was walked to the coffee shop near her work. Her hair was in a neat chignon and she wore her mother's blue drop earrings which complimented her blue suit. She studied her reflection in a shop window and was satisfied that she looked sophisticated. Roger stood up when she walked in and held the chair out for her. They spoke little of Sir Rupert but instead discovered that they had a lot in common. They both loved fine dining and travelling and they had the same sense of humour, they were both divorced and had both come from humble beginnings. Roger had two grown up children and a granddaughter called Carrie and he was about to become a granddad for the second time.

The following morning, a dozen red roses arrived at Foreman and White's solicitors. The card read, *To Annie, may we have wonderful adventures together R xx*

Annie cradled baby Rose, and was enthralled by her tiny fingernails and rosebud mouth. Two year old Carrie came running in with her arms up. Annie passed the baby over to her granddad and sat Carrie on her lap.

Carrie stared at Annie with enormous dark eyes and looked towards the baby and said, "She's not going to be your bridesmaid as well is she?"

Annie laughed "No, it's just you and Ruth."

"Do you promise?"

"I promise," and to confirm it, they hooked their little fingers.

Annie smiled as she remembered her mother saying, "Love is the most important thing and if you find it don't let go of it."

Well, she had found it, and she would *never let it go.*